Love in Maine

Love in Maine

A NOVEL

Connie Falconeri

NEW YORK

THIS LABEL APPLIES TO TEXT STOCK

For Molly,
In spite of our differences.

And for Sonny,
In spite of everything.

Asked, "Who is the rich man?"
Epictetus replied, "He who is content."

—Epictetus

Love in Maine

CHAPTER 1

How hard could it be? It's just taking orders from hungry people and bringing them food.

"Yes!" Maddie lied. "I've worked at a couple of different restaurants and bistros here in Maine. I have tons of experience." (She might have overdone it, she realized, with the "tons.")

The middle-aged cook was tired and skeptical. He'd obviously just finished a busy breakfast shift and he was looking over his shoulder away from Maddie to make sure his line cook was prepping for the lunch crowd. The small city of Blake, Maine, was a working-class, riverfront town that had been building boats for the Navy since the middle of the nineteenth century. A diner like this one tended to survive the ups and downs in the economy by sticking to the basics.

"Bistros?" the cook scoffed, looking at the young woman more pointedly. One of the men at the counter laughed behind his newspaper. "I don't need any fancy-pants college kid sticking her nose up at the customers around here." He turned to leave.

"I'll wash dishes, I'll chop onions, I'll marry the ketchups!" she cried after him. Her friend Kara had told her about how the restaurant manager at the place where she worked on Nantucket made her take the leftover ketchup from one bottle and marry it into the other leftover ketchup bottles so they looked full the next day.

The burly cook turned slowly around. "You'll do *what* to the ketchups?" He looked furious.

"I'll marry them?" Maddie knew she should have sounded more convincing, but he looked like she'd just insulted him.

"If you ever try that at this place, I'll fire you so fast you won't be able to work in this town again."

She looked quickly over his shoulder at the boarded-up storefronts across the street. It wasn't Madison Avenue. If someone was going to threaten her with never working in a town again, crossing Blake, Maine, off the list wasn't the end of the world.

"Well . . . I didn't realize—" she tried again.

"This is a clean place. It might be a bit worn around the edges, I know the linoleum could use an update, but I've never mixed old ketchup bottles together, and no one's ever gotten sick from eating at Phil's."

"I wasn't suggesting—"

Phil stared down at her. She noticed the tattoos on his forearms, indicating he'd probably spent some time in the Navy. She had to really concentrate in order not to stare. It wasn't the type of thing she saw every day at close range, ancient green tattoos of mermaids and anchors and crazy sailor stuff.

He sighed and looked back at the kitchen, seemingly resenting the time Maddie was taking up that could have been better spent prepping for lunch. He curled his lip as if he might have a bit of fun at her expense. "All right, Miss Ketchup. I'll let you show me your stuff during lunch today. I keep the tips."

"Well . . ." Maddie looked down at her khaki skirt and white-collared shirt. She was interviewing. She had dressed to be interviewing, not waitressing.

"You can change in the back. That your bag?" His eyes skimmed over to her worn-out L.L. Bean duffle with the cracked leather handles. It was the closest thing she could find to casual in a closet full of T. Anthony luggage and Gucci loafers at her parents' home in Boston.

"Yeah. I'm renting a room from a lady in town, but I haven't been there yet. I came into the diner right from the bus station when I saw your Help Wanted sign in the window."

"Who?"

"Who what?"

"Who is the lady you'll be living with?"

"I think her name is Janet Gilbertson. Do you know her?"

Phil smiled for the first time since she'd been there, and it had been a while. When Maddie first came into the diner, Phil had been swamped and asked her to take a seat until he was done with the final breakfast orders. Thirty-seven minutes later, he'd come out from behind the stainless-steel pass-through window and he hadn't smiled once that entire time.

"Yeah." His smile was full now. "I know her."

"Is she funny?" Maddie tried to get in on the joke. "Why are you smiling like that?"

"Oh. No reason. Just curious, anyone else boarding over there at Janet's, or just you?"

"Oh. I hadn't thought to ask. The ad on Craigslist said, 'Single room available in safe respectable home,' so I figure I'm the only boarder. Why?"

"No reason." Phil turned back toward the kitchen and then called over his shoulder, "Follow me."

Maddie picked up the duffle and followed him to the kitchen.

Four hours later, she was nearly dead. What a ridiculous fool she was to think she could just traipse into a diner and . . . do anything. Phil had finally relegated her to the dishwasher after she nearly spilled a cup of coffee on a really nice old lady. Maddie managed to get most of it on herself instead, so at least she avoided a $10 million lawsuit from a burn victim, but even the dishwashing had turned out to be really stressful. It just went on and on, and everyone was in such a rush. She kept wanting to text her college roommate about how crazy it was to be washing dishes at a diner in Maine and how funny that was, and then she would remember that her brother Jimmy had taken her cell phone—along with all of her other electronics—as part of their little bet.

"E-mail us from the public library," Jimmy had ordered, "like everyone else in the world who's got a hundred bucks to their name, Sis."

If—no, *when*—she won this wager, she would make sure her pompous older brother Jimmy never, *ever* called her 'Sis' again.

Maddie put the last rack of dishes away and looked up to see Phil with his meaty, tattooed forearms crossed in front of the old white T-shirt covering his barrel chest. She tried to repress a smile over how much he was like Brutus in those old Popeye cartoons. All he needed was a pipe and a cockeyed cap on his head.

"What's so funny, Miss Ketchup?"

He'd started calling her Miss Ketchup and hadn't stopped. She kind of liked having a nickname. And a boss. Who would pay her money.

"Oh, nothing," she said. "Just what a lousy dishwasher I am."

He liked her honesty. For a few seconds he smiled, then scowled.

"Maybe I'd be a better sous-chef or server?" Maddie offered quickly.

Phil burst out laughing. "This here is a diner," he said, like the native Mainer he was (*This hee-yuh is a die-nuh*). "We do not have

sous-chefs. We do not have servers. We have cooks and dishwash-
ers and waitresses." He took off his filthy white apron, pulling it up
over his head, wadding it into a ball, and tossing it handily into the
laundry bin by the back door, like a basketball shot.

"Nice three-pointer," Maddie complimented.

"You a basketball fan?"

"I have brothers." She shrugged.

He turned off the lights where they'd been standing in the
kitchen. "I'm not sure this is going to work." He kept walking into
the main part of the diner. The other cook had left, and the last
waitress had finished wiping down all the tables and the countertop
and had called good-bye as she let herself out the front door a few
minutes before.

"I will try really hard," Maddie pleaded. "I swear. Please give me
a chance. You don't have to pay me—"

He swung around fast. "What do you mean, I don't have to pay
you?"

"I mean . . ." Shit. What an idiot. Maddie's dad had always encouraged her to go for unpaid internships and that sort of thing,
but how the hell was she going to pay her rent if she didn't make
any money? Idiot!

Phil kept staring at her.

"I meant, you don't have to pay me for today."

He nearly choked on his short laugh. "Yeah, that's pretty much
a given."

"But seriously, I am—not that it's your problem—but I am really strapped right now and I will work really hard for you."

"You're not pregnant, are you?"

Maddie looked down at her flat stomach. "What? No! Why
would you say that?" She felt like telling him he could get himself

thrown in jail for that chauvinist crap, but she left her politically correct ego at the door.

"Well, you said you were strapped . . . pretty girl like you . . ." He raised his shoulders and raised his eyebrows in what Maddie supposed was a kind of patronizing apology. He was probably about her father's age and thought he was being kindly. "I mean, you don't *look* pregnant," he added.

Oh, great, Maddie thought, now he's embarrassed. "Look, Phil. I need a job. Plain and simple. You need someone to fill in for your regular waitress while she's away taking care of her sick dad. I'll work all summer, really hard. Come on. Just give me a chance."

He stared at her a few long moments. "All right, Ketchup. You're hired. But no screwing around. You need to be here at five o'clock tomorrow morning for an eight-hour shift. You good with that?"

"Yes! Yes, I am so good with that!" Maddie was bouncing up and down on the balls of her feet.

Phil kept staring at her. "You are going to be washing dishes and sweeping the floor and cleaning up after a bunch of slobs. You got that part, right?"

"Yes!" She was so excited she couldn't help it. She forced her body to still and her face to fall. "Yes." She tried to act more subdued.

He shook his head. "All right, then. See you at five. And you might want to wear a black T-shirt next time."

She looked down at her shirt and realized it was covered with a muddy rainbow of grease, juice, coffee, and unidentifiable muck. "Will do!" She saluted him for some reason, then felt like an even bigger idiot. "I mean, will do," she repeated, keeping her hands firmly at her sides, tamping down her enthusiasm.

Phil showed her out the front door and stood holding it open for her for a few seconds. "You know how to get to Janet's from here?" he asked.

"Yes. I think it's just up that street, and then on to the left . . . Is that right?"

"Yep. That's right." He looked at her again as if he were going to ask her what the hell she was doing in Blake, Maine, in the first place, then thought better of it. "Say hi to Hank for me."

"Who's Hank?"

But Phil was already shutting the door, and she only heard him laugh and lock it as he pulled the old horizontal blinds down and flipped the sign to "Closed."

CHAPTER 2

"Henry Van Rensselaer Gilberston. You do not speak to me in that tone of voice."

"Come on, Mom. You don't need to speak to me like I'm twelve, either, but this is crazy."

"I am not crazy. We settled that years ago. I have the paperwork to prove it." She winked at her handsome son, then tried to stay mad at him, which was always impossible. At twenty-eight, after ten years in the Army, Henry could never hold his mother's wrath for long.

"I didn't say *you* were crazy, I said *this* is crazy," he said. "I will get a second job or do some part-time work cleaning yachts over in Back Cove. There is no reason for you to be taking in strays."

"You make it sound like the city pound. I think Maddie Post sounds like a perfectly nice lady. And someone I can talk to, unlike you, with your buttoned-up, I-just-want-to-be-left-alone thing you've got going on."

Hank turned away from his mother and tried to figure out the best way to tell her he was not about to let some old cat lady from who-knew-where live in his mother's house for a few hundred dollars a month.

"You are charging her way too little," Hank tried, turning back to face her and folding his arms in defiance. "Donald's got a roommate who pays six hundred bucks a month."

Janet Gilbertson folded her arms as well. They looked like mirror images of one another. Rather, they looked nothing like one another, Hank being bulky, tall, and stock-still, and Janet being tiny, birdlike, and fidgety. But their stubborn scowls were identical.

"Well, that's just ridiculous," Janet said. "Who would pay six hundred dollars to live in my guest room? In Blake, Maine. That's just plain old silly."

"Mom! Are you doing this to make money or just to piss me off?"

She let her hands drop to her sides and turned toward the kitchen. "Are you staying for supper?"

Typical, he thought. Subject change. Ten years gone and everything stays the same. "Well, yeah. I am now. You think I am going to let you welcome some Lizzie Borden into this house without getting a good look at her and running a security check on her later?"

Hank had followed his mother into the kitchen. Oh, the scenes he'd endured in that kitchen. His mother and father drunk as loons, kissing or fighting or passed out. The fear of what he'd find when he came home from a friend's house during high school. The desire to bolt, finally achieved when he enlisted on his eighteenth birthday. The mottled yellow Formica of the countertop was like a visual cue that set all those memories into motion. He still wasn't used to being here, even though he'd gotten back from his final deployment nearly four months ago.

"Hank?"

"Yes, Mom?"

"She's just a woman looking for a place to stay for the summer,"

Janet said gently, holding out a glass of iced tea for him. "I want some company." He accepted the glass and took a sip.

"You always knew how to make the best iced tea, I'll give you that."

They heard the slow steps of someone on the path to the front door before they could see the much-anticipated Maddie Post. Janet had let the hydrangeas grow to massive proportions, concealing the few visitors she had until they were right at the front door.

"We need to cut those shrubs back, for security," Hank grumbled.

"Oh, hush. We don't need security on a little side street in the middle of nowhere. You cut that out and be nice." Janet walked to the screen door at the front of the living room and pushed it open. "Well, hello! You must be Maddie Post! Aren't you just cute as a button!"

Henry groaned in the shadowy corner of the living room, waiting to see some little old lady come in with her carpetbag.

"This is my son, Henry."

Hank stepped forward into the center of the living room and lifted his chin in silent greeting. He felt sucker-punched. She wasn't little and she wasn't old.

Maddie hoisted her duffle bag higher onto one shoulder. "Hey! I didn't realize you had a son, Mrs. Gilbertson!" She looked at Janet, then extended her hand to shake Henry's. He hesitated for a split second before taking it. Her face screwed up for that tiny moment of confusion, then broke into a big smile when he took her hand after all.

"Whew! I thought for a minute you were going to be all stormy and moody like Phil down at the diner." Hank pulled his hand away after they'd finished shaking.

"Oh, have you met Phil already?" Mrs. Gilbertson asked, steering Maddie away from her moody, stormy son. "Come this way, dear. I'll show you your room. I hope you like it. I didn't want to make it too cluttered, but I wanted you to feel welcome, if you know what I mean, and it doesn't look like you've brought too much stuff, so . . ."

Henry listened as the two women went up the stairs and his mother kept a constant stream of her trademark prattle going. He set down his glass of iced tea, let himself fall into the big armchair, and stared up at the ceiling. He could follow their movements by the sounds of creaks and cracks created by their footfalls across the floorboards of the 1920 home.

What the hell was a hot woman like that doing renting a room in some stranger's house in—he had to admit his mother was right—the middle of nowhere? Maddie Post looked like she should be on the cover of some glossy woman's magazine with a headline that promised seventy-four ways to satisfy your man. Long chestnut hair. Dark violet eyes above wide, high cheekbones. Full, promising lips. Her messed-up shirt and disheveled ponytail only served to make her look more . . . accessible.

Raking his nails through his buzz cut and along his scalp, Hank tried to ignore the sound of the mattress springs as Ms. Post bounced up and down on the bed to make sure it was to her liking. With everything he'd been going through since he got back from the Middle East—trying to remember what it was like to be a normal person in a normal town—the last thing Henry Gilbertson needed was to be thinking about some fresh-scrubbed college girl alone and rolling around in his childhood bedroom.

He hoisted himself up from the chair and went into the kitchen to see what he could do to help get dinner ready.

After a shower, Maddie felt almost human again. She unpacked her bag in about four minutes and pulled on a pair of low-slung Brown U. Women's Crew sweatpants and a white tank top. She assumed that Hank the Grump would be gone by the time she went back downstairs, so had to hide her surprise when he was sitting at the kitchen table. He looked peevish and impatient when she walked into the room.

"Oh! Hi! I figured you didn't live here . . . I mean, nice to see you again." Maddie suddenly felt like her sweats and workout tank were some kind of seductive get-up, the way he was sizing her up from head to toe. She pushed her shoulders back out of habit, to steel herself, and tried to act like it was perfectly normal for her to be walking into a strange person's kitchen.

"So, Janet, shall I go to the grocery store and stock up or can I just give you money for my share of the meals?"

"Yes!" Grumpy barked over his mother's joyful, "No!"

All three of them looked at each other, then Maddie looked at the stove and the sink and anywhere else she could without looking at Henry Gilbertson. He was too big for the room. For any room. He was all muscle-y and corded, and even his breathing seemed more like a dragon exhaling smoke through his nostrils than a mere man releasing oxygen. And what did she ever do to him, anyway? Maddie wondered. He'd been rude since the moment she walked in.

"Janet," Maddie asked gently, "are you sure this is okay? I'm sure I can find another place—"

"Not for two hundred bucks a month you won't," Grumpy said.

"Excuse me?" Maddie had had just about enough crud flung at her for one day and she decided she didn't need to take any more of it from this guy. Sure he was hot, but, well, so was she!

"I said," Henry repeated slowly, for the resident dimwit, "you are getting quite a bargain to live here for two hundred dollars a month."

Maddie chose to ignore the taunt. Having three older brothers had taught her the power of silence. "Janet, I'm so sorry. I'd be happy to pay more if that's not enough. I would never try to—"

"Of course not!" Janet shook her head. "That's absolutely what we agreed on and I think it's perfectly fair." She stared at her son to quiet him down. "Hank's just a bit . . . protective, aren't you, dear?" Janet patted his clasped hands and got up to see to the meal.

"Please let's all sit down and have a nice supper. I made some corn on the cob and a big salad and some pie for dessert. I'm mostly a vegetarian . . . I hope that's okay!"

Henry rolled his eyes. Maddie ignored him.

"Totally fine!" Maddie said. "I'll definitely need to get some protein sometimes—I have to stay in shape for my final year of sports at college—but I'll make sure to eat my share of T-bones at Phil's or wherever, if you don't want the smell in the house."

"Oh, it's not that, dear. Please don't go to a restaurant, that's just silly. I just meant I won't be serving it or eating it."

"Well, after tonight I wouldn't expect you to be serving me anyway—"

"Yeah, right," Henry mumbled.

Maddie sat up straighter. She was not going to let this guy get to her. So he didn't want a stranger in his mom's house. Okay. Fine.

Janet rolled her eyes as she finished putting dinner together. She stood at the stove and plated the food. "Just ignore him, Maddie. He's very suspicious these days." Janet spoke as if her enormous son were not even in the room. "I like you. That's all that matters. Henry doesn't live here, so he can just mind his own business."

The ignored Henry stared at his mother's rigid back. The room was silent, and even the nighttime insects outside the screen door and open window over the sink went quiet.

His voice was low and steady when he replied, "You *are* my business, Mom. Or so I thought." Then he got up and walked over to the stove to give his mother a kiss good-bye. "You enjoy your dinner and I'll see you tomorrow."

Janet turned to face her son, and Maddie tried to make herself invisible. "Hank, don't worry, sweetheart. I'll be fine. We'll all be fine." She reached up and patted his cheek. It looked like it was about all the physical contact he could stand. "You go on home and get a good night's sleep."

He nodded once, then turned to the left and showed himself out the back door off the kitchen.

Janet and Maddie listened to his hard, sure footsteps as they faded into the night.

"Wow. He's quite . . . something," Maddie said.

Janet smiled a sad, dispirited smile. "He's had a rough go, so I probably spoil him. He's gotten a little protective in return. He'll come around. Not to worry. Now, let's enjoy our delicious dinner." Janet had set down two plates piled high with fresh leafy vegetables, grilled corn on the cob, and a hunk of what looked like freshly baked bread. Maddie had never tasted better food. Washing dishes for four hours straight had turned her appetite into something formidable.

Turned out that washing dishes and waiting tables eight hours a day, five days in a row, turned her appetite into something resembling a ravenous beast. She finally had to tell Janet that she needed steak and fish and chicken, and lots of it, and of course she would buy it herself. But since Maddie hadn't gotten her first paycheck yet, she asked Janet if she could pay her for her share of the food on Friday night when Phil was going to pay her. She was down to twelve dollars, after giving fifty as a down payment to Janet and spending very carefully on food that she had to buy when she wasn't at Phil's.

Luckily, Henry Gilbertson hadn't crossed her path since that first awkward night. Janet talked about him all the time, as if the three of them were great old friends, but Maddie figured Henry was avoiding her and that was fine by her. It turned out Henry lived in the apartment over Janet's garage, but it was far enough away that Maddie never actually saw him. Apparently he worked twelve-hour days, most of it underwater in two-hour shifts.

Janet went on and on about what a successful career he'd had as an engineer diver in the Army. And then she went on and on about how smart and wonderful he was. At first Maddie thought she was trying to play matchmaker, but eventually she realized that Janet was just insanely proud of him, so she let her rattle on. If half of what Janet said was true, he was a pretty intense guy. Maddie promised herself that she'd try to give him a second chance the next time she saw him. As long as he wasn't a total jerk again.

Friday afternoon Phil handed Maddie her first paycheck. For some reason, she wanted to take the sealed envelope home and open it in private. It felt special. Hers. She had gotten paychecks before, obviously. She'd worked at lots of killer jobs, most recently at the campus human rights league, doing paralegal work that a regular paralegal could have charged two hundred dollars an hour for. But this check felt like she had actually earned it. She wasn't quite sure how to explain it, but it felt like real money for real work.

Maddie practically skipped home and smiled at how Janet's

house was already starting to feel like home. She'd made it five days on her own. Six, counting Sunday when she'd first arrived. But she didn't really count Sunday because she didn't make any money that day. She'd done just fine. Her brother Jimmy could take his pontificating self-righteousness and stick it. Maddie didn't need to be coddled by her parents and her wealthy upbringing.

She got to Janet's and let the screen door slam behind her. Somehow that seemed less rude than screaming through the house, "Anybody home?"

It was only half past three and the house was quiet, so Maddie peeked into the kitchen and was about to turn back into the living room when she realized Henry Gilbertson was standing near the back door. He looked like he'd been about to dart out and been caught. He stood so still that, in the shadows cast from the afternoon sun, Maddie couldn't quite convince herself that he was really standing there. In the flesh. There was something invisible about him, about his stillness.

"Oh. Hi, Henry." Maddie put one hand on her hip and leaned against the doorjamb. She was flicking the envelope—*Hello! My first paycheck!*—back and forth like a swishing cattail. He didn't say a word.

Maddie decided it might be fun to push his buttons a little. He was so gruff and manly, he was really a caricature of himself. She walked into the kitchen and headed for the refrigerator. She opened it and bent down to see what she could have to drink to celebrate. Soda. Soda. Juice. Soda.

"You know what I'd really love right now?" she twisted her face around to peek at Henry over the top edge of the old yellow refrigerator, but most of her was still bent over and, apparently, distracting him. His eyes, which Maddie now noticed were a stormy green, were definitely taking her in. Maybe he wasn't such a stoic after all.

He shook his head to silently acknowledge that he had no idea what Maddie would love right now. Something hot and fast crackled between them when Henry moved his head, but he kept his eyes fixed on Maddie. The bastard had hit Maddie's flirting slow pitch right out of the park.

Maddie tried to weigh her options. She supposed she could forego pesky considerations like . . . sentences longer than two words . . . or common courtesy. For a taste of those wide stern lips or a chance to get her arms around those enormous shoulders, she thought she could make allowances. He was so . . . big. So unlike any of the cool, polished guys she'd dated at Brown. He gave confidence a whole new meaning.

Summer fling, Maddie thought, *here I come.*

She stood up slowly, and rested her elbows on the top of the fridge door.

"What I'd really love is . . . a friend." Maddie surprised herself as much as she seemed to surprise Henry with her choice of words. What she originally thought she wanted was an ice-cold beer. Earlier in the week, Janet mentioned that she'd been sober for years, and Maddie wasn't about to stock the refrigerator with beer.

But a friend? What was she thinking? She already had tons of friends. Not that she was the most popular girl in town or anything, but she had her share of really great friends. But that's what had come out of her mouth. A friend. Maybe on some level she really did want him like that, platonically. Maybe zero communication with the outside world was beginning to rattle her. Maybe she was a bit of a social media addict after all. She certainly felt like she had tons of free time with no iPad, no iPod, no iPhone . . . no i-anything. The silence lengthened between them.

The refrigerator moaned back into service from having the door left open too long. Maddie smiled and tried to think of what she could do to get him to talk. Or at least to kiss her, if the talking didn't pan out.

CHAPTER 3

D amn it. Did she have to be so breezy and confident? Madison Post made Henry feel like he was being rude when he was try-ing to be polite, or at least appropriate. She was overly familiar in that way that always put him off. She was too young. Too smart. Too everything. He'd come over to grab a couple of sodas from his mother's fridge after a grueling day in the cold water. Was it too much to ask to be left in peace?

"What are you really doing here, Maddie?"

She shut the door to the refrigerator and stood about two feet in front of him. Her black T-shirt was snug and almost military. She had on super-short khaki shorts above long, tanned legs and a pair of sneakers. She had great ankles. On anyone else it probably wouldn't have looked like the sexiest outfit, but Maddie Post did it justice. She was fanning her face with a plain white envelope that didn't do anything to diminish the light sheen of sweat across her cheeks.

"Just looking for something cool to drink," she said slowly.

What the hell was she trying to pull? If Henry didn't know better, he'd think she was making a move on him.

"How old are you?"

She stopped fanning herself and leaned one shoulder against the refrigerator. "Why? Afraid of robbing the cradle?"

Hank felt another pull of sexual tension that he hadn't seen coming. And he always saw it coming.

"Don't flatter yourself, Sis."

Her face clouded. "Don't call me that, Gilbertson."

"Okay, Post." He smirked and she smirked back. At least the sexual tension was gone, Hank thought with a grateful sigh. "Have a good weekend, then." He turned and made for the back door.

"Aw, come on," she said, slapping the envelope against her thigh. "I just got my first paycheck and I want to celebrate. I don't know anybody here and your mom's not around to raise a glass of iced tea."

Hank left one hand resting on the handle of the back door. "I'm not really the friend type, Post." He gestured with one palm out, almost guilty. "I'm what is commonly known as a loner."

Maddie tilted her head and narrowed her eyes slightly. "Couldn't you make an exception, this one time?"

Henry stared at this woman, basically offering herself to him. What was his problem? She'd be gone in a few months. Maybe they could have a little . . . arrangement. He let go of the door handle and felt like he was letting go of a whole lot more.

"How much have you got to blow on this celebration of yours?" His voice was low and suggestive as he walked the few steps back into her personal space. He liked the sound of her nervous inhale as she tried to conceal the thread of excitement that having him so close caused. He could deny a lot, but he couldn't deny the raw sexual energy that snapped between them.

"I—I don't know—" she stuttered.

Henry reached out to her and looked like he was reaching for her chest, but he whipped the white envelope from her hand instead.

Maddie inhaled. "Hey—"

"Well, let's see how much that cheapskate Phil paid you for your troubles—"

"Give me that—" Maddie cried. "That's my paycheck."

Henry held it out of her reach easily. He was a good five inches taller than she was and it wasn't much trouble to keep the envelope above his head while he looked up and tore it open.

Maddie stopped reaching for the envelope when she realized she was backed up to the refrigerator and rubbing herself up against Hank in her effort to grab the paper back from him. His stomach was as rock hard as she'd imagined it would be, especially against the bare skin of her belly . . . which had become exposed when she stretched up to try to get her check back.

They were both staring at each other and breathing hard. Maddie pulled her T-shirt back into place.

"Two hundred and thirty-seven dollars." He whistled at the paltry amount.

"What?" Maddie yelled and forgot about her wayward T-shirt, giving one last jump and snatching the check from his hand. She stared at the curly ballpoint pen of Phil's penmanship. "Two hundred and thirty-seven measly dollars?"

"And eighty-four cents," Henry whispered as he crowded her closer to the refrigerator.

She looked up and her dark violet eyes flashed and registered that he was really close.

"And eighty-four cents," she whispered and licked her dry lips. "I'm not sure how much of a good time we can have with two hundred dollars . . ."

"I think we can have a little fun . . . don't you?" Henry let his index finger trail across the smooth skin of her stomach. It was only an inch or two, but she gasped at the contact.

"Yeah . . . probably . . ." Maddie's voice was scratchy as she reached up and touched his rough cheek. He'd come straight from work and he hadn't shaved for a couple of days. "No money fun," she added.

Henry smiled at that, and it sliced through her. It might be for the best after all, Maddie thought, that Henry Gilbertson kept that smile to a minimum, because when he let it loose, she pretty much lost her mind. She put the edge of her thumb at the corner of his lips. "You have a great smile."

He leaned in and put his lips across hers, tentatively. His grip on her hip firmed, and his other hand reached up to the back of her neck and held her. But his lips stayed light, in a maddening counterpoint to the hard, controlling pressure of his hands.

Maddie dropped the check and brought her hand up to hold onto his strong neck, before her legs gave out.

Henry heard the screech of the front screen door open first. He pulled away quickly, almost shoving Maddie. She jerked against the refrigerator and looked up at him in startled silence. Her mouth was slightly open, her lips plump and wet, her eyes glassy.

"Do something with your face!" Hank muttered harshly, turning toward the back door, but he didn't make it in time.

"Oh! Hi, Hank!" his mother called from the door as she came in from the living room. "I didn't expect to see you here! Will you stay for dinner?"

"I don't know, Mom—"

"Maddie! What are you doing down there?" Janet looked at Maddie crouched under the kitchen table.

"I dropped my paycheck." Maddie peeked out from under the

table. She caught a glimpse of Henry's relieved face when he saw she was looking relatively normal and not all just-kissed. In fact, she looked downright pleased. She stood up and waved the paycheck for Janet to see. "Isn't it exciting? My first paycheck!"

Janet put down the grocery bags she'd been carrying. "Oh! How exciting! Let's go celebrate! Why don't the three of us go to the movies?"

Maddie raised her eyebrows and turned to Henry. "Yes! Why don't we?" Apparently she enjoyed tormenting him. She tugged her T-shirt down at least, so he didn't have to fight the urge to let his eyes wander to that damnable strip of tanned, smooth flesh that he'd only gotten the briefest hint of against his rough palm.

"Hank?" his mother prompted.

"Huh?" He swung his gaze from Maddie.

"Do you want to come to the movies with us?"

Jesus. Was he living in some sort of teenage hell? Going to the movies with his mother? "I don't know, Mom. Why don't you two have a girls' night out?"

Janet finished putting away a few cans of soup and folded the bags neatly and slipped them between the refrigerator and the wall. She faced Henry full-on. "Because we don't want a girls' night out. Right, Maddie? We want to go out with a big, handsome man." Janet winked at Maddie, trying to get them all to get along. Maddie nearly died of embarrassment.

"Right, Janet." Maddie forced her smile to be tight, because what she really wanted to do was make that big, handsome man across the room blush with embarrassment. He was such an easy mark. "But I really have to shower and change."

"Me too," Henry agreed, reaching for the handle on the back door, as if escape was within reach at last.

"Okay," Janet said, "this is great. Let's all meet up at six, and we'll go see that movie where they blow up the moon and everyone has to live in those weird pod-things."

Henry rolled his eyes. "That sounds realistic."

"It's a movie, silly. It's not supposed to be realistic!"

Maddie smiled and looked at the floor. If she looked at Henry she wasn't sure what she would do.

"Okay, Mom. I'll see you two back here at six," he said.

He couldn't look at Maddie but at least he could say "you two" so she wasn't completely invisible.

"Off you go, then," Janet said to Maddie as the back door slapped shut. "You look a fright after all that dishwashing. Go jump in the shower first, and I'll use my bathroom in a half hour or so, so we're not battling for the hot water."

"Oh." Maddie looked up. "Okay. Thanks. I am pretty wiped. I'll see you at six." Maddie smiled at Janet and turned back through the living room and then walked steadily up the stairs. It took everything she had to keep her pace even, when all she really wanted to do was scream with delight at having just had the most ravishing kiss in the history of ravishing kisses. She made it to her room and turned on the shower to conceal the uncontrollable peal of delight. Maddie pressed her face into the pillow and screamed. Big, bad Henry Gilbertson had just kissed her. Hard.

She caught her breath finally and rolled onto her back. She stared at the white ceiling and breathed deeply, kicking off her sneakers and feeling the memory of his lips on hers, the memory of his hands pushed against the column of her neck. The power of him. Maddie felt her body responding just to the idea of him; she could only begin to anticipate what the reality of Henry was going to be like. She shook herself, like she did after a hard rowing race, when her muscles would be quivering with exertion and she was physically unsure of herself. She peeled off her filthy black T-shirt and sweaty shorts and underwear, and stepped into the old-fashioned white tub and let the spray of the shower momentarily erase the physical memory of Henry from her body.

Two hours later, Maddie was in a pair of linen pants and a T-shirt, sitting quietly in the living room reading one of the novels from Janet's excellent library.

Janet came downstairs a few minutes before six, wearing a pretty summer dress with big blue flowers against a white background, and her white Keds sneakers. "Isn't this going to be fun?"

Maddie looked up and nodded. "You look great. Yeah, I'm excited. Though I have to confess I doubt I'll be able to underwrite all the first-paycheck celebrating with my paltry check."

"Oh, don't be ridiculous!" Janet threw her hand at Maddie. "I wouldn't hear of that." She lowered her voice in case Henry was outside already. "I'm just so grateful that I was finally able to get Henry to leave the house on a Friday night."

"Oh?"

"It's probably to do with you," Janet said with a suggestive lift to her eyebrows. "I think he's been hearing around town about how cute and spunky you are and—"

"What?" Maddie almost laughed. "I'm cute and spunky?"

Janet sat down on the end of the sofa nearest Maddie's chair. "Well, you are, you know. Just adorable. I wish Henry could look at a girl. He'd never look at a girl as pretty as you, of course." Janet looked down at her hands clasped in her lap. "He just isn't

altogether happy anymore." Then she looked directly at Maddie.
"You know what I mean?"

Maddie shook her head no, then nodded her head yes. "I mean,
I don't know him, Janet. So I just can't say."

"Oh." Janet waved one hand again. "Of course. But you will.
And maybe you two will become friends. He's not that much older
than you, you know? He's only twenty-eight. Already served ten
years in the United States Army and he's not even thirty. Isn't that
something?"

"Yes. It really is." *It really was*, Maddie thought. He was an intense, accomplished, powerful human being, and he wasn't even
thirty. Maddie agreed with the woman, but she was finding it hard
to make small talk with her when she couldn't forget that Janet was
the man's mother. The man who had just pushed her up against a
refrigerator and kissed the living daylights out of her. And would
he kiss her again? Would he try to paw her in the movie theater?
Or would he sit on the opposite side of his mother, like a chauffeur
or something?

Janet nodded. "I am proud. I know. I'll try to give it a rest."

"No, you don't—" Maddie said too quickly. "I mean, you have
every right to be proud. He's a great guy." Janet looked at her more
closely. Maddie tried to recover. "I mean, I'm sure he's a great guy."
Luckily, said "great guy" was walking up the back path and calling through the screen door.

"You ladies still primping, or are you ready for a big night on
the town?" He swept through the kitchen, and Maddie felt most
of the air leave her lungs. He looked so fine. So clean, she thought
stupidly.

Both Janet and Maddie stood up at the same time. Maddie set

the book down on the coffee table, carefully putting a piece of scrap paper into the fragile paperback to keep her place.

"Uh-oh," Hank muttered.

Maddie looked up, worried. "What?"

"Are you a book princess?"

Janet started laughing.

"A what?" Maddie asked, looking from mother to son.

"A book princess," Janet reiterated. "Hank and his father always made fun of me for how carefully I treated my books."

Maddie smiled. "Then, yes. I am a book princess. I never crack a spine if I can help it. Especially not on something that's forty years old and in perfect condition."

"See?" Janet said. "I told you. Maddie is the perfect . . . renter."

A small silence hovered, then Maddie spoke to end the awkwardness. "So, let's go have our night on the town, shall we?"

Henry held the front door open for Janet to pass through first. When Maddie passed in front of him, he put his hand on her lower back and she turned her head to look at him. "Hey," he said so only she could hear.

She kept walking, but the goofy smile was unpreventable.

"Let's take your car, Henry."

"Okay, Mom. It's open. Hop in."

Janet stood by the front door of the cab of the big pickup truck. It was superclean, and she gestured for Maddie to climb in. "You take the middle, sweetheart. I'm too old to be riding around like that."

"Oh. No, I'll ride in the back—" Maddie peeked in and saw a pile of diving equipment on the seat where she'd offered to sit.

"Do you want me to move that?" Hank asked across the hood of the car.

"Of course not," Janet said. "Maddie, sweetie, just hop in. It's only a few minutes to the theater. He's not going to bite."

Maddie looked at Henry for a split second, and it was a split second too long. He gave her a half-smile that pulled his cheeks up just enough to crinkle his eyes with the promise of all sorts of . . . biting.

"Oh, all right. I don't want to be difficult," Maddie finally agreed. She didn't think that Janet was trying to foist her on her dark and stormy son, but it was starting to feel like it.

Henry got into the driver's side of the cab and sat down, taking up more than his share of the seat. He was just too damn big. His shoulders were . . . ugh, Maddie stopped herself before she started to sound like she was making a laundry list of his stellar masculine attributes. Janet got in and pulled closer to Maddie as she reached around to get her seat belt. The movement pushed Maddie closer into Hank's side, and he breathed slowly through his teeth, just this side of a hiss.

"Off we go!" Janet cried.

Henry almost growled. Maddie reached between her left thigh and Henry's right to find the seat belt.

"What are you doing?" he asked, his voice full of impatience.

"Looking for the seat belt," Maddie said innocently, far more innocently than she felt. He was all freshly showered and smelled like something woodsy and male, and the khakis he was wearing were straining around his leg muscles. How was she supposed to *not* be hyperaware of him? Maddie finally managed to get the buckle into the receptacle and exhaled. "All set." She smiled a wide fake smile for his benefit.

He drove the car like he seemed to do everything else, slowly and carefully, but with that underlying power humming just beneath the surface. In about fifteen minutes they'd driven to a nearby town, and Henry had parked cautiously a few rows away from any other cars, ignoring the closer available spots by the front of the theater.

"Here we are!" Janet proclaimed. She pulled on the door handle, but it was stuck for some reason, and out of habit Henry leaned across the front seat—and across Maddie—and pushed the door open for his mother. Maddie was frozen to the back of the leather seat, trying to control her breathing. "Jesus, Henry," Maddie whispered.

"Sorry," he muttered under his breath, before stepping down from his side of the truck. Maddie took a deep breath and got out behind Janet.

"You okay, honey?" the older woman asked. "You look a little rattled."

"Oh, fine," Maddie lied. "Sometimes I get a little carsick."

"You do? How awful. Also, you haven't had anything to eat in a couple of hours. You probably need some food. Let's get you some nice buttery popcorn."

Great. Did Janet have to make it seem like Maddie was an animal at the zoo that needed to be fed at regular intervals? She looked up to see Henry smiling at his mother's comment and then quickly looking away so he wouldn't catch Maddie's scowl.

"I think I'll survive on a bag of popcorn until my next feeding, Janet."

The three of them were walking across the parking lot. It was still almost broad daylight despite the late hour. These Maine summer days seemed endless. Janet looked mortified that she had insulted Maddie. "Oh, dear. That must have sounded awful. I'm so sorry. You have a healthy appetite, that's all—"

"Mom." Henry patted her back. "You might want to quit while you're ahead."

Maddie looked at the asphalt, then up at Henry. She shook her head at him. Why was he trying to make his mom feel bad about some stupid, offhand comment? It was almost like he was defending Maddie. Which made Maddie feel suddenly warm inside.

"It was nothing," Maddie said. "I'm sorry I was snippy . . . I'm probably hungry." They all laughed, and Janet looked relieved and started talking about the movie, and how she wanted to treat the three of them and insisted on buying the tickets. All Maddie could think about was how much she hoped she got to sit next to Henry and to sneak the occasional touch of his forearm or shoulder.

Henry was in hell. He had Janet sitting on his right, incessantly asking questions about every plot element, which were usually answered about four seconds after she had asked them, in a loud stage whisper. He remembered why he never went to the movies with his mother. He'd told her it was because dark, crowded places made him uncomfortable. Everything seemed nefarious. But the real reason was he couldn't stand the constant yammering.

To make matters a million times worse, Maddie Post was on his left, all freshly scrubbed, with her long, chestnut hair smelling like some lemony shampoo that made him want to rip her shirt off and attack her right there at the multiplex. His shoulders and neck were so tense from *not* touching her that he was probably going to cramp up at work on Monday. She made matters worse by letting her upper arm push into his when something funny or ridiculous happened on the screen. Not that Hank paid even half a mind to the plot of the inane summer blockbuster.

Of course there was some absurd military element to the story, about how some Special Forces team had to swoop in and rescue some of the pod people. All very dramatic and life-and-death. Constant action. Men of action. It was only a movie, Henry reminded himself, but it still pissed him off. The overriding sentiment of *his* military experience had been a nearly incessant boredom, punctuated by moments of intense paranoia, and very infrequently, mortal violence.

He tried not to be such a wet blanket and forced his shoulders to relax. Maddie immediately relaxed into him, leaning her shoulder gently into his and somehow snaking her left hand under her right arm so she could touch his exposed skin, where the short sleeve of his T-shirt ended.

So much for relaxing his shoulders. He turned to face Maddie in the near darkness. Her eyes sparkled off the reflection of the screen.

"What?" she mouthed. And the way the word framed her lips made him nuts. Just like a kiss.

"Cut. It. Out." He wasn't joking.

Maddie looked like he'd really hurt her feelings, then must have seen the heat in his eyes. She dipped her lashes, touched his arm one last time, and then whispered, "All right already. Sheesh."

Good lord, when would this movie end? Henry wondered more than once over the following hour. The credits started to roll as the movie star marine pulled the Hollywood starlet into a sunset-framed kiss and the screen faded to black.

"Whew," Henry said so that only Maddie could hear, then stood up quickly.

"Wasn't that fun?" Janet said.

"Thanks so much, Janet, it was great," Maddie added.

"Yeah, great, Mom."

"Oh, stop it, you big lug. It was just meant to be fun. Not everything is supposed to have some big meaning, you know."

Maddie looked up and teased Henry, giving him a small punch in his rock-hard bicep. "Yeah, Henry, not everything has to be a big deal."

He looked at Maddie as his mother bent down to collect her purse and popcorn container, his green eyes dancing with a combination of impatience and, Maddie had to call it what it was, raw lust. "Just because something is meant to be entertaining doesn't mean it needs to lack . . . attention to detail." His big body was blocking them from Janet's view, and he reached his hand around and squeezed Maddie's behind, right there in the movie theater. He pulled his hand away so quickly it was as though it hadn't even happened.

"Ach—" Maddie gasped.

Janet's head flew up from where she was rustling around on the floor to make sure she had collected everything. "What is it?!"

"Oh," Maddie said, "I almost slipped on some rancid soda spill or something. It just startled me for a second . . . I almost lost my balance."

Henry smiled in that provocative half-smirk and continued up the gentle slope of the carpeted aisle that led out of the theater.

The three of them went for a few slices of pizza at the shop two doors down from the cineplex. Maddie and Henry split a huge, four-meat pie, and Janet ordered her four-cheese. They rolled into the driveway at Janet's around ten.

"That was just about the most fun I've had in years," Janet sighed. "Thanks for hanging with the old lady, you two."

"Oh, Mom. Cut it out. You're not *that* old."

Janet laughed. "Thanks for that *that*, Hank!" She tugged on the car door and was able to push it open this time. Maddie was wondering whether she'd been able to open it all along and had merely feigned weakness earlier so that Henry would have to stretch across Maddie. "Do you want to come in for an iced tea?"

Henry had locked the truck and was standing at the path that split right to his garage apartment and left to the main house. "No, but thanks, Mom. It was good to be out." He leaned in and kissed his mother on the cheek. She smiled up at him and he realized he needed to be a little less of a hard-ass. It probably worried the hell out of her that he was always alone in his apartment or at work.

"I'm so glad, honey." Janet reached up and patted his cheek the way she always did. "Sleep well."

"Good-night, Hank." Maddie tried to sound casual.

"Yeah, see you soon, Maddie." He turned and walked up the wooden steps that led to the upstairs apartment.

CHAPTER 4

See you soon? Was that an invitation? Did he want her to sneak over to his place after his mom fell asleep? Maddie followed Janet into the house and watched as she latched the lock on the back door. Damn it. That was going to make a noise if she let herself out later. After a week in the house, Maddie had a pretty good idea of where the tricky floorboards were that would announce her treachery, but she just didn't feel right about actually unlocking that back door and sneaking out.

Maddie collected her novel from the living room. "'Night, Janet. I'm wiped from work this week. I think I'll turn in."

"I understand, honey. I'm just going to watch a show on the TV down here until I settle. You have a good sleep and enjoy your first day off tomorrow with a good lie-in, eh?"

"Will do," Maddie said. That was probably the biggest lie of all the white lies she'd told this week. The chances of Maddie sleeping a wink when the hottest, sexiest man she'd ever (briefly) had her hands on was about fourteen feet away as the crow flies. She chuckled to herself, picturing the two of them with a pair of soup cans and a string so they could talk to each other across the driveway.

After brushing her teeth and washing her face, Maddie went

back into her bedroom and gave the soup can idea a new think. She'd always been a blackout shade kind of sleeper and had kept the curtains and the horizontal blinds totally closed this entire week. The longest day of the year was in a few days, and even the middle of the night only felt like dusk.

She pulled back the heavy fabric curtains. They looked like they'd been hand-sewn many years ago, weighted down with a thick liner to keep out the cold in winter and the heat in summer. Like so much in Janet's house, it reminded Maddie of the lyric from that Neil Young song. Old but good.

She lifted up the horizontal metal blinds as quietly as she could, and voilá . . . there was a dark window into Henry's apartment, about fifteen feet away, across the air above the driveway. For all she knew, it was only the stairwell or a closet window. She kept staring at it, hoping it was his bedroom.

Ping. The light flicked on and Henry walked into his bedroom. How had Maddie gone a whole week without looking into this guy's apartment? The light in her room was off, but he must know she was there. Or maybe not. She saw him look out his window toward the first floor of his mother's house, probably seeing the telltale flicker of the television and assuming Maddie was down there with Janet. Maddie watched as he paced back and forth at the end of his bed a couple of times, then raked his fingernails through his buzz cut. Maddie felt it deep in her core. She had touched that hair, and the muscles beneath it, a few hours ago. She wanted those hands on her again.

Was she really going to sit in a dark room and watch a grown man get undressed? Was it really wrong? Or just pervy?

She sat down slowly on the end of her bed, which happened to be conveniently located by the pervy window. Maddie slipped off her sneakers quietly and then reached under her shirt and unhooked her bra. She was just getting ready for bed.

She slipped the straps down off her shoulders, then pulled the whole bra off without removing her shirt. She wasn't going to get naked and roll around alone while she watched Hank get undressed. That would have been so porny. She was going to leave her clothes on.

Henry looked across at his childhood bedroom. He thought he'd seen some movement in there, but the light was out and it looked like Maddie and his mom were downstairs watching television. He stood at the window for a while, trying to perceive the imperceptible in the yawning darkness behind the open window of Maddie's room. He pulled his T-shirt off, crossing his hands in front of his chest and peeling it over his head. He stood there by the window, holding the shirt in his hand for a few seconds, staring into the darkness. He shook his head at his own idiocy and turned to put his clothes into the laundry basket. He left the bedroom to wash his face and brush his teeth, then came back after double-checking the lock on his front door and turning out the lights in the living room and kitchen.

He turned on the bedside lamp, then went back to the switch by the bedroom door and turned off the ceiling light. The evening air was cool and he wanted to feel closer to Maddie somehow, if he was being honest. He went back to the window. He stood there in his boxers, listening to the fleeting night sounds of Maine that had always soothed him.

Henry touched the dog tags that still hung around his neck. He didn't feel like they were representative of any great experience he'd had in the Army, but after ten years it just felt weird when he didn't have them on. Like he'd forgotten to brush his teeth or something. The light from the television disappeared from the downstairs window, and Henry waited for the back porch light to turn off a few minutes later. Which it did.

Despite complaining about his mother's crazy idea to take on a boarder, Henry knew Janet could take care of herself. He wasn't going to be some weird serial killer who lived in his mother's basement—or garage, for that matter—well into his forties, but it worked out for both of them to have him here for these few months after he returned from active duty.

He waited a few more minutes, hoping that Maddie's light would turn on. He could hear the final sounds of his mother getting ready for bed, then both houses settled into total silence. Yet he kept standing there.

Maddie must have been in her room that whole time, watching him get undressed before, he thought. He smiled and took off his boxers. He heard the tiny gasp across the small distance that separated them.

"Sleep well, Maddie," he called quietly out the window.

He heard her giggle, and it was a great way to end the day. He crawled into bed, enjoying the feel of the sheets against his naked body. He turned off the bedside lamp and turned into his pillow. Life wasn't all that bad.

Janet left for her job at the library at eight o'clock Saturday morning. Henry was surprised that he'd slept so late, when the sound of her car's engine startled him awake. The type of work he did meant that he worked five days on and five days off. He'd been thinking he might head up to Millinockett to do some backcountry canoeing. But—

The light knock on his door interrupted his thought. He pulled on a pair of loose shorts and walked through his apartment to answer it. Maddie was standing at the top of the wooden stairs, holding two cups of steaming coffee.

"Hey . . ." She didn't look like she'd gotten much sleep. Good, thought Henry, served her right.

"Hey," he answered, without moving aside to let her pass.

She extended her arm, offering him one of the mugs. "Coffee?"

"Sure." He took the mug from her and stood his ground. She was beginning to get distracted by his bare chest. He watched as she took a sip of her coffee and kept her eyes peering over the rim without meeting his eyes.

He took a sip of his coffee. The hot comfort of that first contact made him close his eyes for a second. "Good coffee," he said slowly after he opened his eyes and saw that Maddie was mesmerized, staring—gawking really—at his lips.

"Are you going to invite me in?" Maddie asked, without looking at his eyes.

"Why? You can stare at me just fine here."

She smiled and looked him right in the eye that time, then reached out her slim fingers and touched his chest. "But I don't want to look," she said. "I want to touch."

"Jesus, Maddie." He pulled her into his apartment, doing a quick double take out the front door to see if any nosy neighbors were watching.

She put her mug down on the kitchen counter. It was a marine wood, maybe teak or mahogany, that had been shellacked to a high sheen. "Wow, nice kitchen."

"Did you think I lived in a shed?"

She turned slowly to face him. "Don't be churlish. I came all the way over here, all forward and timid—"

He barked a laugh. "Timid my a—"

She smiled, then punched him lightly on the arm to stop him from finishing the sentence. "I might look all confident and fabulous, but it still takes a little gumption to walk up those steps and knock on that door. Admit it."

He set down his coffee cup. "Maybe I need more convincing . . . about how shy you are . . . Like would you let me do something like this?" He reached around her waist and pulled her flush up against him. She gasped at the loss of air, and from the feeling of being so close to him. She inhaled him.

"I just about died in that movie theater last night," she whispered into his bare chest. She kissed the muscled skin across his pecs. "You smelled so good. I kept trying to take little hits of you. It was awful." She breathed deep again, her nose against his neck. "You are amazing."

He reached his hand into her pajama bottoms and pulled it quickly out when he felt her bare skin. "God, Maddie, are you naked?"

She smiled up at him after kissing his clavicle. "Aren't we all? Under our clothes, I mean."

He pushed her back toward the countertop, putting his palms on the wood behind her and creating an inescapable perimeter around her. She was wriggling in the confined space, kissing him and trailing her light touch all along his ribs and his back.

"How about a few ground rules?" he asked.

Maddie's hands slowed. "I should have figured you'd be a rules guy."

He smiled and kissed her neck, then pulled away. "Rules are good."

"Debatable," she said, standing on her tiptoes to trail her tongue around the edge of his ear.

"Maddie!" he groaned, then grabbed her long hair into a tight knot in his fist and swept his mouth over hers. He could feel the tips of her fingers trembling against his back and pushed the kiss deeper than he should have. She made him crazy, with that combination of bravado and tenderness.

He stepped away from her after a few minutes or hours, he had no idea. "Hot damn, Madison Post."

She smiled at him, all moist and open like she'd been the afternoon before, when his mom had nearly walked in on them kissing by the refrigerator.

"You were saying something about rules." She reached for the hard plane of his stomach. He swatted her away and stepped another few feet out of her reach.

"Yeah." He stretched his neck right and left, then put his hands on his hips. She pictured him doing that in his Army uniform, with dust and sun and slow-motion chaos all around him. Then she looked into his eyes and they were stormy in a way that almost frightened her.

Almost.

"What is it?" Maddie asked, standing up straighter.

"I don't want to sleep with you—"

Maddie stiffened. "Oh, well, okay—"

"Jeez, Maddie. I meant I don't want to sleep with you right away. Let's just hang out and get to know each other better for a little while, okay?"

Her face cleared. "Yeah. Okay. I just thought, you know, that you didn't want to sleep with me . . . ever."

"You're like every man's friggin' dream come true, why would you think that?" He had pulled her into a tight (damnably platonic) hug, so she couldn't see his eyes when he said that part about being his dream come true . . . or every man's, or whatever. She hugged him back.

"No reason," she said into his chest, and started hugging him tighter and moving her hips in a little inviting—

Henry laughed and set her away from him again. "I was thinking of going canoeing this weekend. Want to go?"

"Canoeing?" Maddie asked.

"Yeah. Canoeing. You know. A boat. With a couple of paddles. Maybe a few beers and sandwiches and a tent and—"

"Ooh. I like the tent part."

"Get your mind out of the gutter, Post. I am trying to be a good guy, here. Doesn't every woman want a man who wants to get to know her before he slams her into bed?"

"Slams?" Maddie whispered with wide-eyed hope.

"You are impossible. Do you want to go camping this weekend or not?" He'd reached for his coffee cup and was waiting for her answer while he took a sip. "Or would you rather get a mani-pedi or something on your days off? Chick stuff. Maybe the paddling will be too hard-core for you."

He smiled as he sipped his coffee and watched her face go from dreamy seduction to competitive ferocity. "Too hard-core? Do you know who you're talking to?"

He shook his head no. "But I'm sure I'm about to find out."

She pointed at her chest. "I am one of the top five rowers in the NCAA Division One rankings."

"Is that where you all pull at the same time and someone calls out from the front of the boat? Sounds like synchronized swimming compared to crossing the English Channel." He shrugged his shoulders. She was so easy. He watched her violet eyes darken and the pupils tighten.

"Synchronized swimming? I bet I could kick your ass—"

He looked down at his muscled torso then across at her lithe, sinewy abdomen.

"Not in a fistfight, you jerk!" she exclaimed. "Endurance. Something that would really compare apples to apples."

He stared at her breasts through the thin, ribbed tank top she was wearing. Her naked breasts. Naked under her clothes, he amended.

"Look at me," she demanded.

"I am looking at you." His eyes slid slowly up from her breasts to meet her tempestuous eyes. "Right. At. You."

"Ugh! Men are impossible. All right. Fine. I'll go on your manly canoeing expedition. And I'll kick your ass. Down in front in twenty, soldier." She pivoted to grab her coffee cup and stormed out of his apartment.

Twenty minutes later, she came out of his mom's house in another pair of those too-short khaki shorts and a clean black T-shirt.

"How many of those black T-shirts you got, Post?"

"None of your business. I'm at a bit of a disadvantage since I only have my duffle bag. Would it be cheating if I asked to borrow a backpack so I don't have to hike into the backwoods of Maine with a useless piece of luggage over one shoulder?"

"Sure. And it's not a competition, you know? We're just going camping."

"Yeah, whatever, Henry."

He laughed as he went up the stairs to get a backpack. He was back in a few minutes and tossed Maddie the old blue one he'd used as a book bag in high school. She held it up. "Is this from this century?"

"You know what they say about beggars and choosers, right? Maybe you want to stick with your duffle?" He reached for the blue pack, and she pulled it out of his reach.

"Never mind," she grumbled. "Thank you."

She started pulling a couple of T-shirts and underwear and her bathroom stuff out of her duffle and transferring it into the small backpack. In her rush to get ready, she had forgotten to zip up her cosmetics bag and a strip of six condoms fell out like a tiny accordion, the shiny metallic wrapper catching the morning sun.

"Maddie!"

"What? I might meet someone while I'm camping." She reached down and grabbed the packets. "Best to be prepared, my mom always said."

He burst out laughing and went back to organizing the camping gear in the backseat. He'd pulled the canoe out of the garage and set it into the flatbed of the truck, securing it with some rope and bungee cords.

"Done packing, Post?"

"Yes." She threw the blue pack into the backseat, then picked up the empty duffle. "Let me put this back up in my room and leave your mom a note. She'll be fine if we're gone when she gets home from work, right?"

"Are you kidding? She'll be thrilled. She'll have us married with children by Monday morning."

Maddie kept walking toward the house without looking back. She was mildly disconcerted by how Henry had said "married with children," as if it were the most laughable prospect imaginable. She tried not to let her mind wander into the strange paranoiac minefield of thinking about whether he was opposed to married-with-children-with-anyone or married-with-children-with-Maddie. As if that would ever be her problem. She shook her head and jogged up the stairs to the second floor to toss her useless duffle into her closet, went back to the kitchen, jotted down a quick note to Janet, then locked the back door. She walked around to the front door and double-checked that it was locked too.

"All set," Maddie said. "Let's hit it."

Hank was leaning against the cab of the truck with his arms folded across his chest, watching her move with all that restless energy.

"Come on!" She snapped her fingers up close to his face and he grabbed her hand before she realized he'd even moved. He pulled her fingers to his lips. "Relax, Post."

She took a deep breath. "I'll try."

He kept her hand in his. "We'll work on it together. Okay?"

"Okay." She stood there for a few more seconds. "But, we should go—"

"Get in the truck, bossy boots." He opened the door and kept her hand in his as he helped her into the driver's side of the truck and she slid across to the passenger's side.

"Thanks," she said.

❧

Within a few minutes, they were out of Blake and on I-95 heading north into the wilds of central Maine. The trees. That was all Maddie could think about. The trees. The trees. The trees.

"There are so many trees." She must have said it five times already.

"Yeah," Hank agreed for the fifth time, not even making fun of her. "There really are."

He had a satellite radio hooked up to his car and it was tuned to some classic rock station. He reached to change it, expecting Maddie to want some alternative rock or pop, when an old classic came on.

"Wait! Do you mind? I love that song. I love that they make it to Mexico. Is that wrong of me? That they rob that guy and get away with it?"

He turned to face her. Their windows were rolled down and she was lounging against the opposite side of the seat, sort of sprawled out with her back in the space where the seat met the door. She had kicked off her sneakers and her long legs were distracting, one beneath her and one near the suspension ridge in the floor.

"Who wouldn't want them to get away with it?" Hank asked.

"Probably the guy they killed while robbing?"

Hank laughed. "Hey. They only shot him. They never said he died."

Maddie laughed. "An optimist. I like it."

"But you're right, maybe that guy. But everyone *else* wants them to get away. It's like a modern day Robin Hood story. Chicks love that shit."

Maddie stared at his hard jaw and his cocky smirk. "You are

kind of a jerk sometimes. You know you like the song—" She shook her head and stopped talking so she could keep listening to the final chords. The song timed out, and another song came on. Another California '70s kind of rock song.

"Go on," he prompted. "You were going to say how chicks don't love Steve Miller?"

"No, I wasn't going to say that. I was just going to say that you didn't have to try to belittle everything to be cool." She stopped looking at him and forced herself to look at more trees out her window.

"You think I'm cool?" He prodded her thigh with his right hand. "Admit it. You think I'm cool."

She repressed a smile. He didn't deserve it. Yet. "I'm just saying . . . if one *were* to think you were *possibly* cool, it wouldn't be necessary to be all judge-y about everything to solidify that opinion . . . of your coolness."

He stifled a laugh and kept his eyes on the road.

"Well?" Maddie asked.

"Wait . . . were you speaking English just then? You lost me at something-something cool, then something-something coolness."

Maddie shook her head and her smile widened. "Whatever, Mr. Big Man. You've got everything sewn up tight." She kept looking out the window and missed the way Henry's face clouded at her words. He wasn't sure himself why that sewn-up-tight comment had scraped across him like it had. He didn't like it.

"Let's play some games—" he said.

"Okay." Maddie was like a puppy, practically bouncing up and down in the seat. She widened her eyes and lowered her voice. "What kind of games, Hank?"

He laughed again. "Word games! Are you a nymphomaniac or

something? Has it been more than your usual seven days without getting any?"

He was still smiling, but she took it wrong. He thought he was still being funny. Sort of. Shit. He should have known she wasn't going to like him basically calling her a two-bit whore.

"Sorry. I didn't mean that like it came out," he tried.

"Whatever, Hank. You're safe with the sex-starved co-ed. Not to worry. I'll get my daily dose in town behind the diner like I've been doing this past week."

"Maddie, c'mon. It was a joke. The condoms falling out of your bag and all that. Lighten up."

All of his suggestions that she relax or lighten up or take it easy were starting to set Maddie off. "You know what, Hank—"

"Oh, here we go—"

"Yeah, here we go—"

He slowed down the truck. "Am I going to need to turn around, because this is as good a place as any—"

"Darn it, Hank! What is your problem?" Maddie felt frustration welling up. Why couldn't this guy just be normal?

He continued to slow down the truck. "This was a bad idea."

"No it wasn't. Keep driving. Cut it out. You are being such a baby."

"*I* am being a baby?" But he started to accelerate again.

"Yes, you are being a baby. We were going to have fun and relax, remember?"

"Yeah, I remember. I suggested it. So why did you have to go and get all sensitive about me accusing you of being a hooker?"

She whipped her head around and was ready to rip his head off, but he was smiling that secret, really good smile and she just shook her head and looked at him instead.

"What?" he said, still smiling.

"I bet you get a lot of mileage out of that smile."

"As a matter of fact, I do."

"You're like one of those girls who just bats her eyelashes and everyone does what she wants . . . no effort."

He flexed his biceps by squeezing the steering wheel and dipped his chin close to the bulging muscle, showing off like a body builder. "Oh, there's plenty of effort. You don't get to bat these eyelashes without being able to bench two-fifty."

"There's no way you bench two-fifty," Maddie scoffed. "That's just something guys say at bars."

"You calling me a liar?" He was challenging her, but the smile was there and she felt more like she wanted to kiss him than kill him again.

"Maybe a little white liar. But yes. My brothers always say stuff like that, and it's always a crock. I read somewhere that sixty-nine percent of men think they are in shape and in reality only thirteen percent are."

"Do you think I'm in shape, Maddie?"

He was such a tease. When he talked to her like that, with that deep, rolling suggestive voice, she felt all quivery and shaky inside.

"You know I do." She looked out the window, hating to admit how attracted she was to his body. It seemed wrong, somehow, insulting to him, to just be hot for him because she wanted him for sex.

He laughed. "See. That's the great divide, right there."

"What is?"

"You probably feel guilty because you only want me for my body and you shouldn't. Feel guilty, I mean."

She smiled her encouragement. "Go on."

"I don't feel the least bit guilty for wanting your body . . . and you probably think I should. Feel guilty, I mean."

He kind of had a point. She twisted her lips the way she always did when something rankled. "But . . ."

"Mm-hmm." He looked at her for a few more seconds, then focused back on the turn that was coming up after the straightaway that had taken them through the wide valley north of Bangor.

"I think it's the 'only' that's the sticking point."

It was his turn to encourage her. "Yes?"

"Yeah. I mean, think about it."

He smirked. "I'll give it a shot, Post."

"You know what they say about hiding your lamp under a bushel, Gilbertson."

"Point taken. Go on. I'll try to keep up."

She rolled her eyes. "I just mean telling someone that you *only* want them for their body is kind of like telling a chef how to cook. It's a package deal. It's a whole recipe. You can't just walk into a restaurant and stroll into the kitchen and say, more oregano, I hate onions."

"Sure you can. People order like that all the time."

Maddie smiled. "But they don't really like to eat."

He laughed hard. "You might have a point."

"Seriously." She was warming to her theory. "If you want to bang some chick—"

"Maddie—"

She swiped her hand to cut him off. "You know what I mean. One night stand. Whatever. Don't trip me up. I'm on a roll."

He smiled. "Go on, then."

"I mean, if you want to just *use* someone for sex, there has to be something about *them* that you want . . . not just their flesh."

"This is a deadly dangerous conversation. You might be painting me into a corner so I'll say something you'll use against me."

"Oh, cut it out. Consider this the all-clear or whatever you would call it in the Army. All bets are off. Say what you will. I won't hold it against you."

"Women always say that."

Maddie shook her head in dismay. "Darn it, Hank. Who are '*all these women*' that you keep talking about? It's so annoying!"

"Simmer down, tiger. I just meant, that's always the way when *the women I have dated*—and banged—in the past drew me into the quicksand of let's-have-a-real-discussion type discussions. Maybe you are different."

"Talk about quicksand. If I say, 'Yes, I am so different from other women,' then I am some arrogant twit. If I say, 'No, I'm just like that. Tricky. Wily. Trying to trap men into saying all sorts of stuff they don't really mean . . .' Doesn't leave me much wiggle room."

"Okay, okay. Go back to your theorizing. At the very least, I like to hear your voice and watch your lips twist around when you're trying to get your mind around an idea."

"You're impossible."

"Totally," he said with another smile. "But you like me this way, so keep going. Please."

"Oh, all right. It sounds stupid now that we've lost track of what was really just a little aside. But here's the thing: by saying I just want someone for x, y, or z it's like you are totally denying that they are a whole person. They are just some object. A tool."

Hank tapped the steering wheel for a few minutes. Thinking. Finally he started talking. "But. Now hear me out. Sometimes you need a tool. I use very specific tools on my job. There are very specific wrenches and gauges and valves and—"

"But those *are* objects!" Maddie said over a laugh.

His smirky, wide-eyed look silenced her. "May I finish?"

"Yes," she said, chastised.

"And sometimes people *want* to be used like that. To be taken in hand."

Oh, Jesus. He did it again. The slow, deep, suggestive, this-means-nothing, this-means-everything voice. Maddie felt like she might melt right into the seat of the car.

"Yeah? And?" She tried to sound blasé.

"Yeah and nothing. It's just a fact. I think people sometimes just want the cigar. It doesn't need to be all Freudian and meaningful. It can be great and not be attached to everything that ever happened in the universe. It can just be a thing."

"Eloquent." Maddie sneered.

"Preach not to others what they should eat, but eat as becomes you and be silent."

She stared at him. "Picked up a little Epictetus in the Middle East, did you?"

"Something like that." He put his elbow on the edge of his window and looked peevish.

"Something like what? Where did you get the philosophy degree, and why do you act all anti-intellectual and then go and quote Epictetus to me?"

"West Point." He barely said it loud enough.

"Yeah right." Maddie inhaled to laugh and then realized he was serious. "You went to West Point? How? When? I thought you enlisted on your eighteenth birthday."

He looked at her and narrowed his eyes. "My mother been singing my praises to you?"

"Something like that." Maddie smirked back and tried to ignore him. Why would he act all gruff and dumb when he had a degree from West Point?

He rolled up the window and turned the air-conditioning on. "Sorry. It's getting too windy. It's giving me a headache." A negative side effect of being in the water for so many hours a day, Hank's ears pretty much always bothered him.

"That's fine." Maddie rested her hands on her lap. She figured if he wanted to tell her about West Point or any other secret facts about himself, he could do so of his own accord. She wasn't going to pry around like some desperate . . . person.

After listening to the radio for a couple of songs, Maddie started to feel sleepy. "Do you mind if I crash for a few minutes?"

He turned to look at her. "Sure. Are you tired? I thought you went to bed early last night?"

"Very funny. I couldn't sleep a wink knowing you were naked in your bed a few feet away."

He smiled and shook his head. "I don't care if I hurt your feelings, Madison Post, you are a hussy."

She started laughing softly as she nestled her cheek against the front seat. "You're probably right. If wanting you makes me a hussy." Her eyes were closed when she said it, and Hank had to force himself to breathe evenly.

How could she just say everything like that? At some point in Henry's childhood, he had missed that whole chapter on expressing your feelings clearly. Or at all. Maddie just blurted everything flat out. I like you. I want you. You are hot. You are cool.

Hank felt like he was always standing on trial, in the dock, being interrogated, on the record, making it count. He was such a liar for trying to convince her that most people wanted just this or just that for quick satisfaction. That he wanted to use people like he used the tools of his trade. He couldn't even use his own brain openly without feeling like he was a showy bastard.

He turned off the radio and drove the rest of the way in silence, enjoying the slow, even rhythm of Maddie's steady breathing. Especially the occasional sleepy hum and sigh.

CHAPTER 5

"Are we here?" Maddie was groggy. "How long was I asleep?" She looked up at the bright sun reflecting through the tall trees that shaded the car. Hank turned off the engine.

"Hey, did you have a good rest?"

Maddie was slower and softer when she was just waking up. She hadn't had time to marshal her resources, thought Hank. He reached out and caressed her cheek where she'd just lifted it away from the upholstery.

"Yeah." She put her hand over his. "It's nice to wake up to you." She closed her eyes again, still half-asleep.

Hank felt something hot and slow slice through him, like an evisceration. He left his hand on her cheek—mostly because hers had trapped his beneath it—and it would have seemed rude to yank it away. But he wanted to yank it away.

He cleared his throat. She released her hand and arched her back to stretch her neck and shoulders after being asleep in that awkward position. He stared at her chest and then opened his door and stepped out of the car. It was even worse when she wasn't intentionally trying to mess with him.

Walking to the back of the truck, Hank shook his head to clear the image of all that nakedness right there under that T-shirt and sports bra. He started undoing the ropes and bungees that held the canoe in place and then paused to watch Maddie let herself out of her side of the cab, leaving the door open. She bent down and stretched, placing her hands flat on the bed of pine needles—and her ass in the air— and then reached up as high as she could, standing on her tiptoes.

She let her arms down slowly, then turned to look at him.

"So how far are we going?"

"What do you mean?"

"I thought we were going for some kind of deep-woods version of *Camping with the Stars*. I want the full military treatment. I can take it."

"You can, can you?"

"Yeah, no girls on trip."

"What's that?" He was back to untying the restraints. Maddie had leaned into the backseat to start unloading the tent and the backpacks and other gear Hank had brought along.

She leaned her head out so she could see him. "No. Girls. On. Trip."

He started laughing. "What the hell does that mean?"

"It's an old family joke. I'm the youngest. I have three older brothers. And I am a girl." She smirked and curtseyed. "As you can see."

He smiled. "Yeah, I see."

She leaned back in to get the canoe paddles, then shut the car door. "My older brothers used to go hiking with my dad, and when I was about ten or eleven I said I wanted to go, and my brothers started chanting, 'no-girls-on-trip.' So I've got a little bit of a complex, I guess."

Hank pulled the canoe out of the bed of the truck and flipped the gate back up into place.

"Well, I like girls-on-trip, so we're good."

She put her hands on her hips and tilted her head. "You make no sense to me, Henry Gilbertson."

He shrugged. "Oh well. Luckily I never promised to make sense to you."

She smiled, deciding not to get drawn into another nit-picky argument about semantics and who promised what to whom, and tried not to feel sad about promises that Hank didn't want to make.

"Okay, how should we portage?" Maddie lifted up her backpack. "Also, this is really light, so if you want me to carry the tent, I can attach it to the bottom of the pack."

"First of all, *we* are not going to portage the canoe. *I* am going to portage the canoe. And yes, tie the tent onto your pack and I'll take the rest."

Pulling her eyebrows together, Maddie bent to attach the tent to the bottom of the pack. "You don't have to carry it all by yourself. We could split the weight."

"Have you ever portaged a canoe before?"

She wasn't looking at him. Maddie was trying not to pick a fight, but if he wasn't going to let her do her share, it was going to be all wrong.

"Well, not technically."

"What's that supposed to mean?" Hank had moved around to where she was standing and bent to pick up his pack and the two sleeping bags. He used the hood of the truck like a worktable and attached a sleeping bag to either side of his rucksack.

"It means," Maddie flipped her face up to look at him from her crouched position near his feet, "that the place where we usually go camping leaves the canoes for us, so we don't have to actually portage."

Hank smiled and rested one arm on the hood of the truck. "How convenient. And no one ever steals all those canoes just resting on the side of the lake."

Maddie mumbled something indistinguishable.

"What was that?" Hank knew she was embarrassed.

"I said, it's a private lake."

"Like the whole lake belongs to a club or something?"

"Something."

Hank whistled. "You mean, your family owns the whole lake, don't you?"

She shouldered the knapsack into place, trying to adjust it to make up for the drag and awkwardness of the heavy tent weighing it down at the bottom. Maddie tried to busy herself with the straps and the minor modifications to avoid answering the question.

He shook his head and didn't push it. He returned his attention to lashing the sleeping bags. "What's your cell phone number, in case we get separated?"

"I don't have one."

Hank looked up to the treetops, trying not to lose his composure entirely. He exhaled slowly. "Of course you have a cell phone. Did you forget it?"

She shook her head no.

"Did you lose it?"

"No. I just can't afford one right now."

Hank finished attaching the sleeping bags, tugged on the straps to make sure they were secure, and pulled the whole bundle onto his shoulders with an easy toss.

"So let me get this straight. You have an entire lake, but you can't afford a cell phone?"

"That pretty much sums it up. And it's not *my* lake. It's my grandmother's."

They stared at each other, each of them holding their thumbs beneath the straps at their shoulders.

Maddie's gaze slid to the forest floor near her feet and she decided to just spill the beans. "Look. My brother made this stupid bet with me. . . ."

Hank kept looking at her, but his expression changed from humor to wariness. "What kind of bet?"

She took a deep breath. "My brother acts like I am this spoiled brat—and I'll admit it, my mom totally spoils me—but I am not spoiled . . . just because my mother loves me—" She looked up into Hank's eyes and hoped she didn't sound like she was overly defensive.

"Go on."

She shook out her shoulders. "So . . . I think he was just joking when he said he didn't think I could go three months without talking to my mom, or asking for money, or buying a new pair of shoes just because I felt like it. . . ."

Hank's eyes narrowed. "And?"

"And when I said I actually wanted to do it he started backpedaling and I held him to it and—I was angry and I wanted him to pay up—so we made a bit of an insane wager. . . ."

"How insane?" Hank asked quietly.

"Fifty thousand dollars of insane."

Hank coughed to cover his disbelief. "Your brother is going to pay you fifty thousand dollars to be a normal person for three months?"

Maddie burst out laughing. "Well . . . yeah . . . when you put it like that it's even more ridiculous. But, yes, that's pretty much the crux of it." She kicked the dirt at her feet again then lifted her eyes to his. "And he's not giving the fifty thousand to me. He's going to have to give it to some worthwhile charity . . . I'll think of something good."

Hank stayed quiet and Maddie started to question why she had told him at all. She tried to stuff the realization that she wanted him to know everything about her. She wanted to open herself to this guy in a way she had never wanted to open up to anyone.

"You think I'm ridiculous." She said it with a quiet resignation, as if all the grit and heart she was trying to prove she had was never going to be enough to earn the respect of Hank Gilbertson.

"I don't think you're ridiculous, Maddie." She had started to turn away and he pulled her back with a gentle hold on her upper arm. "Come on." He pulled her into a quick hug, then released her. "I still wish you had a cell phone, though . . . it's not safe."

Maddie held his gaze. She might have been five inches shorter, but she was not going to be the one to lose this battle of the wills. Hank finally relaxed his shoulders. "This is such a bad idea, but okay."

"Good!" Maddie's smile beamed, and he had a hard time staying irritated with her. She was too damned cheerful.

"Moderately good," Hank added.

"Okay, fine. Moderately good!" But she said it with all the enthusiasm she felt.

She loved camping.

A few hours later, she conceded that he was right about the portaging. He had rigged up his canoe with some sort of head strap thing and he carried it like an African woman might carry water from a well. When the paths were wide enough, she walked beside him, but for the most part she stayed behind him and enjoyed the incredible smells and textures and sights all around them.

Despite her initial excitement and enthusiasm, Maddie had calmed. She'd always loved the woods and found it settling and reassuring on some deep level to just walk through tall trees or paddle through quiet lakes.

By two o'clock she was starving.

"Hey, can I have one of the sandwiches? We don't need to stop."

Hank had been leading them through some old path that was apparently one of his childhood favorites. No one was anywhere in view or within earshot. She had a momentary flutter of fear—who the hell was this guy anyway, and what was she doing with him alone in the middle of nowhere? It wasn't even the middle of nowhere. Blake was the middle of nowhere. This was like a three-hour drive and a two-hour hike from the middle of nowhere.

He tipped the canoe over and set it down easily on the ground in the small clearing. "We can stop. I'm hungry, too, and my neck could use a rest."

"Okay." Maddie peeled off her backpack, the hot, sweaty T-shirt and skin beneath cooling as soon as the air made contact. "Man, that feels good."

"We're almost there. It's worth the hike."

"Hey. You're funny."

Hank pulled out two of the peanut butter sandwiches he'd made that morning and handed one to Maddie. "Bon appétit."

"Are you fluent in French as well as Epictetus?"

"Very funny."

She sat cross-legged on the ground, then looked up at him and used the back of her hand to push a strand of chestnut hair out of her eyes. "Are you going to sit down?"

"Wasn't planning on it."

"Okay." She opened the ziplock bag and took a grateful bite of the sandwich. "Yum!" she moaned around the food. "What is this?"

He liked the sound of her satisfaction. "Secret ingredients."

"It's awesome. Don't you love how food tastes outside? Why is that? Food just tastes better outside." She took a swig off her water bottle and then another bite of the sandwich. "Honey?" she said through a mouth full of food.

Hank nodded and watched her eat. Her mouth was the worst. The best worst. Totally distracting. He couldn't really look at her because he kept staring at her lips and not listening to what she was saying. And despite his devil's advocacy in the truck, at base he agreed with her that thinking it was ever cut-and-dried to have sex with someone and never think about it (or them) again wasn't really his style.

She popped the last bite into her mouth and wrapped her lips around her index finger to get the last crumbs. "Yum! That was just the best. Thank you." She slapped her hands on her thighs and then stood up. "Are you going to eat yours?"

Hank looked down and realized he was still holding his sandwich in his right hand, the bag unopened.

"Now that you're done watching me eat mine?" The witch gave him a saucy wink and wandered deeper into the forest. "Nature calls! I'll be back in five!"

And she was gone. His immediate response was a little patter of panic. He hated that she didn't have a cell phone. He would have brought his walkie-talkies if she hadn't been such an airhead and had remembered to tell him before they'd driven the full three hours. He'd heard all sorts of stories about how disoriented people could get in the woods. The slant of the light, the trick of the shadows: it could all wreak havoc on even the most accomplished outdoorsman. Hank had orienteered in all of these woods and wasn't worried, but Maddie was so easily distracted, what if she—

"Hey. Why do you look so serious? And eat your sandwich already. I want a swim."

Oh, Jesus. Just what he needed. He was almost certain he hadn't spotted a bathing suit when she was transferring her clothes from her duffle into his backpack. She was going to go all Hero and Leander on him. He scowled at the idea of having to watch her nubile body pulling effortlessly through the steely blue lake water, then ate his sandwich in a few unsatisfactory gulps.

"You don't lie. This is awesome." Maddie dropped her bag.

"Almost there" had meant another forty-five minutes through the forest. Her body was warm and humming.

"Do you want to canoe for a bit now?" Hank asked.

"Shouldn't we set up camp first?"

"We can, but it stays light up here for ages. Hours more."

"Oh. Okay. Then sure, let's get the canoe in the water already."

They were on the edge of a huge lake that wove through a series of gently sloping hills. "Are those mountains?"

"I guess they once were. They've worn down over time. I think they're Devonian."

"You think they're what?"

"Devonian." He pronounced it slowly, each syllable overly accented.

"What the heck is Devonian?"

"It was about halfway through the Paleozoic Era. About four hundred million years ago. Give or take."

"Do you just keep stuff like that in your brain?"

He shrugged. "I tend to remember dates."

Maddie laughed and it sang out onto the lake and rose clear above them. "Four hundred million years of dates? That's a lot to remember."

"Are you making fun of me?"

She stopped smiling. Completely. "What? No." She looked at the ground. "I like you." She looked back up to look at him. "Why would I want to make you feel bad?"

God. Damn. It. Hank wasn't sure how many more of these gut-piercing truths he was going to be able to stand. Yes, Hank. Good question. Why would you want to make someone feel bad? Who would do such a thing, Hank? Hmm? You would.

He took a deep breath. "Sorry. Forget it. Let's get in the canoe. This'll be great."

But it wasn't. It wasn't great at all. Because if there was one thing Maddie could bring to the party it was her share of endurance and upper body strength, and she pulled too hard on her strokes.

"Cut it out!" Hank finally called out.

"You cut it out!" Maddie snapped back. "I keep trying to go on the opposite side from where you're going so we can keep heading in one direction and then you switch sides and I feel like we are going to go in circles so I switch sides and then you do it again! Just pick a side already!"

This did not bode well. If she was this bossy in a boat, Hank could only imagine how bossy she'd be in bed.

"Why don't I just sit here in the back and let you paddle for a while, Post?"

"Good idea," she said on a huff and began pulling them along at a steady clip toward the far end of the lake.

Hank sat with the paddle resting across his thighs and stared at her back and her hips. He was momentarily tempted to set down his paddle and do something about the aching pull that was starting to gather in his lap. Maybe letting her take charge wasn't such a bad idea. In the boat or in the bed, he thought, then smiled because he felt like a Dr. Seuss character.

"Are you laughing at me?" she asked, without looking over her shoulder.

"I didn't make a sound."

"I know. But I can sort of feel you smiling back there."

"I'm happy. What else do you want me to do?"

She held up the dripping paddle and they coasted quietly through the water. Maddie turned her head slowly so she could look at him over her right shoulder. "You're happy?"

"You don't have to sound so surprised, you know?"

"Okay. I'll try not to sound surprised. I know we only met a week ago, but you didn't strike me as the *happy* type." She had turned back and resumed paddling. "More grudgingly accepting than happy, I'd say."

"How miserable. Is that how I seem?" It was easier talking to her straining back, probably because he didn't have to see her curved lips. She shrugged, and he liked the way the movement pulled her T-shirt up so he could see the skin at the small of her back.

"How should I know? It's not like you set your emotions out on a platter."

He laughed a little. "Now that's probably true."

She smiled over her shoulder and winked. "I'm not a total airhead."

He didn't think he had actually called her an airhead out loud, but he felt guilty for thinking it just the same.

"Should I start paddling back to camp?"

"Probably. I'll need to go catch dinner."

"Oh, how primitive. I love it. Did you bring a bow and arrow? Are you a trapper?" She kept paddling, and he had the wonderful vision of being a trapper, in another time, with his little Sacagawea guiding him through the wilderness.

"Nothing so heroic. Just a fishing rod."

"Oh. Well, I suppose a girl has to make allowances." She kept pulling the canoe with strong, confident strokes.

"You're good with the paddle."

"Thanks."

The silence of their voices let the sounds of the lake blossom around them: the gentle slap of the water against the edge of the canoe, the little brushes of noise near the shore, the occasional loon crying out for his mate. It was beautiful in that spiritually calming way that Maddie only found in these rare moments of pure, deep silence. "Thanks," she repeated, in a reverent whisper this time.

"You're welcome," Hank said with a gentle nod to the sloping hills in the distance. He was glad he'd brought her here.

CHAPTER 6

The lake was so remote and so full of fish, they caught four in ten minutes. *They* didn't really catch them, Hank did, and he held them up by their gills and taunted her. "You know how to clean these?"

She put her hands on her hips. "As a matter of fact I do." She took the fish from him and made a bed of leaves. She set them down carefully on the makeshift tray and took out her Swiss Army knife. Hank stared, probably waiting for her to screw it up, she thought skeptically. "Part of no-girls-on-trip training. Worms. Fish. Squirrels. Pheasants. You name it, I had to gut it."

"That might be the sexiest thing I've ever heard."

Maddie looked up and blew that strand out of her eyes again. "Ew. Why would that ever in a million years be sexy?"

Hank rinsed his hands in the lake, then walked over to their packs and started to undo the tent bag. "I don't know, maybe some caveman response to you being able to feed me." He pounded his chest twice with his fist.

She kept looking at him and the obvious turn of her thoughts from gutting fish to having him do something crude and caveman-like to her body crackled between them. He kept staring at her. Maybe now that they'd made it through the Nemean Lion of a three-hour drive without her asking for a pit stop, and the Lernean

Hydra of portaging, and the Ceryneian Hind of canoeing, and now the Augean Stables of fish-gutting—just maybe they could skip right ahead to the part where Hercules is granted immortality, forgiveness, and a bride in the bargain. A weekend bride.

"What are you thinking about?" Hank asked. He was driving the tent stakes into the ground with a small hammer and not looking at her.

"The Twelve Labors of Hercules."

"Of course you are."

She smiled and kept her attention on the fish. Maddie had already removed the heads and tails, cleaned all the guts, sliced off the little fins, and deboned them to splay them out into filets the way she liked.

"Did you bring a pan?" she asked.

"Nope."

"Okay." She went to the water's edge and rinsed the cleaned pieces of fish and wrapped them up in the leaves. "I'll be right back."

Hank looked up from the last tent stake and watched her amble off into the dimming forest. "Don't go far!" he called.

"I won't," she called back, her voice floating from the dense emptiness.

She returned several minutes later with a few long sticks, then proceeded to sit on a rock by the edge of the lake and whittle the bark off the ends of a few of the sticks. Then she created eight shorter sticks, smooth and sharp. She retrieved the fish and pierced them, creating two perpendicular pieces that fit neatly into the end of the longer stick. When put together, the whole thing became a rough-hewn frame into which each of the filets was elegantly secured. When she was finished she stood all four sticks in the soft ground. "Bon appétit!"

"I have to say, I'm impressed, Post."

"Thanks, Gilbertson."

She looked down at her hands and her dusty self. "Do you mind if I go for a swim?"

It was turning into a gorgeous early evening, the purples and oranges of the sky beginning to rise up from the horizon to crowd out the piercing blue of the late afternoon sky.

"Sure. I guess." He stood staring at her.

"Want to come?"

His stomach coiled tight. Did he want to come? Was she joking? He honestly didn't know. If she was joking, that is.

"Sure. I'll swim."

"Awesome!" She reached for her backpack and he thanked everything that was holy when she whipped out a bikini.

"Back in a flash!" She jogged off into the forest again and was back a couple minutes later looking as hard and ready as an Olympic swimmer on the starting block.

"Jesus, Maddie."

She looked down at herself. "What?"

"Nothing." He scowled and pulled off his shirt, then bent down to take off his hiking boots and socks. Still in his cargo shorts, he waded a few feet into the freezing water, then dove long and elegantly across the surface and below.

Maddie took a moment to appreciate him in his natural habitat. He was definitely meant to be in the water. His long body rose to the surface and swam with long strokes, about a hundred feet out into the lake. He turned back to face her, treading water. "It's amazing! Get in here!" he called.

She took it back about the happiness thing. He definitely knew how to be happy. Apparently he just had to be wet.

She stepped onto the cool, wet stones at the water's edge and then walked a few feet into the shallows. It took every bit of control she had in her to resist the urge to scream at the icy temperature.

"Too cold for you, Post?"

"Nope!" she cried, way too quickly. She sounded like an auctioneer yelling sold.

"What are you waiting for?" he prodded.

She took a deep pull of air, relaxed her shoulders, and dove in. When she came up for air, she was beyond caring. "Oh my god! This is freezing!"

Her lips were trembling, and she swam to him as hard and fast as she could to try to raise her body temperature. "How long before we die of hypothermia?" she asked through chattering teeth, when she reached him.

"Come here." He pulled her hard and fast against him. His body was so warm and strong compared to the arctic deep that touched her everywhere she wasn't touching him. He held her firmly under her arms, his arms snaking around her back. He could almost cross his forearms behind her.

"You feel good," he whispered.

She reached her hands up to circle his neck. "So do you." For some reason, she didn't want to initiate the next move. She wanted to kiss him so badly, but all that hooker and hussy talk had gotten under her skin. Maddie wrapped her legs around his hard middle, linking her ankles together at the base of his spine. He made treading water appear effortless.

"Am I too much?" she asked. She hadn't meant it as a double entendre, but of course it came out that way.

"Probably," he said over a groan, then took her mouth in a possessive, demanding kiss.

The freezing water swirled around them, and the warmth of his mouth and his skin seemed so hot by comparison. Maddie felt everything in the extreme: the cold of the water, the warmth of his skin, the slick welcome of his mouth. His lips started roaming down her neck, and her head dipped back into the water. His hand was there to cradle the back of her skull. He pulled her tighter against him and began to breathe harder as he kissed her neck. Hank moved his lips back up to the lobe of her ear, his legs never stopping the continuous scissoring stroke that kept them both afloat.

"Still cold?" he whispered with a near-painful tug on her ear.

"Not on that part of my ear at least."

His laugh rumbled deep in his chest, and she felt it thrum through her. She pushed her breasts more firmly against him.

"My front half is pretty warm too," she added.

He kissed her again, taking his time, feeling the bend and ease of her spine as he found the edges and dips of her desire. His tongue traced the line of her jaw. "Mine too," Hank said.

"Come on, you're starting to get too cold. I'll race you." He pushed her away from him, catapulting her toward the shore. She kind of adored how he could toss her body around like that.

She could feel his presence behind her and pulled harder to beat him to the shore. Maddie ran out of the freezing water and dove into her backpack to take out the small face towel she'd packed. It was enough to pat herself dry. She hunched over her bag and tried to casually take her freezing wet bikini off without making a big deal about it. She pulled on her sweatpants and then pulled the sweatshirt over her wet top, then reached under and removed the wet bathing suit, keeping herself covered with the loose hoodie.

"All set?" Hank asked. She turned to face him and realized he was still standing there sopping wet and must have been staring at her the whole time.

"Yeah. Did you enjoy the show?" She hoped he did.

"One good strip deserves another, right?"

Maddie caught her breath when she thought he was going to give her a full Monty right then and there. He must have followed her salacious train of thought. He shook his head right and left. "Not now, Post. I meant last night when you were watching me under cover of darkness."

She smiled and folded her arms across her chest. "You obviously wanted me to watch if you were going to stand there by the open window and pull off your underwear for the whole world to see."

He walked toward her, then bent down to pick up her damp face towel. "May I?"

"Sure, go ahead."

He began to dry off his neck and then his arms and then under his arms. Maddie was mesmerized. She loved the way the fabric rode across his muscles. She loved the way he touched himself with such deft efficiency. She wanted to be the frigging towel.

"You all right, Post?"

"Yes." But her voice cracked.

He laughed and dried off his insane abs. She kept staring. He reached the towel around to his lower back, slowing down a bit to give her a little extra time to focus on his stretched hip flexors. She bit her upper lip and pulled her folded arms tighter into her breasts.

"You sure?" he asked.

"Yes. I'm sure. Go on."

He stood there for a few moments, deciding what to do next.

"Yes, ma'am." Hank snapped the small towel over one shoulder, then slowly unbuttoned the wet fly of his cargo shorts. The water had tightened the buttonholes, and it forced him to slow down his pace. Once he'd gotten them all loose, he reached his thumbs into the waistband of his boxer briefs and pulled the whole wet mess off. He walked naked over to one of the rocks and bent over to lay the clothes out so they might be drier by morning. Chances were slim that they'd dry, but he had another pair of shorts and a larger plastic bag to put this pair in if need be.

When he turned back to face her, Maddie was frozen in place.

"You are really something, Hank." He looked down at his nakedness, as if seeing himself through her eyes.

"Not a lot of big lugs like me at Brown?"

She'd decided about ten seconds ago that he could say any stupid incendiary thing he chose to and she was absolutely, 100 percent *not* going to come up for it. "Oh, there are plenty of lugs."

Maddie couldn't really catch her breath. His legs and thighs were so strong and solid. His hips like some ancient Greek statue. His shoulders—well, she'd seen those already, she supposed, but they were still amazing. And he was so comfortable in his own skin, just prowling around the campsite as if it were perfectly normal for him to be buck naked in the middle of the forest. Maybe it was.

"Do you go naked camping a lot?" she blurted.

"Do I what?" He was crouching by the circle of rocks he'd just finished building for their campfire and was snapping small twigs and throwing the bits of kindling in.

"Do you come out into the wild so you can roam around like a big old naked caveman?"

"Maybe?" He said it like a question, but he was smiling. "I'm just more comfortable like this, I guess." He shrugged, and she watched the muscles in his back shift and glow in the early evening light.

"Well," she chuckled, "you certainly don't need to put on any clothes on my account!"

She walked over to where he was busying himself with the fire. He'd already gotten a small flame going, and she stared at the flickering light against the planes of his face. She lowered herself to sit next to him, then reached out hesitantly to touch the muscles on his back. His eyes closed at her tenderness, and she felt a tingling sensation in the palms of her hands. She felt like St. Jerome with the lion. Hank could turn on her at any moment, but when he was pliant like this, it was incredibly powerful. She leaned in and kissed his upper arm, then rested her head gently against his shoulder. He leaned his head against the top of hers, and they both stared into the growing flames.

Maddie heard the steadying pace of his breath and tried to calm her skittering heart. Despite her possession of condoms and sharing banter about hussies and hookers, the truth was that Maddie had never quite gotten around to losing her virginity. She wasn't saving herself or anything, but it had just never happened. She was always perfectly happy fooling around and doing what her roommates used to call "any old thing." But that next step always felt just too emotionally perilous.

And Hank . . . well, he was probably the most emotionally perilous person Maddie had ever met. She wanted to kiss him and touch him so badly, but there was no way she would spend the rest of her life having to confess—if only to herself—that she'd lost her virginity in a tent with some guy she would probably never see again after this summer.

Her heart was calming down. She reminded herself that a summer fling and the-first-man-I-ever-had-sex-with were two entirely different concepts. She needed to keep Hank firmly in the summer fling department. For both of their sakes.

She took a deep breath and relaxed closer into him.

After a few minutes of what Maddie could only vaguely describe as communal bliss, he kissed her forehead and said, "I think the fire's ready for the fish. If you want to set it up."

"Sure." Maddie answered but didn't move. She didn't want to break the spell of the two of them just sitting there next to each other like that, without any banter or misunderstandings or anything, just being like that. Together. She took a cleansing breath and stood up to get the fish.

Hank watched her walk barefoot across the pine needles that created a soft bed underfoot. "You should probably put some shoes on," he said.

"You should probably put some clothes on," she volleyed back, without looking at him.

He laughed and rustled through his backpack before finding the pair of sweatpants that he'd packed all the way at the bottom. He snapped the elastic waist and turned to face Maddie as she worked on placing the fish-stakes at different angles over the flames. She looked up and smiled. "You look great."

"You too," he said quietly.

The fish was done quickly, and they ate it with their hands, right off the sticks, like melted marshmallows.

"So, good, right?" Maddie was in the food zone again, relishing every taste that went into her mouth.

Hank nodded and went back to his new favorite pastime of watching the way her mouth moved when she chewed. She licked every bit of fish off the smooth spikes she'd whittled, then tossed the wood sticks into the fire. "Now, that's what I call a good dinner!"

"You are one cheap date."

Maddie rolled her eyes at him. "I know it's probably a lot to ask, but could you try, for like a few hours, to keep the cheap whore jokes to a minimum?"

"I didn't mean it like that!" He laughed.

"Sure, you didn't!" But she laughed, too. He finished eating, then tended the fire to make sure there were no stray branches that could catch a spark. He'd unrolled the two sleeping bags earlier and set them into the tent side by side.

"How cozy," Maddie said as she passed in front of the triangular opening.

She used a bit of water from her water bottle to moisten her toothbrush and quickly brushed her teeth. When she turned back to Hank, he was in the midst of strapping up his backpack on a high branch away from where they were sleeping.

"Bears," he said, in a pedantic, leave-it-to-me tone of voice.

"I know."

She crawled into one of the sleeping bags and shook her legs down into the end. A few minutes later, Hank joined her in the tent.

They were only a few inches from one another, the small space not allowing either of them any privacy. Hank was kneeling awkwardly, trying to get into his sleeping bag.

"Are we going to fool around?" Maddie asked, trying to sound nonchalant.

"You are such a piece of work." He shook his head.

"Why? I just want to know. Because if we're not going to, then I'll just fall asleep and not lie here wondering."

"Wondering what?" He started moving again, working his way into his sleeping bag. The moon was bright and the tent was barely dark. After a few seconds, they could see each other's faces easily.

"You know, stuff like: Is he asleep? Is he going to reach over and hug me? Is he going to kiss me? That sort of thing." She turned on her side so her face was only a few inches from his profile. She kept her hands to herself, tucked up to her chest inside the sleeping bag. When he didn't make a move, she yawned. "I'll take that as a no," she said, yawning a second time.

"Get some sleep, Post. You've had a long week."

Her eyes were closed and she felt safe next to this strong, caring man. Even though he wasn't really touching her, he created this vibe around her that made her feel totally protected. Maddie fell quickly into a deep sleep.

They both woke up just after five, the sun barely beginning to peek over the horizon.

"Hey," Hank said softly, touching her cheek.

She opened her glassy eyes, then closed them again, turning her lips to kiss his palm. "*Mmmm.*"

There was nothing "*Mmmm*" about how much he wanted her, thought Hank, it was more like hell.

She rolled away from him—good, he thought, I'll be able to escape—then she shimmied her entire body against his—her back to his front—and made that disastrous "*Mmmm*" sound again. Obviously she felt him against her; how could she not?

"You feel good," she added sleepily, swiveling her backside into him.

He threw his left arm over her hip and pulled her roughly against him. He'd kicked off his sweatpants in the night and he was naked against the slippery nylon inside the sleeping bag. Hank made an unintelligible sound of frustration. Maddie looked over one shoulder.

Delectable. All half-asleep and willing.

Hank's heart began to pound.

"What is it?" she asked, without a hint of irony. "Are you okay?"

He pulled her around to face him, then pinned her to the ground with his body, both of them still in the sleeping bags. She strained her neck up to kiss his hard chest and felt it deep inside when he gasped in response.

"Maddie . . ."

"Hank, please let me . . ." He was still trying to hem her in with the cage of his strong arms, but she was slipping around in her sleeping bag and managed to get her sweatshirt off while they were sort of wrestling like that.

"Oh, Jesus . . ." His voice trailed off when he looked down at her exposed body. She shook her mussed hair out of her face and arched up to him.

"Please, Hank."

He dipped his head down toward her, and she felt like he was in slow motion. Like he was underwater. He would make love like he was in the water. With natural power and grace.

"*Mmmm!*" She was holding her lips tightly closed between her teeth, trying to silence her piercing reactions to his kisses along her body.

"I want to hear you, Maddie. No one's around for miles. Let me hear you."

She didn't need any more encouragement to let her voice, and her body, do as he bid.

She was so immersed in his touch, reveling in his exquisite attention, that she lost her focus entirely. Her fingertips slipped along his back in a dreamy near-touch, trembling along with his strained muscles. He was methodical. Competent. Thorough. She almost started laughing when she realized he was going to take her to the heights of sexual pleasure just like he did everything else: confidently.

And then she was gone, her head flung back, her eyes staring blindly at the seam along the top of the tent, her body sizzling and heating up higher and higher as Hank worked his way down her stomach with possessive kisses. When his face reached the edge of elastic at the waist of her sweatpants, he bit the fabric and tugged it down with a low growl.

Everything stopped. She gasped.

"Maddie?" There was a tenderness in Hank's voice that shifted everything. Suddenly, she wasn't sure she wanted him tender. Tender was complicated. For all her talk about being opposed to some two-dimensional hook-up, Maddie realized she didn't want to have an emotional quagmire on her hands, either. That's what she kept telling herself, at least, because the alternative—that she was already starting to care way too much about the mess of feelings that swam behind this man's eyes—was not an option. She needn't have worried.

He yanked her sweatpants all the way off and drove all thought from her mind, kissing his way up her thigh.

When her final piercing cry reverberated through them both, Hank slowed down his pace, drawing out her pleasure. He softened his hold on her hips and caressed the inside of her petal-soft thighs with his thumbs, then kissed his way back up her rising and falling abdomen.

"Good morning," he said with a smile of arrogant satisfaction.

Maddie panted and smiled back with a little nod.

"Good. Speechless. I like it." Hank trailed his palm back and forth across Maddie's bare stomach, watching the skin pebble and ripple in the wake of his touch. "Amazing skin."

After one long exhale, Maddie finally started to come back to earth. "Hey." She stared at his buzz cut and the two-day growth of whiskers and the tiny scar on his left cheek. She touched the scar with the tip of her index finger, just to feel it. She had no mind for curiosity. Everything had been reduced to physical sensation. Starting with the contact of that one fingertip, her body began to wake up to the possibilities of Hank's entire body at her disposal. She pushed him onto his back and straddled him.

Maddie's head almost touched the top of the tent when she was astride him like that. She placed her palms on his chest, then leaned down to enjoy every square inch of this man's hard, toned body.

As she learned to map the areas of his greatest response—the pale flesh of his ribs, the turn of his neck, his sensitive ears—Maddie gradually moved down his body, just as he had moved down hers.

"You don't have to—"

Maddie was so close, hovering between his navel and her objective. Her hair fell along his hip, a silky panel.

"But I can if I want to, right?" She stared at him, waiting for him to answer. "I mean, you'll try to like it, right?" She'd already begun touching him lightly between his legs.

His voice was thin. "Only if you want to."

Maddie wanted to. Badly. So she did.

After, the two of them lay there breathing hard, Maddie's cheek against his lower belly. Hank's hand slowly loosened its grip in her long hair and he massaged her scalp absently. It felt like gratitude.

They both fell back to sleep.

When Hank woke up an hour later, he was naked and alone on a pile of empty sleeping bags. He rummaged around until he found his sweats, pulled them on, and ducked his head as he moved out of the tent opening and looked around for Maddie. She was sitting on a rock near the edge of the water, facing toward the long, narrowing end of the lake, where the sun was making its slow ascent. He intended to leave her alone, but she must have heard his rustling and she turned to face him over one shoulder. Her face was the picture of peace, angelic, with the new sun creating a golden glow across her wide cheekbones and gently curved mouth.

Hank's immediate reaction was to walk backward, very slowly, like he'd been trained to do if he happened upon a suspected land mine. Danger! Danger! That look of satisfied harmony that emanated from her was like a spike in his gut.

"I'll break down the tent," he said, turning away from her and getting busy.

She shrugged and went back to watching the day explode before her eyes.

They had a couple of energy bars for breakfast and spent the rest of the morning in the canoe. What had happened in the tent had made Maddie far softer, compliant. She didn't fight him on the direction of the boat or the pace of their paddling. The two of them moved around the lake in easy symmetry, exploring small coves, pausing to listen to the slap of a jumping fish or the slow awakening of the insects and small creatures that lived in the woods. Around noon, Hank said it was time to pack it in and head back to the trailhead. Three hours of portaging and three hours of driving still lay ahead of them.

Unfortunately for Hank, Maddie's sense of peace and ease seemed to deepen in inverse proportion to his anxiety. On the drive home, he pecked at her with little jabs of repartee, and she just smiled at him and said mild things like, "Don't be such a grump." Or "It's no big deal." Or "Maybe you're hungry." He was far more comfortable when she was chatty and confrontational—it kept things light to have that banter between them. This new turn of events was starting to feel like the beginning of that most dreaded of all words in Hank's vocabulary: A Relationship.

Vague. Unpredictable. Amorphous.

Hank spent the final hour of the drive home silently convincing himself that Maddie had fallen in love with him in that damned tent, and that he was going to have to spend the rest of the summer trying to avoid her and, more importantly, any of the feelings she stirred up in him.

By the time they pulled into the driveway in Blake, Hank practically dove out of the car. Maddie pulled the blue backpack out and lifted it onto one shoulder, easy as you please.

"Do you want me to help you unload the stuff?" Maddie asked. Neutral.

He was already untying the cords from the canoe. He might as well have been welding the most complicated rigging at fifty fathoms for all the attention he was giving the mundane task. "No. I'm good."

"Okay."

Here we go, Hank thought. The thank-you-for-the-most-wonderful-weekend-of-my-life speech. He looked up finally, feeling her still standing there waiting for him to say good-bye or something. He supposed he could look at her while she spilled her heart to him.

But she didn't do that at all.

He would always look back on that moment as one of his greatest lapses into solipsistic egomania: He was the one who was in danger, not Maddie. He was the one who was going to crack apart if this progressed any further. She was light as a feather. Whole. Normal. She just smiled that small, satisfied smile and turned toward the back door of his mother's house.

"Have a good week, Hank," she said, raising one hand in a half-hearted wave and keeping her back to him. "I'll see you around."

CHAPTER 7

Hank almost slammed his forehead against the prow of the canoe where it extended near his face. Several times. Hard. Stupid. Stupid. Stupid man.

Instead, he took a deep breath and found a small thread of comfort in breaking down the camping equipment and putting everything away with the precision and exactitude that always made everything else seem bearable. Maddie's blasé departure was what he had been secretly hoping for, wasn't it? No big deal. Just a cigar and all that.

Just to be sure, he kept his distance. When he got to work the next morning, he signed up for two extra shifts so one of his co-workers could go to his grandmother's ninetieth birthday over in Wiscasset.

"You stockpiling hours to go on a vacation or something?"

"Nah, just nothing else going on, so might as well make the extra cash, right?"

"I guess." Ned Pendleton was a single, ill-tempered former Marine. He always tried to make jokes about how Hank was an Army grunt and too bad he couldn't make it into the *real* military.

Hank ignored him.

The week improved the longer Hank was away from Maddie.

He didn't risk going into his mother's kitchen to steal a few sodas; he went straight from his apartment to his job and back again, grateful that his seven o'clock morning departure was a few hours after Maddie left to start her shift down at Phil's.

By Thursday afternoon, he was feeling almost even-keeled. So they'd rolled around in a tent. So what? He shook his head and smiled at his own maudlin stupidity. It didn't need to be anything more than that.

Hank was in the locker room getting out of his deep-sea gear when Ned poked his head around the wall from the shower area.

"Hey, Gilbertson, you want to go grab a beer? You look like you're finally over your little snit of the week."

What a tool. Hank should have punched the bastard in the face, but it seemed lame to punch someone for being right.

"Sure. Why the hell not?"

Ned pulled back behind the wall to finish drying off, but kept talking. "Have you seen that new collegiate piece of ass working at Phil's yet?"

Hank reconsidered the punch. Sometimes being right was even more of a reason to knock someone's head off. He ground his teeth together.

"Yeah, I've seen her, asshole. She's renting the guest room at my mother's house."

A low wolf whistle came from behind the white tile. "You mean to tell me you got that flat stomach and those perky tits right upstairs, and you haven't done anything about it?"

Hank slammed the metal locker door and finished buttoning up his shorts. He leaned into the part of the room where Ned was standing so he could see his face. "Go drink your beer alone, dickwad."

"Testy! Testy!" Ned called out as Hank left the building, the jerk's mocking laugh fading behind him.

It was about half past eight on Thursday night when Hank pulled into his driveway. He killed the engine and sat in the truck for a few minutes. The light was on in his mother's living room, and he could see the silhouettes of his mom and Maddie reading or talking through the old embroidered sheers. Before he realized how long he'd been sitting there, he saw the silhouette of his mother rise from the sofa and wave to him.

Shit.

She opened the front door and called to him. "Hey, sweetheart! I haven't seen you all week. Want some supper?"

He opened the car door and flipped his keys around his index finger. Busy man of affairs and all that. What a tool.

"No. I've got some stuff to catch up on." His eyes darted to the back of Maddie's head—perfectly still, not turning to look at him—diffused through the gauzy curtain.

"Oh. Okay, then." His mom was trying not to sound disappointed. "Do you have plans this weekend? Do you want to go to the movies again tomorrow night?" She spoke quickly, before he got away.

"Sorry, can't. I have to work a couple of extra shifts this weekend." He thought he saw Maddie's shoulders lower a tiny bit—from relief or frustration, he had no idea. He didn't want to know.

"Okay, then." His mom tilted her head slightly. "You okay, honey?"

He puffed up his chest and tossed the keys a little higher. "All good, Mom. All good." He turned and took the wooden steps two at a time and was relieved to feel the pressure of his mother's concerned gaze leave him when he shut the door to his apartment.

He was screwed. There was no way he could go on living in his mother's garage no matter how much space she gave him. He needed to get on with his own life, and that was never going to happen with her concerned questions waiting for him every time he pulled into the driveway. Coming back to Blake—trying to be normal—had always been a temporary solution. To help him reintegrate or some damn thing. Meeting Maddie was making it worse.

Everybody talked about what it was like to go back to "normal life" after all those years in the military. He was dealing. He had been dealing just fine before Madison Post showed up. Now he was starting to feel all fractured again. He hadn't seen the kind of action he knew other grunts from his class had run into, in Somalia and Afghanistan and every other fucked up place on earth. The fact that he'd probably killed more people than all those guys combined was another story altogether.

Maddie's shoulders relaxed all the way when she heard the door to his apartment close. What the hell was a grown man doing living with his mother anyway? He needed to get his own place. And stop driving Maddie insane with all his around-but-never-around nearness. She didn't know if what they had started was just a fling or if it was going to lead to anything, but all of his special-ops-evacuation-stealth-invisibility-maneuvering was turning their whole fun time together into something tawdry and regrettable. Maddie was beginning to feel like maybe, on some level, he was the innocent and she was the hussy after all. One way or another, they were going to have to have it out; there was no way either of them could go on like this indefinitely.

Maddie closed her eyes and tried to compose herself when

Janet came back into the living room. She immediately shoved her nose into the nearest book on the coffee table.

Janet locked the front door and turned slowly to face Maddie. "What happened on that canoe trip, Maddie?"

Maddie's heart began to hammer, and a light sheen of sweat bristled on the back of her neck from the spurt of adrenaline. Janet had become a friend. Maddie really believed that she wasn't asking as Hank's mother, but as a concerned friend. But Janet was always going to be Hank's mother first. Always would be.

"I thought we had a good time," Maddie said.

Janet sat back down on the sofa, but at the edge, not like she was going to settle back into her book, the two of them drifting back into the friendly silence that had come to define their evenings together.

"Maddie?"

Pulling her lips tight between her teeth, Maddie did her best to answer. "*Mm-hmm?*" She kept looking at her book.

The silence spread, slow and cold, through the room.

Finally, Maddie looked up and met the older woman's questioning eyes.

"Are you okay?" Janet asked.

Oh, Jesus. She was asking *Maddie* if she was okay? *Take. Take. Take.* That's what her brother Jimmy always accused her of. Maddie felt the shame of how she had selfishly pushed things forward with this woman's beloved son, and couldn't look at Janet anymore. "I'm sorry."

"Oh, sweetie. What do *you* have to be sorry about?"

Maddie couldn't breathe. "This is wrong. Because you're his mom. And I know you sort of thought it might be sweet if we, you know, got together or whatever, like when we were at the movies and it was all fun, but—" She was talking too fast, the words were coming out against her will. She continued in a frantic whisper, worried that Hank was up at his window listening to her strange, guiltless confession. "But he acted like he wanted to just have fun. I mean, oh gosh, this is horribly weird, and I'm sorry, but we didn't have sex, just for the record, and I thought, well he *made* me think, that it was just fun and games, and then he changed and became all silent and moody again, and now I feel like I've done something selfish that has triggered something angry or unhappy in him and I wasn't trying to be selfish—for once!—and it turns out I might as well just revert to type if I'm going to end up in the same place of feeling like everyone thinks I am just this selfish . . . bitch."

Janet kept staring at her, but in a caring, listening way rather than in that questioning way she'd been looking at her before. "Are you done?"

"Isn't that enough?" Maddie made an attempt at a little laugh but it came out wrong, and she reached up to her eye to wipe the moisture that she hadn't realized was there. She pretended she was just exercised, as her grandmother would say.

"This is when I am so grateful that I don't drink anymore," Janet said. "I mean, if I was drunk right now, I would have missed all of this. But I can see you, Maddie. And I have always been able to see Henry, even through the fog of alcohol, I could always read him. I think that's why he had to get away. Who wants to be known and observed like that? It's too much sometimes."

Maddie nodded.

Janet continued. "Well, it's none of my business. I promised Hank that if he moved in over the garage, I would never ask him a single word about where he was going or what he was doing." She sat up a little straighter. "And I said he wasn't to ask me any of those types of questions about my private life, either."

Maddie's eyebrows lifted. "Really?"

"You don't have to look so surprised. I have someone I like to see sometimes, but it's a little complicated, as they say these days, so we're pretty quiet about the whole thing. And I certainly wouldn't want *his* mother asking me what I'm doing with *him*."

Maddie smiled her gratitude. "Thanks."

"I wasn't ever going to judge you or anything. I can see now that neither of you are trying to be hurtful."

"Ha!" Maddie laughed once. "Yeah, not on purpose, at least. Sins of omission and commission, right?"

Janet smiled. "There's a reason they're both sins, don't you think? Because we feel bad afterwards, whether we meant to or not. Or, at least, I hope we feel bad after. Otherwise, we're really in trouble."

"You're a really good person, Janet. How did I get so lucky to find you?"

Janet stood up and turned off the light next to the sofa. "Some things are just meant to be, I guess."

"Thanks again for the talk."

Janet paused at the bottom of the stairs, then turned her face to Maddie. "Don't be too hard on him."

Maddie exhaled. "I'll try. Seeing as I'm so much bigger and stronger than he is."

Janet smiled at the irony. "Good-night, Maddie."

"Good-night, Janet."

The next day, Maddie's new best friend at work, a thirty-eight-year-old mother of two named Sharon, was bemoaning the fact that she and her husband never got to go out anymore.

"I'll babysit for you," Maddie said.

"Oh, I can't afford a sitter."

"You don't have to pay me. I'll think of something nice you can do for me. Give me a manicure or something. I'm crap at that. Let me do the babysitting. I feel like such a waste of space when I'm not at work."

Sharon stared at her.

"What?" Maddie looked up to meet her eyes. The two of them were sitting in one of the back booths cleaning all the condiments before the weekend closing.

"Why aren't you out on a date?"

"With whom?" Maddie laughed.

"With any of the nine hundred guys who've been coming in here the past two weeks checking out your short shorts!"

"They have not!"

"Oh, cut it out. It's me, Sharon, remember? I know what it's like to have long firm legs and like the feel of a man's eyes on them. Cough it up. Who's the guy?"

Maddie's stomach fell. "Who's what guy?"

"The guy you must be thinking about to ignore all those other guys."

"Who says I'm ignoring anyone?"

Sharon rolled her eyes, then stared at Maddie with wide-eyed meaning. "I heard you tell that guy Ned that you were a lesbian!"

They both started laughing. When she'd calmed down enough to talk, Maddie stammered, "With him as the only alternative? I probably am!"

The infectious laughter spread between them, and Maddie felt *good* for the first time in a week, the carefree kind of *good* that was her usual default. None of that broody Hank Gilbertson crap weighing her down.

"Just let me watch your kids, and you go get all dolled up and surprise that cute husband of yours."

"He *is* pretty cute, isn't he?"

Cute was an understatement; Sharon's husband was superhot. He came in for coffee every morning after dropping the kids off at day care. Left twenty minutes later after reading the paper and blowing Sharon a kiss. He worked at Bath Iron Works, and they'd just bought the house of their dreams, a run-down Victorian over near Janet's house.

"Come on, admit it. You want to go to the movies, then make out with him in the parking lot."

"You are such a bad influence, Madison Post!"

"That she is." The deep voice came from the front of the diner, and Maddie's head swung around so fast she almost pulled a muscle in her neck. She leapt up from the table and ran into the open arms of the tall, handsome man by the door.

"Jimmy! You jerk!" She hugged him and didn't let go for a long time.

"Hey. You okay? Let me look at you . . ." He held her chin between his index finger and thumb. "What's going on? Ready to come home?"

She leaned her face into his palm and closed her eyes. He smelled like home. Like the laundry detergent they'd all grown up using and Ivory soap and family.

A few seconds passed, and she stood up straight. "No. I'm not going to lose this bet!" she whispered, then poked him in the chest. When she was done poking him, she straightened the Windsor knot of his Hermès tie and pulled his hand into hers, tugging him down the length of the restaurant to introduce him to Sharon.

"James Post, this is Sharon MacKenzie. Sharon, this is my pain-in-the-ass brother Jimmy."

Sharon looked momentarily disappointed, then stood up and shook his hand. "Nice to meet you, Jimmy. What brings you to Blake?"

He pulled Maddie close and draped one arm possessively around her shoulders. "Had to see how H-R-H was surviving."

Sharon cocked an eyebrow. "H-R-H?"

"Her royal highness," Jimmy said.

"Not literally!" Maddie laughed. "It's just a hideous nickname my brothers use to torment me."

"Oh." Sharon looked from Maddie to Jimmy and back to Maddie. "I get it. I thought he might be the guy who was keeping you from the rest of the guys." Sharon smiled and sat back down at the booth to finish with the condiment bottles.

Jimmy widened his eyes to question Maddie. "Guy?"

"Don't even think about it!"

"Okay! I won't pry. Want to go out for dinner, Mad?" Jimmy asked.

"I can't. I just offered to babysit for Sharon while she goes on a much-needed date with her husband."

"Why don't the four of us go out?" Jimmy asked, trying to be inclusive.

Sharon stared at the man standing there in front of her, who looked like he'd just walked off an Italian menswear fashion runway. She read *People* magazine. She knew Prada when she saw it. Which had been never, in real life, until right now.

"I'm not sure—" Sharon answered slowly.

Jimmy interrupted Sharon with a quick lift of his chin. "Come on. It will be fun. We can go to the big hotel over in Wiscasset, then I can leave straight from there—"

Maddie pinched him hard on the side of his stomach before he finished that sentence with the fact that his private jet was in the Wiscasset private airfield, waiting for a call from him to start the engines.

"Ow, what was that for?" Jimmy asked.

"Just stop being so bossy!" Maddie replied. "Sharon is going out with her husband. I am babysitting. You are leaving."

"Wow. Some welcome wagon. I was up at the Universal Paper factory—"

"Enough!" Maddie knew all about Universal Paper, and every other factory in Maine that her family owned. "Get out of here. I'm fine—" She pulled away from him and threw her arms wide. "As you can see."

"All right. I'll tell Mom and Dad I saw you, and you are the same loose cannon you always were—"

"Hey! That is so not true. Tell him, Sharon. I'm a good worker, right?"

Sharon watched the verbal sparring and put her hands up, palms out. "I'm not getting into any sibling rivalry. Maddie's a great waitress. That's just a fact."

"Okay, okay." Jimmy shook Sharon's hand. "Nice to meet you. Have fun on your date tonight."

"Thanks. I think we will."

Maddie took his elbow and steered Jimmy back toward the front of the diner. "Thanks for checking on me." She squeezed his hand.

Jimmy paused and turned to face her. "It was just a silly bet, Maddie. You don't need to turn it into some big thing."

For some reason the mention of "some big thing" threw her into a slew of memories about Freud and Epictetus and Hank. And kissing. She shook her head.

"It's not a thing. I'm having a really great summer. You were right; you might as well rub my nose in it. I needed to work like this. I'm good at it."

Jimmy stared at her, assessing her. "Okay. But don't—"

"Stop." Maddie laughed. "I'm fine. I promise I'll call if I get hit by a bus or something, I'm not going to chew my own arm off to prove a point."

He smiled then, and she stood up on her toes and gave him a kiss on the cheek. "I'm really glad you found me. Give a big hug to Mom and Dad for me."

"Will do. Bye, Sis."

She rolled her eyes at the despised nickname and held the door open for him to leave. He got into the chauffeur-driven black Jaguar, and she couldn't see the slightest hint of him behind the blacked-out window tinting once he shut the door.

When the car pulled away, she happened to look across the street, only to see one pissed-off Henry Gilbertson sitting in his truck, staring at her. He shook his head once, started the engine, checked his rearview mirror, and pulled onto Main Street . . . without looking at her again.

She shut the door to the diner and flipped the deadbolt. She turned the "Closed" sign to face out and let the horizontal blinds drop the length of the door with a satisfying metal clatter.

Good, she thought, let Hank think I've got some sugar daddy who swoops in to visit; he already thinks I'm a tramp anyway.

"I'll babysit anytime you want," Maddie offered when she sat back down. "Why don't you and Gerry go away for the whole weekend?" Anything to keep me away from the Gilbertsons, Maddie thought desperately.

Sharon looked at Maddie. "You okay?"

"Why does everyone keep asking me that?!" Maddie was too loud and too mad for it to sound offhand. "I mean, probably not. But yes, I'm fine."

Sharon reached across the table, their chore finished. "Come on. Let's go back to my house and have a glass of wine. I'll give you that manicure and pedicure this afternoon before I get all dolled up for tonight."

"Thanks, Sharon. That sounds perfect."

The two of them took off their short, black, pocketed aprons, tossed them into the industrial laundry container, and let themselves out the back. The heavy metal door locked automatically behind them.

CHAPTER 8

The house was dark when Hank finally pulled into the driveway. He'd driven on back roads for a couple of hours to erase the vision of Maddie straightening that bastard's tie with that dreamy, faraway look in her eyes. Hank could see from across the street that she felt relieved to be back in his arms. Why wouldn't she? He looked rich enough. And, if Hank was honest, he looked like the type of guy who would probably make an effort to talk to her after spending one of the best times he could remember wrapped in her arms.

So she'd been slumming it all along, just like he'd suspected. Hank tried to thicken his defenses. She was obviously using him and her job at the diner and the middle-class town of Blake and her whole summer vacation to do some sort of sociology project for her final year at Brown. He could just imagine her thesis title: "How I Spent My Summer Observing the Little People."

Janet's car was gone, and he figured the two women had taken his advice and gone for a girls' night out. They wouldn't be home for at least another hour. He took his chances on getting some leftovers out of the fridge in his mother's kitchen.

The small light over the stove was on, and the purple shadows of the outdoors were enough for Hank to walk in and open the fridge without turning the overhead light on. He pulled out a soda, popped the top, and took a big pull. He rummaged around in the fridge and pulled out a drumstick and a glass bowl of his mother's famous coleslaw. He kicked the fridge shut with his foot and left the house.

Two hours later he heard a rumbling engine—definitely not his mother's small, Japanese compact and definitely not that other guy's chauffeur-driven Jaguar from this afternoon—and then the singing strains of Maddie's voice.

"I had a great time. I mean it, if you want to have fun again tomorrow night or next weekend, just let me know."

A man's deep grateful voice replied in syllables Hank couldn't make out. He couldn't see the car without craning his neck out his bedroom window, and there were depths to which he would not stoop. That was one of them.

She laughed into the night. "I'd love that, too. Have a great rest of the weekend."

She slammed the door of the guy's car and called out, "Bye! Thanks for the ride!" Maddie was probably watching the new man in her life pull out of the driveway, savoring every last glimpse of the latest bastard to come through her revolving bed.

Hank knew he was being an idiot. Nothing made sense any-more, especially when he thought about Madison Post. He was scraping his nails against the bristled texture of his scalp when a fist pounded on his apartment door.

"Who is it?" he asked as he pulled the door open.

She slammed the flats of her hands into his chest. He was sur-prised by the force of her, and stumbled back a step.

"What the *hell* is your problem?!" she cried. She shoved him again, further into the room. "You never kissed a girl and just acted like a normal human being after?" She pushed him again, but he caught her wrists this time. Maddie tried to pull her hands free then realized the futility of the effort.

"Stop hitting me," Hank said softly.

Her lip started to shake and she tried to pull her hands again. She needed them to cover her face. "Don't talk to me in that soft voice, you bastard." The fight was draining out of her.

"How do you want me to talk to you, Maddie?" He hated himself, knowing that she'd been with those two other guys today, but he couldn't bring himself to care. When he felt the pounding beat of her pulse, where his thumbs were resting against her wrists, it pounded into him as well. "How do those other guys talk to you?"

"There are no other guys. How many times do you need to hear it? That was my *brother* at the diner today. And that was Gerry MacKenzie dropping me off just now after I babysat for his daughters." His grip loosened as he realized the extent of his paranoia, and Maddie quickly pulled her hands from his grasp.

Hank stayed quiet, then finally started to register her wacky appearance. Maddie had glitter all over her face and stickers on her ears, and her hair was wrapped in about fourteen rainbow dreadlock things. He couldn't help smiling.

"Don't you dare laugh at me! The MacKenzie girls gave me a makeover."

"Hey, come on. So I got a little freaked out and gave you some space for a few days—" Hank reached out to touch her upper arm.

She wheeled away from him. "You couldn't even say hi to me in passing? I mean, it's just so juvenile! We didn't even have sex—"

"Whoa! What?!" Hank was incredulous. "Of course we did."

"Well, I mean, not technically."

It wasn't helping matters that she looked like she was about sixteen and some kind of naughty Pippi Longstocking after a night in a mosh pit. "I don't know what technical manual you're working from," Hank said, "but in a court of law I would definitely be perjuring myself if I said I did not have sexual relations with *that woman*." Hank pointed at Maddie as he said the last two words.

"Ugh." She sighed. "Quit trying to derail me. This isn't about penetration or whatever—"

"Ouch," Hank said.

"Just cut it out. It's about you being a total horse's ass and freaking out because . . . because . . ."

"When you figure it out, let me know." He leaned back against the kitchen counter.

"Because you made me so happy. I think that's what it was. And you got all—" she scrambled her fingers around her skull like a crazy person "—messed up in the head because you thought I was going to melt into your arms or slobber all over your perfectly ordered life or something."

She looked around his apartment while he processed what she was saying. Maddie was totally fired up. "Seriously." She gestured around the immaculate space. "Just look at this place. Are your spices alphabetized?" Her chest was pounding, and her brow was sweating. She tried to put her hair behind her ear, but the wraparound string thing made it too unwieldy to stay put. She took a deep, frustrated breath into his silence.

"Okay." She shrugged, holding her shoulders up for a few seconds, then letting them drop. "I guess I've had my say." She turned to go and then turned back. "One more thing—"

He smiled at her. "Yes?"

"Just to be perfectly clear, me freaking out right now is not me freaking out about you giving me the best sexual experience of my life, and me having these unrealistically high expectations that it will always be like that, or that you will always be the one to do that for me, or any of that crap. Me freaking out right now is about *you* freaking out after all that other stuff happened. Got that?"

"Yeah, I got it. Freaking blah-blah best sex blah-blah freaking blah-blah."

"Oh my god. You really are a Neanderthal. We are going to have to talk about our feelings at some point, aren't we?"

"Not if I can help it," Hank said.

Maddie stared at him, then shook her head in disbelief. "Well, I guess that settles that. No feelings. Is that it?"

"Yeah. That's pretty much it." He didn't look smug or sad or anything. He just looked like he was telling her the truth.

"Okay. Maybe an uncomplicated hello every once in a while?"

He smiled, and she thought she might survive, because it was a good smile, not a pacifying one like he'd been giving her earlier. "Sure. I can handle an uncomplicated hello every once in a while."

"Well, that's progress. Bye, Hank."

"Bye, Maddie."

She let herself out and trotted down the stairs, feeling unburdened and relieved for the first time all week. It wasn't a glorious reunion but at least it was détente.

She opened the back door and let herself in, turning to lock it behind her. She slid the chain for good measure, just in case the boogeyman over the garage got any funny ideas about coming over to pay a midnight call.

She flipped the light on in the kitchen and saw a slip of paper on the farm table.

Dear Maddie (and Hank if you happen to see this),
I switched out my shift for the weekend and decided to go visit

my sister in Albany. Please call me on my cell phone
if you need to reach me. I will be back late Sunday night.
      xx Janet

Maddie stared at the note then read the postscript:

PS I made a batch of my famous coleslaw for you to try.

Maddie, suddenly ravenous, pulled open the fridge. She could actually picture where the now-missing coleslaw bowl had been sitting. Did she care enough to go back up to Hank's and demand that he return it? She felt like an idiot.

She shut the refrigerator door, turned off the overhead light, and walked heavily through the living room. She picked up her good friend, Ken Follett, on the way, and plodded up to her bedroom to spend the night in bed with a good book.

The curtains and blinds in her room had stayed firmly shut since she'd gotten back from their canoe trip on Sunday night. No more prurient peeping escapades for either of them. Maddie put the book on her bedside table and walked into her bathroom. She turned on the light over the sink and had to cover her mouth to silence her cry of shock. She looked like a wreck. Her hair was going in seventeen different directions. The wraparound string things were jutting out at odd angles that made her look like she might be receiving alien transmissions right there through her scalp. Her ears had rainbow-colored star stickers all over them. And her face.

Maddie's face had been covered in about four pounds of sparkly liquid blush that had solidified into a waxen sheen.

"Oh, Jesus," she said aloud. If Hank thought she was wacky before, he probably thought she was certifiable now. She smiled at her reflection, shook her head, and began the lengthy process of de-princessing herself.

Saturday morning, Maddie decided to go for a long run. She also needed to find a gym or other workout place where she could row. She'd amassed a stunning fortune: nearly five hundred dollars. Phil stopped making her split her tips after the first week—a deprivation that had probably been one more of his trials by fire, Maddie suspected—and it had made a considerable difference in her take-home pay, so she could afford to join a gym, finally. She also needed to go to the library and use the Internet—or, gasp!, a real book—to begin her preliminary research for her senior thesis.

She finished eating a bagel and a cup of coffee, then tied on her favorite sneakers. Hank's truck was gone; she'd heard him head out a few minutes before, to go back into the murky depths for another shift. Or to get away from her, more likely.

Maddie headed up the hill in the opposite direction of I-95, which Hank had taken her on the previous weekend. The street narrowed within a few minutes, as she got farther out of town, and gradually began to wind into a beautiful rural expanse. After about twenty minutes, she decided to head down a single paved lane that wended its way through the dappled trees. The morning was cool and refreshing, and the heat her body was generating gave her a feeling of deep satisfaction. She didn't need Hank and his stupid lips on her body. She didn't need anyone. That was the whole point of this summer, wasn't it? Freedom. Independence.

She kept running, enjoying an easy, consistent pace. If she kept her wits about her, she could probably do ten miles. She followed

the road until it came to a dead end that split off into three directions. The driveways were unpaved and unmarked, but there were
three mailboxes indicating that three different people lived farther
along. Maddie jogged in place, looking up at the canopy of trees,
deciding she'd be a fool to trespass on someone's property, and was
about to start heading back out the way she came when a black SUV
nearly crushed her as it came barreling out of the center driveway.

She leapt away from the middle of the road and tripped on a
tree root, falling gracelessly on the ground, near the edge of the
pavement where it met the woods.

A young guy, maybe late teens, early twenties, Maddie thought,
slammed on the breaks and whipped the front door open.

"Holy shit! Are you okay? Oh my god, my mother is going to kill
me if I hurt you in her car. Seriously! Can you talk? Say something!"

"Denny?"

"Madison?!"

They both started laughing. Dennis Fullerton was her roommate's ex-boyfriend from their freshman year at Brown.

"Holy crap. You scared the shit out of me. What are you even
doing here?" He sounded so relieved he was sort of half-laughing/
half-talking and rubbing his forehead. "I honestly thought I'd
killed you, and I was going to have to bury you in a shallow grave
or something."

Maddie brushed off the palms of her hands where they'd gotten
a bit scratched from trying to break her fall. "I think I tripped. You
certainly didn't hit me."

"Oh, thank god!" He looked at his watch. "I'm late. As usual.
Want a ride somewhere? It's the least I can do after giving you a
near-brush with vehicular manslaughter."

"Nah, you go ahead. I just started running a little while ago."

He smiled with a knowing smirk. "Meaning you've already gone ten, or you're aiming to go ten?"

"You got me. I'm aiming to go ten. But now I've lost my rhythm. I'll ride back with you, I guess. Can you drop me in Blake?"

"Sure, hop in."

They got in the car, and Denny drove like a little old lady, sitting up extra straight and clutching the steering wheel.

"Relax," Maddie said, pushing his upper arm casually. "I'm alive, remember?"

His shoulders settled a bit, but he didn't lean back altogether. "I think I'm pretty freaked out. I've got that acidy residual adrenaline thing going on right now." He turned to face her. "You sure you're okay? I don't want Zander to beat the crap out of me if I've hurt you."

She looked out the window. "Would you give it a rest about Zander? We broke up ages ago."

"That's not what he thinks. He said you were taking a break over the summer but that you were still totally together for senior year. And since you're running down his driveway, he might appear to be right."

"Whatever," Maddie replied. The thought of Zander Dalgliesh put her in a foul mood. "What did you say?" she asked suddenly.

"What do you mean? I said you don't have a very strong case for wanting to be broken up if you're traipsing all over Maine after him."

"I am not traipsing anywhere." Maddie was about to kick somebody's ass, more like it. If Jimmy had made her go to Blake, Maine, out of some misguided attempt to get her back together with Zander, she was going to scream. "What the hell are *you* doing here is the better question?"

"A bunch of us rented that big rambling place that leads down to the water back there, and we're painting houses and buying kegs and just, you know, having our last summer of freedom. We're having a big party tonight, you should come."

"I think I'll pass."

"You always were a bit stuck up, Post. Why don't you loosen up a bit?"

"Stop the car, please."

"Relax." Denny shook his head and slowed the car to a stop on the side of the road.

"You know what, Denny?"

"No. What?"

"I think you better just forget you ever saw me, all right?" She pulled the handle on the door and realized that it had auto-locked when he'd accelerated. She couldn't find the lock button and she tugged harder on the handle.

"Chill, Post." He clicked a button in the center console. Something about Denny Fullerton driving a brand-new luxury SUV and painting houses for fun just rubbed her wrong all of a sudden. She got out and held the door open to finish talking to him.

"I am perfectly *chill*, Denny. I wanted a summer away from anyone I knew. I had no idea you and Zander and all the guys from your fraternity were going to be here."

"Whatever," he said with no intonation, then turned to look back in the direction they'd been heading. "You coming or going? I'm late."

"What a gentleman. You practically kill me with this ridiculous beast of a car and then you tell me I need to lighten up." She slammed the car door, and he drove off before she'd finished with-drawing her arm.

Shit.

Maddie paced back and forth a few times, unsure if she wanted to try to go back to her run or if she was too rattled. She stopped pacing when she heard a rustle in the woods. Hands resting on her hips, she turned slowly, feeling the gaze of another creature. She didn't see them at first, through the camouflaging shadow and light of the trees. Then the sun caught the mother's eyes. Two moose, a large female and a young calf, stood frozen in place about twenty feet away from her. Maddie exhaled and let all thought of Zander and Denny and her final year of university and the stupid brute of a man she was falling for who was probably submerged in a dark silent world as she stood on the side of the road. She just stared at those black eyes and then at their ears. The young one twitched a muscle on its neck, but otherwise remained beautifully still.

She didn't want to pet them or befriend them or throw a rock to startle them and shoo them away from the dangers of the road. Maddie just wanted to remember every single detail about them, every eyelash, the way the sun made their velvety noses shine, the tender breathing of the small one, the way their shoulders turned in at exactly the same angle.

Maddie tasted the salt of her tears before she even realized she was crying. Why couldn't she just *be*? Why couldn't she just exist the way these animals did? She felt like such a conniving, demand-ing, controlling human. She felt like she was in a constant whirl of pushing or pulling or getting or spending. She couldn't even stand here on the side of the road without thinking about what it meant to be standing here on the side of the road.

The tears kept coming. The baby moose leaned in closer to its mother. The mother remained perfectly still. Maddie honestly felt like the mother was wordlessly warning her young progeny, "See! See how unhappy they are."

Maddie closed her eyes and took a deep breath. A small car was driving too fast around the curve, and she opened her eyes and stepped slowly away from the edge of the road. When she looked back into the woods, the two moose were gone. She decided to walk back into town rather than run.

CHAPTER 9

Hank almost forgot to set his valve properly. If he made another mistake like that, he was going to tell his supervisor he was too distracted to work. In the world of deep-sea diving, the man who knew his limits was the man who kept his job. Whenever someone saw another diver behaving erratically or even seeming a little tired, the entire team weighed in. The group decided.

On the one hand, it was a really solitary profession. There he was, at that moment, very much alone in the freezing, murky depths. On the other hand, he was inextricably woven into a team of people at all times. The gear, the oxygen . . . the surface team. Everyone else had to be trusted with his life through every step of preparation, through the work itself, and through proper withdrawal.

His team had been called out to do a preliminary inspection job for a wind turbine company. The US was way behind the leaders in this particular alternative energy solution. Countries like Denmark and the UK had been putting both human and financial resources into offshore wind power for over a decade. The US had yet to cut through the political, environmental, and aesthetic quagmire.

Hank settled into the tasks at hand, measuring the proposed area, providing geological samples of the ocean floor where the future base's construction units would be installed. His breathing and the strange noises of the deep mingled and worked their usual magic. He had to focus too hard to think about anything else. Being in the deep like this forced Hank to clear his mind of the little splinters of things and deal methodically and carefully with the whole.

He felt useful. Which was good.

He felt terribly alone. Which was fine.

At the end of his shift, Hank drove back to Blake in silence. Oftentimes after a long day in the sea, the radio grated on his nerves. It sounded too loud or too tinny. It sounded fake. And he craved real.

Or so he thought.

Hank pulled into the gathering darkness at nine o'clock on Saturday night. He could see the lights coming from Maddie's window. More accurately, he could see the tiny perimeter of light that escaped through the closed curtains and closed horizontal blinds that Maddie had firmly shut across the window. He sat in the silent truck for a few minutes, staring up at the second floor of his mother's house.

He knew Maddie didn't have any music or earbuds or anything to distract her, so she must have heard his truck pull in. What was he waiting for? For her to run breathless down the stairs, flinging the front door open and falling into his waiting arms?

He let his head hang forward. He told himself it was a matter of stretching the sore muscles at the back of his neck and shoulders, but it was really shame. He knew Maddie was right. He could pretend that he needed the extra hours at work or that he wanted to help out a colleague, but the fact was obvious. Hank couldn't stand being around Madison Post. She was too alive, too receptive. She was always "on."

He was off.

Lifting his head and reaching across the seat to grab his back-pack, Hank resigned himself to having to keep his distance from anyone who expected him to thrive like that. He was keeping it together. That was enough for now.

After he opened the car door and shut it, he felt her simmering behind him. He didn't turn around.

"I want the coleslaw."

Hank turned on his heel and faced her. She was in those demonic pajama bottoms with the waist that folded down and the ribbed white tank top that left that mesmerizing inch of skin visible above her waistband.

She tugged on the tank top to cover the skin. "Did you hear me? Your mom made that coleslaw for me."

He stared at her. Obviously, this had nothing to do with coleslaw.

"And don't stand there and try to make this about something other than the coleslaw."

"I'll be right back." Hank's voice was raspy from little use.

She folded her arms and shook her head in irritation.

He kept walking. On the third wooden step leading up to his door, he stopped. Hank rested the palm of his hand against the gray paint of the clapboard garage. It was like being dragged across a bed of nails on his stomach, but he could do this. He turned back to face her. "Do you want to come hang out? Watch a movie or something?"

She tightened her crossed arms and lifted her shoulders, folding herself in, away from him.

"Or not?" he asked.

He waited for her to answer.

"Are you trying to be normal?"

"I guess I am."

They stood looking at each other for a while longer.

"All right. I think I would like that." Maddie pulled the front door of Janet's house closed behind her and walked barefoot across the gravel driveway.

Hank had turned back, continuing slowly up the steps. "Doesn't that hurt the bottoms of your feet?" he asked, without looking back.

"No. My feet are shot. Running. Rowing. Skiing. My toes are a mess. I'll probably have arthritis by the time I'm twenty-five."

Hank slipped his key into the lock and opened the door, letting Maddie pass in before he did. He reached behind her and flipped on all the overhead lights at once. It was really bright, especially after the darkness outside.

"Sorry, that's a bit harsh." He flipped down two of the light switches and the areas in the two far corners of the room fell back into shadow. "I'm going to go change and put my work stuff away. I'll be right back. Grab yourself a beer in the fridge if you want."

"Okay. Thanks."

When Hank came out of his bedroom ten minutes later, Maddie was holding a cold beer and leaning over his drafting table. She had turned the two corner lights back on and was taking her time nosing around all his stuff.

"Find anything good?"

"Shit!" she grabbed the beer bottle a split second before it slipped out of her hand and spilled all over his blueprints. "You are so effing quiet. Have you always been like that or is it a military thing?"

He shrugged. "I guess a little of both. You definitely learn how to make yourself scarce with parents like mine used to be . . . or when someone's trying to shoot you."

She relaxed her hips back against the edge of the tilted work table and held the beer casually with one hand. "You've been shot?"

"No. I've been shot *at*." He walked over to the refrigerator and pulled out another beer. He popped the top off with the opener Maddie had left on the countertop, then returned the metal device to the drawer where it was supposed to be.

"Sorry I didn't put the bottle opener back. I figured I was probably going to use it again fairly soon."

"No problem. Just habit. A place for everything, and all that."

She took a long, satisfying pull off the beer bottle. Hank stared at the curve of her neck and the rise and fall of her throat. When she finished the sip, she smiled at him. "So, what movies do you have?"

He came around from the kitchen island and walked over to the big sofa.

"Have a seat?" He gestured to the blue-denim slipcovered sofa, then went over to the television and grabbed a remote.

He settled in on the sofa a few feet away from her and swung his feet up onto the big square ottoman that doubled as a coffee table. He reached forward and opened his iPad, made a few swipes across the screen with his fingers, then passed the tablet into her hands. "Here are the movies."

She looked down at his spreadsheet with about six hundred movies listed in alphabetical order. "Oh my god. This is like the little box of three-by-five notecards in *When Harry Met Sally*. You are such a girl."

He looked down at his very un-girl-like self, then raised an eyebrow and took a sip of beer without breaking eye contact.

"Let's watch *Troy*. I haven't seen that in ages."

"Cool." He got up and opened one of the cabinets beneath the television to retrieve a black notebook filled with DVDs.

Maddie smiled at his totally meticulous level of organization and decided not to dwell on it. She let her eyes meander around his place. The ceiling beams were exposed and painted a bright, cheerful white. A retro fan—kind of aeronautical brushed metal, maybe 1940s or '50s—spun way up at the pitch of the roof. There were a couple of skylights over the kitchen and a couple over the seating area.

She looked at the large-scale photographs on either side of the flat-panel television. The whole place was such a contrast to the old-but-good feeling that his mother's place exuded. Everything here was considered. Clean. Nothing without a purpose.

"Where'd you get those photographs? What are they?"

He was slipping the disk into the player and looked up to see where she was looking. "Just water. I took them." He went back to cueing up the movie.

She stared at the abstract blues and grays of the pair of photographs. He had taken care with the framing, the wide, black trim painted to a shiny perfection.

Hank fiddled with a couple more knobs, then walked over to the front door and flipped all the overhead lights off. "Too dark?"

Maddie slipped deeper into the enormous sofa. "No! This is perfect! No wonder you don't ever want to go to the movies." The opening menu was already up on the screen. "This is better than any movie theater."

"Thanks. You ready for another beer before I sit back down?"

She looked over the back of the sofa. "Sure. I'd love one." Maddie heard the pop of the next beer and let the vision of a naked, sated Brad Pitt fill her field of vision as the movie began playing.

Hank returned to the sofa and set her second beer on the small trunk that served as a side table next to his side of the couch.

"Ooh, I love this part!" Maddie cried as Achilles went flying through the air and slayed his opponent.

Hank looked at her profile in the bright glow of the screen. He marveled at the way Maddie felt everything so completely, how she let the world and all of her experiences and reactions explode like that. Why would anyone do that?

She shook her head and took the last sip of her first beer, setting the empty bottle on the floor to her left. "I'll take that other beer now . . ." She extended her hand to him without taking her eyes from the screen. He put the cold glass against the palm of her hand without letting his skin touch hers.

"Here you go." Thankfully, she wasn't trying to be suggestive or teasing with a scrape of her fingers across his.

"Thanks," she replied vaguely, her attention entirely focused on the movie.

She didn't rattle away like his mother always did, but he could see by the slight nods and turns of her head that Maddie was utterly engaged. Every ten or fifteen minutes she would say something harsh, when something exceeded her patience. "Oh, come on! That is so unrealistic!"

Hank laughed.

"What?" She turned to face him. "It is. They didn't have that technology until at least two hundred years later. That's like . . . Google-able. Never mind."

He stared at her with renewed interest. "What do you know about the technological advances of antiquity?"

She shrugged. "I'm a classics major."

He laughed. "You're a what?"

She kept her eyes on the screen. "I. Am. A. Classics. Major."

He shook his head.

"Pause the movie, please," she said, sounding like she was at the end of her rope.

"What?"

"You heard me. Pause the movie."

He leaned forward and hit the "Pause" button on one of the myriad remotes.

"What did I say?"

"You shook your head in that doleful way that made it perfectly clear you think a classics major is some stupid, useless—"

"You are so defensive. Of course I don't think that. Epictetus, remember?"

She narrowed her eyes and stared at him. "I always feel like you're making fun of me."

"Why?"

"Because a lot of the time you are. And my brothers always make me feel sort of . . . frivolous. And I don't like it." She kept staring at him.

"Well," he moved his beer back and forth at the neck of the bottle, "I'm not those guys. I think it's cool."

"Oh." Maddie looked down at her lap. "Sorry. I guess I am a little defensive."

He held up the remote. "May I?"

Maddie smiled. "Yes. Please."

He pushed the button, and the roar of a crowded Trojan street scene filled the room. They watched the rest of the movie in friendly comfort. When the final credits began to roll, Maddie yawned and stood up. She bent down to pick up the two empty beer bottles she'd set next to the sofa. Hank had to look away before he got caught staring at her round backside. He walked over to the kitchen and then to the door to turn the lights back on.

Maddie put her two empties into the sink. "Thanks, Hank. That was great." She walked to where he was standing by the door. She yawned again, then rubbed her upper arms where they had begun to chill. "May I give you a quick kiss good-night before I leave or will that make you uncomfortable?"

He didn't know whether he loved or hated her practicality. He'd given her every reason to be cautious, so he couldn't very well turn around and accuse her of being cautious.

"Sure."

She kept her arms folded in front of her chest and leaned forward on the balls of her feet. Leaning into his neck, she rested her barely parted lips against the smooth, warm skin just above the hem of his T-shirt's collar. She took a deep inhale, then began to pull away. She dipped in for a quick follow-up peck.

"Thanks. I'll see you later. Okay? We'll be normal, right?"

"Sure, Maddie. We'll be normal." He reached up and put his thick fingers through the strands of chestnut hair that were coming loose from her braid at the nape of her neck. He didn't pull her against him or dive at her. He just wanted to feel the texture and warmth of her skin there. He stroked that tender part of her neck for a few seconds and watched as her shoulders relaxed and her eyes dipped. Hank pulled his hand away gently. "Thanks for coming over, beautiful."

She opened her eyes and stared at him with gentle sweetness. "Thanks for inviting me, handsome." Then she pulled open his door and let herself out.

Maddie only made it about halfway down the steps before turning abruptly back. "Hey! I forgot—"

Hank was standing at the top of the stairs, holding the glass bowl with his mother's coleslaw.

"—the coleslaw."

She walked back up the steps. "Thanks. I'm starving."

She took the bowl and went back to Janet's house to eat coleslaw in the yellow kitchen and then go up to her bed and wonder about whether or not to open her curtains again. Or if maybe her imagination was a safer option.

CHAPTER 10

Maybe Madison Post was a gift, Hank thought to himself later that week, back at the bottom of the ocean. The wind farm company had put Hank's diving team on retainer. There was going to be lots of work for the next few months.

His shift was about to end, and he was trying to let his thoughts about Maddie sift into something recognizable, like the way the disturbed sand around his heavy feet would resettle when he left the ocean floor. Not a good analogy, he chided himself. The ocean floor tended to capture everything and keep it perfectly preserved for centuries. One of his Army buddies had just e-mailed him about a private salvage group that was looking for experienced divers to work on a shipwreck that they'd dated to the fourth century BC. What happened on the ocean floor stayed on the ocean floor . . . forever.

He double-checked his valves and gave the signal that he was going to begin his ascent.

Hank got home a few hours later and saw the light on in his mom's kitchen. This week had been much better in terms of, as Maddie would say, acting normal. He turned off the engine of his truck and smiled to himself that the idea of *normal* still felt like acting. And maybe always would. He knew he was running out of time before he was going to have to go see someone at the VA hospital. He'd promised himself six months for reentry, to be a normal civilian. For normal to seem normal. But it didn't seem to be happening. For the most part, Hank still felt awkward and isolated when he was around other people. He hated crowds, like that night at the movie theater. He hadn't had any panic attacks or flashbacks. Yet.

Shutting the car door behind him, he walked around the narrow path that led to his mom's back door. He tapped twice on the wood frame next to the screen and made a note to repaint the door this weekend. "Can I come in?"

Maddie and Janet were sitting at the farm table and looked up at him simultaneously.

"Sure, sweetheart. Come on in. We were just trying these vegan cookies I made."

He rolled his eyes.

"What?" Janet said. "They're good, right, Maddie?"

Maddie was eating one just then and mumbled something that sounded like "Yes" around her full mouth.

Hank pulled a soda out of the fridge and sat at the far end of the six-foot-long table, a few seats away from Maddie.

She finished swallowing. "I mean, at first they're kind of . . . like . . . twigs . . . but then they're really pretty good."

Hank smiled at Maddie, then reached for one of the cookies. "Twigs, huh? Sounds delectable."

Janet smiled down at the table. "Well, give me a break, you two. How in the world am I supposed to make something without butter?"

"You're not!" Hank cried as he tried to get past the initial twiggy bite.

Maddie smiled at both of them. She didn't want to intrude; she could tell that Janet wanted to spend some time with her son. But Maddie just loved being in the same room with him when he was easy like this. He'd been much more relaxed this week. He'd wave or call hey when they'd passed each other. He'd come into the house once or twice just to say hi. Normal. Or what she hoped would be normal. She got the feeling that Hank didn't always do normal. Or maybe never had. He was seriously buttoned up.

"Okay, you two," Maddie said, standing up, "I'm going to head up to bed. Have fun without me."

Janet looked up, a curious look in her eyes. "Oh, so soon? Okay, then."

"Yeah, I'm wiped." She was. The summer crowds were starting to pile into the diner in the mornings, and her tips were starting to mount up. "But at least I've got a little bit of cash to show for my efforts." She held on to the back of the old kitchen chair. "So I'll see you guys around." She smiled from Janet to Hank and tried not to acknowledge the slow roll of what must be desire as he smiled at her and said, "Sleep well."

Maddie took the stairs two at time and walked quickly to her room. Her attraction to Hank didn't seem to be going anywhere except up. Maybe he'd been right to try the amputation approach after they got back from canoeing. She stood in the middle of her room, holding the flat of her palm against her fluttering stomach. She was seriously crazy about the guy. She knew she acted like a silly puppy when she was excited, but she couldn't help it. She knew it bothered him. She could feel Hank looking at her sometimes when she was particularly happy or exuberant about something. She could feel him judging her while they'd watched *Troy* the previous weekend. She could feel his judgment like a palpable thing between them that night.

But if Maddie claimed to want "normal," she had to try to understand what that meant for Hank. She got ready for bed and picked up her Agatha Christie as she slipped into the cool sheets. She sniffed the smell of sunshine and fresh air that clung to the old floral sheets. Janet had changed her linen that day. Maddie reminded herself to thank her for that.

They were all puttering around Janet's for the rest of the weekend. Hank had taken it upon himself to remove all the screen doors, strip and repaint the frames, and replace the screens. Maddie tried not to be too much of a gawker, strolling past Hank in the driveway, where he'd set up a couple of sawhorses to rest the door frames on while he sanded and prepped them.

She wasn't the only one, she realized, when she noticed a couple of teenage girls who just so happened to be bicycling past the driveway. Repeatedly.

"Hey, Hank!" one of them called, then laughed and got all embarrassed.

"Hi, Emily. Say hi to Karl for me."

Maddie was walking by with a box of old clothes from the attic, which she was helping Janet clean out.

She must have laughed or done something to indicate that she'd seen the exchange. After Maddie put the box in the back of Janet's car, Hank said, "What are you laughing at? She's the younger sister of one of my oldest friends."

"Just how all the girls in this town have a crush on you."

"Don't be ridiculous." He scowled and went back to hand-sanding the trim on the door that he couldn't reach with the electric sander. Maddie felt her heart pick up, and her pulse followed the beat of his movements. She was rapidly moving from crush to full-on lust when it came to Henry Gilbertson. He had on his usual fitted gray T-shirt and worn-in cargo shorts. He looked so damn good. So natural in his skin. His shoulders and arms exuded strength and power. His hands held the sander with familiar confidence. His back and neck flexed and relaxed through the repetitive strokes. His hips and—

"Cut it out, Maddie. I can't concentrate."

She must have stared too long.

She shook her head. Guilty.

"Oh, sorry." She walked quickly back into the house and returned to the attic for another box of old junk to bring to the VA hospital thrift shop down in Portland.

About two hours later, Janet and Maddie agreed that they'd done enough for one day. Janet suggested they all three go to dinner in Portland.

Hank had finished stripping and sanding all three screen doors—his mother's two and his own—and the first coat of primer was done, set to dry overnight. He was in the midst of moving all of his tools and the sawhorses back into the garage when his mom came out with a tray of three iced teas for them.

"I don't know, Mom. Why don't you two go on without me." A statement, not a question.

"Because it would be more fun to go all together. You could go shower and look nice and the three of us could go to that great place with that new chef that everyone's been talking about. Phil said it was supposed to be really good."

Maddie looked up from her glass of iced tea. "When did you see Phil? I don't remember you being in the diner this week?"

Maddie realized too late that she had totally violated the

sisterhood of the . . . sisterhood. Janet looked cornered and then overly blasé. "Oh, I bumped into him at the Safeway the other day, I think. I can't remember exactly."

Hank looked skeptical. "Maybe we should invite him to come with us? Even up our numbers."

Maddie looked at him. He was a cruel beast.

"Well," she hesitated, then looked right into Hank's sparkling eyes, "that might be nice."

And there went the air out of the driveway. That might have been all the air leaving the town of Blake, Maine.

"You and Phil?" Hank blurted before he could think better of it.

Janet kept looking at him. She didn't say a word, just nodded. She was steely when she wanted to be, that was for sure. Maddie watched the little power struggle play out, taking a slow sip of iced tea and reaching for an imaginary bucket of popcorn.

Front.

Row.

Seat.

It dawned on Maddie that this was exactly what Janet had been hoping for, to draw Hank into something—anything—that would make him take an emotional stake in life.

He must have seen the trap as quickly as Maddie had, because he retreated immediately. He coiled back into himself just like he had on the drive back from the canoe trip. Total shut-down.

Hank shrugged.

"You three should go. You'll have fun."

Maddie nearly spit her iced tea out. "I'm not going to Portland with Phil Campbell on my night off." She turned quickly to Janet. "No offense! I mean, he's my boss—"

Janet looked at Maddie as if the younger woman had just revealed the details of the Manhattan Project to the Russians. Traitor!

"Oh, fine!" Janet finally conceded. "We don't need to invite Phil. I don't know how I got painted into this corner in the first place. I just thought it would be fun to drop off all this stuff at the thrift shop in Portland and then get a lobster roll while we were there." She shrugged, a blatant mockery of Hank's similar movement. "Call me crazy!" She pivoted on the heel of her blue Keds and stormed back into the house.

Maddie whistled with low accusation. "You are in deep shit, Hank!" Then Maddie laughed; she just couldn't help herself. "Your mom basically just confessed that the secret mystery man is none other than Phil Fucking Campbell and you rained all over that particular parade. Nice going, buddy." Maddie patted him on the upper arm with a dismissive swat. "Good one!"

Still laughing to herself as she walked through the front door, Maddie called out, "Quit sulking, Janet! I still want to go to Portland! Let's leave Mopey home and go have some fun!"

Within half an hour, both women were showered and had changed into casual sundresses and sandals. Hank was sitting on the bottom step of the stairs that led to his apartment, reading what looked to be some sort of mechanical engineering magazine.

He looked up when they walked past him.

"Have fun, ladies," he said.

"Oh, we will!" Janet said with a defiant lift of her chin.

Hank smiled despite himself, feeling a slight tremor of that ephemeral "normal," watching his mother and his beautiful . . . friend . . . get into the small, piece-of-crap Japanese car and drive off like a pair of teenagers on their way to the mall.

CHAPTER 11

The following week was the Fourth of July, and Blake, Maine, had done a little bit of primping. Bunting stretched across the storefronts on Main Street, and sparkling little white lights had been strung from the rooftops on the north side of the street to the rooftops on the south side of the street and back again. The parade was happening on Saturday, and then there were huge fireworks on Sunday over in Freeport.

The sun cast long shadows across the sidewalk on Saturday afternoon. Janet, Hank, and Maddie sat on the curb along with hundreds of other people who'd grabbed a plastic cup from home and come to watch the antique fire trucks and small-scale military bands parade past.

Hank was sitting in the middle, between Janet and Maddie. At one point, he turned to look at Maddie's profile. She was gazing contentedly at the bagpipers from a few towns away. To his right, Janet was talking to a friend of hers with whom she worked at the library on weekends.

"Hey," Hank said softly.

Maddie's head spun to face him. "Hey . . ."

"Really exciting, huh?" He was trying to bait her into admitting how boring their small-town existence really was.

"I love it!" She didn't clap her hands against her thighs or sigh or do anything overly enthusiastic, but her eyes gleamed and, Jesus, if Hank didn't feel it like a punch in the gut. "I am so happy right now. Just to be sitting here."

So much for baiting Maddie. If anyone had been snared, it was Hank: he felt like he'd been hooked and gutted. How could she just feel, and experience, and express like that? It was so foreign to him. And it was beginning to dawn on him that the Army and his deployments might not be entirely to blame. He had never been comfortable around this kind of vitality. It felt messy and threatening. It was like being drunk.

It was like Maddie was drunk.

On life.

That's probably why Janet had come to love her. Because that's what had happened. It wasn't some misdirected mother-daughter thing. Janet just adored the way Maddie looked at life and found it all so exciting and promising. That was the way Janet had probably always wanted to look at the world—through clear-eyed, rosy glasses—but the only way Janet could achieve that was in a bottle. To see someone who did it on the air? That had captured Janet in a way that a bottle of Jack never could.

Hank turned away quickly, pretending that he wanted to pay close attention to one of the vintage fire trucks that had driven over from New Hampshire for the festivities.

"Do you like it, Hank?" Maddie asked in a near whisper.

She wasn't even overly close to his ear. But he felt her close. He felt her voice as if she were breathing hot and tight against him, even when she was a few feet away.

"It's all right, I guess." Remaining ambivalent was becoming more and more difficult. Maybe that was progress. Maybe that meant he was getting better. But he didn't feel better. He felt like he was coming apart at the seams, in slow rips that were going to make all of his insides slip out. And he resented that Maddie was the one who was making him feel that way. He resented that it was so easy for her to be jubilant and connected. To be a part of life.

When he wasn't.

Janet's library friend left and a little while later Phil showed up and sat down next to Janet. At one point he looked past Hank and Janet to make eye contact with Maddie. She smiled, and he winked. Maddie was so happy for Janet, who had obviously been trying to keep their burgeoning relationship under wraps until she knew how far it would go.

From the way the two of them were holding hands in front of the entire town, it looked like things were very unwrapped. And going far.

Maddie had a little shudder as she realized how much she wished Hank would hold her hand like that, to tell the world that they were together (which they weren't), to take possession of her (which he never would), or just to feel the warmth of his skin against hers (which would feel lovely).

She must have sighed aloud. Hank turned to look at her again. She knew her freewheeling, emotional outbursts drove him crazy, but it wasn't like she could change who she was. And he hadn't even seen the half of it.

"You okay?" he asked.

"Sure, fine. Just enjoying the festivities." She smiled quickly and then set her face back to a stony mask, taking in the fire trucks. Concentrating. Watch me be a reliable, unemotional, normal person watching a parade, she thought.

"You want to go out tonight?" he asked.

"What do you mean? We are out—"

He shook his head. "Never mind."

"No." She reached for his forearm—digging her fingers into his skin too hard and too quickly—and then pulled her hand away. "Please. Yes. I would love to go out with you tonight—" Jesus. Why did he have to make her feel so desperate? Maddie wondered. She was going to make him pay for that in bed one day, if she ever got the chance. She would make him beg or cry out or grab at the nape of her neck and demand things of her, things that only she could provide in that moment of wanting. Because right now he was making her feel so needy, and she didn't want to be alone in that.

She knew she'd be alone after. She had spent much of the past few weeks making all sorts of deals with the devil about what she would be compromising if she actually slept with him. The risks were pretty vast. If he bolted emotionally the way he did after the canoe trip, well, she argued with herself, at least she could know that it was all about him and his screwed-up isolation issues. Not about her.

Because that always worked. Knowing it wasn't about her. Yeah, that was so comforting.

Not.

She shook her head and whispered, "Oh, never mind."

He reached over, like a thirteen-year-old boy might reach for a girl's hand the first time he went to the movies without his mom there. Tentatively and so sweetly. So cautious.

He held her hand like that, fingers intertwined, both of their hands resting on his strong thigh, as the fire trucks passed by in a dreamy blur. Maddie had a brief vision of being so unwilling to remove her fingers from his that the parade would finish and the people would disperse and night would descend and the bits of stray garbage would be floating down the middle of the dark street like a tumbleweed in a ghost town, and there the two of them would be sitting, still quietly holding hands on the side of the road. Content.

"I'll pick you up at eight," he said.

She smiled so broadly. It was only half past two in the afternoon. And he was still holding her hand in that public, possessive way that told the world they were *more than friends*. And she could relax into the *now* because he had just offered a beautiful *later*. It didn't get much better than—

"Guess who!" Two strong male hands covered her eyes from behind. She could hear immature masculine laughter and recognized the sound of Zander's voice right away. Hank's hand shook free, and Maddie thought she might burst into tears at the loss of those strong fingers in hers. Then the rage of Zander Dalgliesh spoiling her perfect moment overrode every other feeling.

Maddie pushed the jerk's hands away from her face and jumped up with a spring that years of squats had given her.

"What is your problem, Zander?"

He was looking down at Hank, who was looking at the fire trucks and ignoring . . . everyone and everything.

"Zander!" Maddie barked.

"Hey, beautiful!" Zander reached up to caress Maddie's cheek, and she swatted him away before he could make contact.

"Cut it out!"

"Aren't you going to introduce us to your friends?" He said "friends" in a way that made Maddie despise him. Unforgivably. For the rest of his life. Because he said it in a challenging, collusive way that made it seem like Zander and Maddie were cut from the same cloth and—even though Maddie might pretend to be friends with *those people*—that Zander and everyone else knew that she was always going to end up behind the wheel of a late-model BMW that her husband had bought her for Valentine's Day. Different cloth.

"Yes!" Maddie beamed. "Zander Dalgliesh, this is Henry Gilbertson and his mother Janet. And this is Phil Campbell, who owns the diner here in town."

The other three looked up from the curb, Janet smiling widely and reaching up awkwardly to shake hands with Zander.

"Nice to meet you," Zander said to Janet. He was almost sincere. He turned back to face Maddie with that fake, doe-eyed, I've-missed-you-baby look in his eyes. Maddie could feel Hank's stiff back like a physical thing weighted against her.

"Thanks for saying hi, Zan. Have a good summer—" Maddie tried to fob him off with a quick good-bye, beginning to turn away before she finished speaking.

"Hey! Wait a minute! It's me, baby! Get over here—"

He reached for her waist and tried to pull her into a quick hug. She smelled the beer on his breath and felt Hank rise up behind her and saw Janet's eyes cloud and all sorts of ragged bits of information were pelting her senses and she couldn't process what was actually happening.

"Zander! Stop!" Maddie pushed herself away from him, and then almost fell backward as Hank doubled the momentum of the movement, pulling her flush against him with his strong hands at her hips.

Zander stared at Maddie with a disbelieving look on his arrogant, handsome face. "Who is this guy?" Zander jutted his chin at Hank without ever looking at him.

"Zander," Maddie said, proud of how steady her voice was, and feeling slightly guilty for how good it felt to have Hank's strong, thick fingers digging into the waist of her shorts and his thumbs pressed into the skin at her lower back. "This is my *really good* friend Henry Gilbertson. Get it?"

Zander's expression was incredulous. "You're fucking this guy?!"

Hank's fist flew so fast and so close to Maddie's ear before it slammed into Zander's face that she didn't even understand what had happened. They'd all been standing there and then—*poof!*— Zander Dalgliesh was lights-out on the sidewalk. Denny and two other guys from their frat whose names Maddie couldn't remember stared down at their friend's limp body.

"Whoa," Denny commented. "Nice hit, dude." Then he took a sip of his beer. *What a pal*, Maddie thought. The other two were equally disinclined to bend down and check on their friend's well-being.

Phil and Janet had also stood up, physically and emotionally backing up Hank. Maddie could feel his breath against her neck.

"You okay?" he asked Maddie.

A policeman was making his way over. He'd been standing about ten feet away, talking to Sharon and her in-laws who'd come to town for the holiday weekend. The cop was named Steve, and Maddie had served him coffee a bunch of times.

"Hey, Maddie, what happened?"

"Hey, Steve. This guy kind of grabbed me, and I tried to push him away, and then he said something really rude . . . so . . . Hank punched him."

Steve stared at Hank and Janet and Phil.

"Hank?"

"Yes, sir."

"It's me, Steve. Cut it out with the yessir stuff. What happened? You okay?"

Hank's hold began to loosen on Maddie's waist, and she quickly put her hands over his to keep him attached to her. And to let him know that she was with him. Supporting him.

"It's like Maddie said," Hank told Steve.

Zander was starting to come around. Denny squatted down.

"You got totally nailed, dude."

Zander stared with vacant, disoriented eyes, first at Denny, then up to Maddie. He looked at her with a combination of rage and shame. Then he caught the way Hank was staring at him and he levered himself up to a standing position and dusted himself off.

Denny stood up next to him.

Steve stared at Zander without asking him any questions or encouraging him in any way.

Finally, Steve rested his right hand on the handle of his gun in that quintessential that's-right-I-am-the-one-with-the-gun-here gesture, and said, "You all right, son?"

Steve couldn't have been much older than thirty, so the *son* had a little hint of aggression behind it. Kind of like, *You getting me, buddy?*

Zander looked slightly cornered, and Maddie almost felt sorry for him. But not really. It felt great to see the moment when he realized he was just a prick.

"Yeah, I'm fine. I must have just fallen down."

Denny and the other two frat guys started laughing. "That's for sure." And "You always were clumsy." And "This old sidewalk is pretty uneven. Watch your step next time, Dog-man!" The four of them regrouped and started to walk off.

Lifting his plastic cup in a salute, Denny turned back to Maddie and said, "Always a pleasure bumping into you, Post." Then he turned, and all four guys started laughing again at his rapier wit.

She probably would have run after him and scratched him in the face if Hank hadn't been holding her in place.

"Let them go, babe."

And nothing really mattered after that because he was leaning in close to her ear when he said it, and it was so sweet, and he really cared about her. It didn't matter if he freaked out and ran off and never saw her again, she was going to get this man in bed and make sure he knew how much she cared for him.

She turned out of his hold. "I hate to be a downer, but I think I want to go home and chill out for a little while."

Janet was still standing just beyond Hank, with Phil on her right. "Oh, I'll walk home with you, sweetie. The parade's almost finished."

"No it's not!" Maddie smiled. "There are probably two more hours at least. You all stay. I'll be fine. I just want an iced tea and to be quiet for a little while. I'm totally fine."

Janet looked at Phil. Phil looked at Hank.

"I'm definitely walking home with you. No point in arguing." Hank took her hand in his and then turned to his mom. "Thanks."

Janet tilted her head, and her mouth tightened as she held her emotions in check. "You are a good man, Hank."

He looked embarrassed. "Bye, Phil."

"Bye, Hank. Bye, Maddie," Phil said.

Hank guided Maddie through the crowd in the opposite direction from the one Zander and his friends had taken. They took the first right onto Ash Street, and it was almost immediately deserted. It felt strange to have been in the midst of all those humming crowds and then to be suddenly dropped into this silence. Hank looked mad. He started walking a little bit faster, and Maddie picked up her pace.

She had hoped they might duck behind one of the big oak trees that sprawled in some of the yards on the sloped road that led back up to his place. She wanted to kiss him so badly. It was terrible to admit how that punch had made her want to kiss him. She felt like some vaporish medieval heroine who wanted to give her handkerchief to her knight-errant to carry in battle.

Hank seemed like he just wanted to deliver her home as quickly as possible and be done with the whole stupid fracas.

He was practically dragging her the last few feet up the driveway, and she assumed he was going to lead her into his mother's house, pour her the ameliorative glass of iced tea, and leave her be. She started to let go of his hand and lean toward Janet's front door, but Hank's hold on her only tightened and he pulled her along with even more abrupt power.

Toward his place.

Up the steps.

Pounding.

He didn't let go of her hand when he reached into his front pocket and pulled out the single key to his front door. How he remained so steady, so focused, Maddie would never know. She only knew that her heart was hammering so hard she was beginning to lose some of her hearing. The blood was pounding in a way that made her eardrums throb. *He-wants-me-he-wants-me*, the beat seemed to hammer away. He pushed the door open, pulled Maddie in, kicked the door shut, and tossed the single key into the small bowl on the table next to the front door.

CHAPTER 12

When Hank knew he had her, in his lair as it were, he went into damnable slow motion. The hand that had been holding her like a vise for the past fifteen minutes began to loosen, and then the pads of his fingertips were touching the lengths of her fingers. So lightly, with such gentle intent.

Maddie's breath was faltering.

He brought his other hand around to her back, slipped it under her T-shirt, and then his hand somehow snaked up to her nape. With one firm press of his thick forearm against her back and the tightening grip of the hand at her neck, Maddie was his.

Hank's lips came down onto hers, and there was none of the light teasing that she remembered from some of his other kisses. He was taking her hard and fast this time. And she wanted to give and give. She whimpered at the promise of all that power and strength. She tried to pull her hips away slightly, but his left arm was so relentless at her back. His strength was completely immovable.

"Tell me," he breathed, kissing his way down her neck, nuzzling behind her ear.

Her lips were slightly open, her head leaning back into his strong palm. "Tell you what?"

"Tell me you want this." His voice was deep and far away, muffled by her skin and his desire.

A strained little moan escaped her.

"Tell me!" he demanded, pressing harder into her, crushing her against him.

"Yes. You know I do." The words were stilted and sounded unfamiliar on her lips. They sounded like passion. Not the kind of passion that she'd experienced while rolling around in a tent or making out with Zander after too many beers. This felt like something unavoidable was bearing down on her, pulling her under, pushing her higher.

She felt the floor slip away, not even caring that she'd completely lost control of her own body. Hank was carrying her into his bedroom, and she leaned her face into his tensed chest muscles. Maddie wanted to inhale him, not just the scent of him, but the actual essence of his humanity. She wanted to take and take and take.

She smiled at the irony. There would never be a more generous taking. Maddie was going to make sure that Hank felt the gift of all her taking, of how much she needed and wanted to feel him and appreciate him and know him and love—okay, so yeah, there it was, moving on—*love him*. The perfect giving and taking. And, Maddie hoped, giving and taking and giving and taking, until neither of them could distinguish one from the other. Just as it was in those perfect moments when she was rowing, lost in the natural rhythm, the catch and the extraction of the oars becoming seamless. When the parts became the whole.

Hank was afraid of how badly he wanted her. He needed to slow it down and breathe. She would drown him without even trying. The way she was looking at him just then, when he'd tossed her roughly on the bed and she had laughed her exhale, then lifted herself up on her elbows, her hips tilting right and left, unable to stay still. Her lips were . . . sin.

He stood at the side of the bed, staring down at her, stretching his jaw and placing the flats of his palms against his cheeks, then covering his mouth.

"What am I going to do with you, Madison Post?"

Her face bloomed. Her eyes sparkled with desire and mischief and something much darker. Something that pulled him so far down, way too deep. "I have no idea, but I can't wait to find out."

He looked up at the ceiling to collect himself, then he stared down at her.

"May I take your shorts off?" she asked.

He was confused by her tenderness. It wasn't a sexy submissive thing, either. She was trying to take care, to be mindful. Hank smiled at the realization. "Look who's all relaxed and mellow all of a sudden?"

She bit the inside of her lower lip and looked up at him. "You make me kind of warm and gooey inside. It's like I'm in slow motion when you look at me like that." She was on her knees on his bed, fingering the top button of his fly, reminding him that she was waiting for his answer.

He knew what she was really asking. Was he ready? Was he ready to bare himself to her, to let her really see him and really be with him? He was tempted to push her hand away and shuck off his own clothes in a careless rush, to remove any romantic byplay from the equation.

But.

It was going to feel so good to have her hands on him. To feel the slight quiver of her fingers as she messed around with the buttons and pulled at the elastic of his underwear and touched him. To feel her excitement and have that energy around him and against his skin. To feel her feeling him.

He could deal with the fallout later, but for now he wanted to feel all of that. He wanted to feel, full stop.

"Yes," he answered. His voice was certain, but it was deeper than it usually was and she looked up at him.

"You're sure?"

"Are you trying to protect my virtue or something? Take off my shorts!"

They both laughed, and she began undoing the buttons. Her hands were doing that fluttery thing he had relived again and again since the canoe trip. The way she would become kind of overset with desire or sensation or whatever you wanted to call it, and her fingertips would sort of lose their dexterity, and she would take those little breaths that meant she'd discovered something she liked, and her fingertips would hover and barely touch him.

He reached for her. "Just tell me to stop if I'm too rough or anything—"

"Stop trying to go easy on me, Hank."

"Okay, but just . . ." He was peeling off her tight T-shirt and paused to stare at her purple lace bra. "You wear stuff like this . . . just during the day . . . around . . ."

Maddie was busy leaning in to kiss his neck, and he kept pushing her away to get a better look at her chest.

"Yes, why?" She leaned in again and then stood up on the bed so he could take off her shorts.

"No reason . . ." Her shorts were just below Hank's eye level. He kissed her navel then undid her shorts and pulled them down the length of her smooth, tanned legs. He left on the matching purple lace underpants.

"Honestly, Maddie. You are amazing . . ."

She had draped herself over his shoulder and was kissing his spine and shoulder blades. "So are you," she whispered, moving her kisses up to his neck and around his ears.

"Be careful . . ." he whispered.

"I know," she said. "I'll be gentle with you." He knew she was referring to his ears and how tender they were from all the years of diving, but he felt like she might not rip his heart out either. That she would be good to him.

For now, he amended. She would be good for now. No pressure.

He must have stiffened at the thought of some kind of long-term provision. She stood up, flipping her hair down her back and enjoying the stretch.

"It's kind of fun being up here, six inches taller than you are."

He looked up into her eyes as he began to work his hands up her legs, massaging deep strokes and rising higher each time. "It is, huh? You like to be above me?"

"I like to be anywhere near you . . ." She pulled him toward her and bent forward so she could fit her mouth into the crook of his neck.

He adored her in that moment. Way more than he ever thought he could adore another human being. Way more than he would ever allow himself to feel after the hours or days they spent in this room. Because they both knew he wouldn't be able to sustain anything like this level of intimacy.

"It's just for now. Okay?" Hank blurted.

She smiled at him, and he thought he saw a sheen of emotion

across her eyes. Maddie looked to the ceiling for relief from the pressure of Hank's eyes, then took a deep breath and stared him down. Down deep. "Whatever you can spare, handsome."

He crawled onto the bed and put one leg over her hips. She wriggled under him like she had in the tent, enjoying the confinement of his arms and his body. "Don't say it like that, Maddie. I don't mean it in a scrimping way. I just mean . . ."

She was touching him again, and the words started to evaporate. "I just mean . . ."

Her hands were everywhere. "It's all good," she whispered.

"I just can't give you anything more than this . . ."

She stopped kissing and touching and moving all over and against him and grabbed his head in her hands. "I want whatever you can give. Nothing more." Maddie pulled his face to hers and kissed him with everything she had, she wanted to give him everything. He could go on telling himself it was just for now, just for today, just for this week, just of this summer, but Maddie knew in her guts, in all of her tingling nerve endings, that—for her—this experience would never be limited by time or distance. She would never look back and think that Hank had given her anything less than . . . everything.

Maddie's possessive hold on his skull loosened and her hands fell away, resting easily on the pillow by her face. She bit her own knuckle and tried to get some of her hair to cover her face. She felt scared all of a sudden. Not of him or what was to come, but of revealing herself, of the vulnerability of it all. She was trying so hard to relax, but it was all becoming real.

Hank's face shifted slowly into one of his movie-star smiles. "Are you getting nervous all of a sudden?"

She froze under him, trying to let the pain abate. It was nothing really. It was fading already. Maddie was already beginning to feel the spread of warmth that meant she would be feeling the bliss and abandon of release—

"Maddie?" Hank's voice was stern, like it had been that first night she'd ever met him. "Open your eyes and look at me."

She opened her eyes.

"Are you a virgin?"

"No . . ." The unspoken "*not anymore*" hung in the small space between them.

He ground his teeth but didn't move. Maddie put her hands on his hips to hold him in place, just in case he got any crazy ideas to get all dramatic and not finish what they'd started . . . just barely scratched the surface.

"Maddie?"

"What?" she whispered. He stayed silent. She persisted. "Please don't make it a thing, okay?" It was a legitimate question. She was asking him politely. Please. Please don't turn it into something that it's not. She had agreed to do the same for him, hadn't she? In that weird way, they were both asking one another to move forward without any judgment—about the past (in her case) or the future (in his).

He huffed a small breath and began to move. It felt so amazing, so complete and whole. He made her feel intensely *right* in the world . . . on the planet. Like a natural creature. No getting or spending. Just being.

He began to move, but slowly. Probably way more slowly than he was planning on way-back-when, ten minutes ago, with all his promising talk of stop-me-if-I'm-too-rough and all that.

Holding her eyes—then losing his focus when his care of her began to increase his own pleasure—he began to bring her back to him.

"You're coming with me," he ground out.

"I don't know if I can . . ." She felt so out of control. All of the other non-sex sex she'd had in her life had been more manageable, somehow. This just felt completely out of her jurisdiction.

"Stay with me . . ." Hank took one finger and pushed her chin so she was forced to face him. He kept up the slow, relentless rhythm. "Stay with me, Maddie."

She knew what he meant, to keep her focus on him, to look at him in that moment of joint ecstasy, as both of them rose and shared the intensity of it all. But the possibility—however remote—that he might one day say that and mean it literally, that he wanted her to stay with him for the rest of their lives, *that* made Maddie realize she might have stepped into an abyss.

Maddie saw in that moment that he was the most beautiful creature she had ever happened upon. Together they were beautiful. Complete.

Then she began to shake.

Not just a slight trembling, but an all-over-body, uncontrollable shaking. Hank pulled her into his arms. She was beginning to curl into herself, and he pulled the sheets and the light cotton blanket over them both and just held her like that until her shuddering body recovered from the shock.

It took a while.

She finally fell asleep about an hour later and Hank slipped out of the bed once he was sure she was totally out. Even through her sleep, she made a sad little dreamy sound when his body broke contact with hers. He tucked the light bedding over her and went out to his living room.

This wasn't a disaster, he reminded himself. He had experienced and survived legitimate disasters. This was more of a Terribly Complicated Situation. He opened the refrigerator and pulled out a cold beer. He flipped off the top and threw it into the bin, then reached for the drawer to put the opener away. But he didn't open the drawer. He stood there for a few seconds, then left the opener on the counter. He stared at it. "Why put it back if you're just going to use it again right away?" The memory of Maddie's voice echoed in his mind.

Why put Maddie back? She was a grown woman—they'd both just proven that with flying colors—she wasn't trying to lure him into anything against his will. If anything, she'd been even more cautious about his feelings than he'd been with her body. They could have a few months of bone-cracking pleasure. Even he could see he'd be a fool to pass up the opportunity. And obviously Maddie could handle it; she'd practically orchestrated this whole damn thing. He finished the first beer and cracked open two more to bring into the bedroom.

Stopping to look at his cell phone on his desk, Hank put the beers down and picked up the device. His mother had sent a brief text asking to confirm that Maddie was all right. Hank texted her back that Maddie was fine. Five seconds later, there was a text letting Hank know Janet was going to dinner with Phil. His thumbs hovered over the phone . . . did he need to reply to that? He finally managed to tap, *Have fun.*

That taken care of, Hank picked up the beers and returned to the bedroom. He set the bottles down quietly and went into the bathroom, then slid back into bed behind Maddie. She hummed her appreciation, settling her backside against him.

He didn't want to wake her, but he couldn't help trailing his palm along the perfect curve of her hip, draped in the white sheet and the pale blue cotton summer blanket.

"Do you want me to leave?" she whispered, not looking at him.

He pulled her quickly around to face him. "What?!"

"You said, *just for now*. So I didn't know if you meant, *just this one time*, or *just tonight*, or what."

She wasn't even baiting him or trying to push him to make a decision. Maddie looked into his eyes with plain curiosity, like she was having to decide on a bus schedule, and needed the facts that would let her move on with her plans.

"Do you want to leave?" Hank realized he hadn't even considered this from her point of view. "I mean—"

Maddie lifted her lips to his, to get him to stop saying all that nonsense. The kiss escalated quickly and she was back to all that faraway moaning and pleading in about five seconds. She withdrew from the kiss, letting her head flop back onto the pillow. "I don't want to leave until I have to be at work Monday morning, and even then I'll be hard pressed to leave if you're still wanting me around."

He stared down into her eyes. "You knock the wind out of me when you talk like that, you know. Every time. All breezy and accommodating and eager at the same time."

She smiled and kissed his cheek. "I thought you hated my enthusiasm."

"You thought wrong." Hank kept her caged in his arms and had the incongruous thought that one day he would like to meet her family, so he could see what it took to instill that level of confidence.

"You are so entitled," he said, caressing her cheek with the back of his knuckles.

Maddie's face turned stormy in an instant. "I am not—"

He kissed her quickly to get her to stop flying off the handle. "I meant," Hank continued, moving so he was back down on the bed lying alongside her, "that you have a wonderful sense of what you are legitimately entitled to. You have certain ideas about what you can accomplish in life, what you deserve. I didn't mean it like you were spoiled. I meant it as a compliment."

She looked skeptical. "I don't think there are many people in the world today who would take 'entitled' as a compliment." Maddie tried to rearrange her arms so she could clasp her hands up near her chin, in a sort of horizontal version of crossing her arms in front of her chest, which would have just been ridiculous.

Hank laughed anyway, and pulled her to him. He began kissing her again and Maddie sank deeper and deeper into the abyss, not caring about the consequences. Not caring about how miserable she was going to be one day in the not very distant future, when Hank just didn't show up or didn't say hello to her when he walked past her window. None of it mattered, because right here in the beautiful present, she was his to do with as he pleased. As he pleased her.

They spent the rest of the weekend in bed, with the occasional foray to the refrigerator or the couch. They watched a movie in the middle of the night, Maddie lounging all over Hank like she had been desperately wanting to do the whole time they had been watching *Troy* the week before.

By Sunday afternoon, Maddie suggested they go down to Freeport to watch the fireworks. They were back in bed, dozing lightly.

Hank didn't open his eyes when he spoke, but his hand tightened gently on Maddie's. "I'm not really good at fireworks."

"Oh." Maddie sounded surprised and a little disappointed. She was having visions of the two of them on a blanket holding hands and looking up at the sky and feeling the pounding, explosive claps in their bones.

"You should go with Janet and Phil. It's supposed to be a really big deal this year."

"I think I'd rather lie here with you," she said simply.

His eyes were still closed, but his lips turned up with a satisfied smile. "I like the way you think, kid."

Maddie rolled into Hank's arms, lining her body up with his, and fell into a blissful nap. It was one of those fairy-tale sleeps where she felt partially aware of the birds outside Hank's bedroom window, and drugged by the smell of Hank's skin on every inhale, but her brain was quiet and she felt like a still peace had settled over her.

A few hours later, they took a shower together and then Hank made a big pot of pasta and they sat at his kitchen counter and ate it with a couple of glasses of red wine.

"I should probably go," Maddie said, after she'd helped him put the dishes into the dishwasher and they'd finished putting away the pots and pans.

"Really?" He looked a little crushed.

"Oh, you better not look at me like that, Gilbertson—what were you, by the way?" He looked confused. "What was your rank in the Army?"

"Oh, that. Major."

"Wow. That's pretty high for someone your age, isn't it?"

He folded the kitchen towel neatly and hung it over the handle of the stove. "Not really."

"Why do I get the feeling you wouldn't tell me it was some huge honor, anyway?"

He smiled and pulled her into his chest. "It's over. It doesn't matter."

"Just because something is over doesn't mean it doesn't matter." She said it into his T-shirt and tried not to think of everything as having two or three ulterior meanings. She pulled herself out of his hold. "But I really do need to go. I mean," she gestured down at her appearance, bare feet and legs leading up to one of Hank's gray T-shirts, nothing more, "I'd really love to show up at work like this tomorrow, but I think a little sleep in my own bed and some clean clothes might boost my tips. What do you think?"

"I think your tips would be off the charts if you went into work exactly like this." He wrapped his arms around her waist again. She kind of loved how he always wanted to touch her, to have his hand in contact with her, while they were eating dinner, while they were watching a movie. And in bed, after the obvious times, he always rested his palm on her or draped his leg over one of hers. It felt amazing.

She started laughing a little, then kissed his neck.

"What's funny?" he asked.

"I was just thinking my body is going to miss your body. All this touching. I'm going to get greedy."

Hank nuzzled into her neck, and Maddie thought it was probably because he didn't want her to see he felt the same way.

"Okay," she tried again a few minutes later, feeling herself getting ramped up all over again, just from those kisses. "Stop!" She laughed again, and he smiled with a hint of guilt, but he certainly wasn't sorry. "Let me go!"

He did as she asked, then leaned back into the refrigerator, sizing her up, his hands pushed into his pockets, making his shorts tug lower.

Maddie shook her head and rolled her eyes. "You don't have to

try to look hot." She gestured toward his broad shoulders and narrow waist. His bare chest was tanned and muscled, his hard stomach going pale where he'd pulled his shorts low.

"I wasn't trying."

"Yeah, right!" Then she squealed as he tried to lift up her
T-shirt for a quick grab before she left the kitchen. She pulled the
fabric out of his hold and ran into the bedroom.

CHAPTER 13

The next few weeks it seemed to Maddie that everything slowed down and settled into a wonderful groove. She woke up at 4:30 a.m. and made it to work by five every day. Her waitressing had become second nature. Her familiarity with the regulars. Her banter with Phil. Her friendship with Sharon. And then: the afternoons. Hank was always there. He was usually back around four or five, which gave Maddie time to go for a run or workout down at the boxing gym she'd joined.

The two of them would fall into each other's arms, usually sweaty and dirty from the day at work or exercise, and none of it mattered because they were desperate for each other. And they'd fall onto the sofa or the bed and replenish themselves with every inch of their bodies after the seemingly endless drought of an entire workday spent apart.

On a particularly sultry afternoon in early August, Maddie turned to him in bed and asked, "Will you take me down to the ocean floor sometime?"

He looked up at the ceiling.

She knew the look. He might want to be touching her all the time, but he didn't like the slightest effort on her part to get into his head. He didn't want anybody in there, not even (maybe especially not) himself.

"Why? It's just dark and cold."

She shrugged. "I don't know. It's just where you are so much of the time. I just want to see what it's like. You know what it's like at the diner."

He grunted noncommittally.

"Don't you ever picture me at the diner, just look at the clock at ten in the morning and think, *Hmm*, I can just picture Maddie at Phil's spilling an iced tea on Dr. Vinton—"

"You didn't?" he asked, his eyes wide.

"No!" She laughed. "But I almost did. I'm too good for that now." She flexed her muscle in her upper arm to show what a pro she had become. "Look at that. I had to start carrying the tray with my left hand because my right bicep was getting bigger than the left."

"Quite the Lou Ferrigno, aren't you?" He squeezed the muscle to test how hard she had become.

"Quit trying to change the subject. I want to go to fifty fathoms with you."

"Why fifty fathoms? Do you even know what a fathom is?"

"No idea. I think my dad has a watch that's called a Fifty Fathoms, and I like the sound of it."

He shook his head and smiled, shutting his eyes at her ignorance.

"Don't scoff like that. How should I know how deep a fathom is? It's probably like a hundred feet or something. Like a league or a score. Or knots."

"You're not even talking about distances anymore. You're talking about speed. And Abraham Lincoln."

She punched him lightly on the arm. "Come on. Please let me! I'll be very obedient. I promise."

He raised an eyebrow. "What's that supposed to mean?"

"Oh, you know. Like when you get on a sailboat, I know how to be all 'Aye-aye, Captain' and 'Full steam ahead,' and all that."

He stared at her. "How can you be so smart and such an idiot all at the same time?"

She smiled. "I know I should defend my honor and call you out for suggesting my idiocy, but I just can't bring myself to care when it makes you smile like that and it brings out those little wrinkles around your eyes . . ." She reached up to lightly trace his eyebrow and he softened immediately.

"Three hundred feet," he said a few minutes later, seemingly out of nowhere.

"What?"

"Fifty fathoms is three hundred feet."

Maddie put her head up on her bent elbow. "Wow. So fifty fathoms isn't that serious."

He laughed. "Yeah. Fifty fathoms is serious."

"How deep is the ocean . . . roughly?"

"About . . ." He did a quick mental calculation. "About twenty-five hundred fathoms. Roughly. Fourteen thousand feet, pretty much. But there are trenches and canyons that are much deeper."

"How deep have you gone?"

"Sorry to disappoint, but I've only hit fifty fathoms once, and that was with Trimix, a special type of oxygen that you need to go that far."

"Oh. Is that all?" She turned away from his body as if his accomplishments were rather paltry.

He pulled her back and they laughed into each other, then settled back into the folds and bends of each other's bodies. Their curves were starting to mesh together with natural ease.

A few weeks later, Maddie had just finished a ten-mile run and was feeling pretty much invincible. She was drinking an iced tea with Janet in the late afternoon on Friday, and they were laughing about Phil trying to tell his ninety-six-year-old mother about the fact that he was dating Janet.

Maddie was still laughing, talking between gasps. "Why does he need to tell her at all?"

Janet smiled. "Because we're getting married."

Maddie nearly choked on her iced tea. "You're what?!"

Janet kept smiling.

"Oh my god," Maddie said, but she was smiling too. Then, "Have you told Henry yet?"

Janet's face fell slightly, and she looked at the back of her hands where they rested on the farm table. "I'm sure he's figured it out."

"Right," Maddie said, "because he's so good at seeing things like that."

Janet looked at Maddie closely. "You've really gotten to know him, haven't you?"

Maddie wasn't embarrassed, exactly. After the Fourth of July, it was pretty much an open secret that Maddie was spending all of her free time with Hank. They were always together on weekends, and Maddie was only at Janet's to sleep on the nights she had to get up at 4:30 for work. Otherwise, Maddie had become pretty scarce.

"Oh, I don't know if anyone can know Hank. Really. He doesn't really want to be known."

"Those are often the people who need to be known the most."

Maddie shrugged. "We don't need to go down that prickly path, Jan. We're all grown-ups, and we're all going our separate ways in September." Maddie took a deep breath, then fortified herself. "Except you! You're getting married! To Phil."

Janet started giggling. "You are so transparent, Madison. He's such a sweet, caring person. He really is."

"I know. Look, I work with him, remember? He's a really good guy."

"But?"

"But nothing. It's just that you seem so sweet and . . . dainty."

"Oh! You are adorable. Dainty?" Janet shook her head, and then her expression turned dour. "I was the town drunk. Do you know what that means in a town this size?"

Maddie felt her heart cramp under the weight of what that must have meant for Hank. And what it meant for Janet, too, of course, but for what it meant for a child to be living with an adult who was—

"It meant that I would walk down Main Street in my pajamas, barefoot. In February. To buy a pack of cigarettes. It meant that I was a screaming, blubbering mess when my husband drove his car into a telephone pole and was pronounced dead on arrival at the hospital, and I had to be sedated because I pretty much lost my mind. It meant that Hank more or less had to raise himself, because his father and I were so far gone down the path of our addictions that we barely even knew when he was awake or asleep."

Maddie was crying, and Janet got up and grabbed a few sheets of paper towel and handed her one.

"You can't think any less of me than I think of myself. Of how I was then, at least." Janet took a deep breath, then continued. "I feel okay about myself now."

"I don't know what to say, Jan. I'm just so sorry. It must have been so hard on . . . everyone."

"On Hank, you mean?" Janet had wadded up the paper towel and put it against the corner of her right eye and then her left. She

smiled and tried to laugh. "This isn't the celebration I had antici-
pated for this weekend! We need to quit all this moping and focus
on the real issue. What did you get Hank for his birthday?"

Maddie's head shot up. "What? When is it?"

"Oh. He is so bad. He didn't tell you, did he?"

"No. But I guess I didn't ask, either. Is it today?"

"No," Janet said. "It's tomorrow, but I thought maybe the four
of us could go out tonight, and then I figured Hank would probably rather go out, you know, just the two of you, tomorrow night.
Or . . ."

"Oh." Maddie was embarrassed again. As much as she and Hank
had slid into a happy routine, they never really made any plans. On
the few occasions that Maddie had offered to babysit for Sharon,
Hank had come along with her. Neither of them were inclined to
spend money on fancy dinners or going to the movies, when they
could be in bed for free. Maddie tried to shrug it off. "I mean,
maybe he has plans. We haven't really talked about anything specific."

The engine of Hank's truck interrupted their conversation. He
flipped off the engine and was in the kitchen a few seconds later.
No more hanging his head over the steering wheel, that much was
certain.

"Hey, you two!" He reached into the refrigerator and pulled
out a soda. He shut the fridge door and leaned against it with an
easy smile as he opened the soda tab. He took a sip, then slowed
down. "Who died?"

"Oh cut that out. I was just telling Maddie that it was your
birthday, and maybe we should all go out and celebrate, with Phil,
and you, and Maddie . . ."

Maddie nearly cringed, sensing the way Janet had almost said "double date" and hurled them all into a pit of embarrassment.

Hank shut down. No expression. No comment.

"Or not," Janet added.

Maddie took another sip of her iced tea and stayed quiet. She heard her father's stern patrician voice in her mind: "You don't have a dog in this fight."

Hank took another sip of his soda and stared at his mother. "Why do you keep trying to get us to go out with you and Phil? It's not like you're going to marry the guy or anything."

The silence fell like that hammer at the high-striker game at the carnival. *Bam.*

"Yes, it is like that." Janet stared back. "I thought you'd be happy for me."

If Hank could have leaned farther into the solid metal of the refrigerator, he looked like he would have. "Sure." He cast the word aside like it was nothing. "Sure, I want you to be happy, Mom. That's great."

Maddie was going to start crying again. She'd never really gotten on her knees and given thanks for the fact that her parents actually loved each other in that totally secure way. Coming and going. Passing each other with quick nods or a quick phone call, but always together at the end of the day, tucked into their chairs in the den, talking over their days and looking up when one of their four children happened into the room for one reason or other. No violence. No secrets.

Well, probably some secrets, Maddie thought. But nothing like this. Nothing that hurt like this. She took another sip of her iced tea to swallow the lump of emotion in her throat.

Hank finished his soda, rinsed it out in the sink, then put it into the recycle bin. "So, you guys have a good weekend. I'll see you later." He walked out the back door, and the screen door closed with a quiet slap against the frame.

Maddie was frozen solid. *You guys?* What the hell was that supposed to mean? Did he mean just Janet and Phil or was he lumping Maddie into their little party?

"That went well," Janet said.

Picking up her glass of iced tea and taking it to the sink, Maddie tried to think of something appropriate to say. It wasn't really one of those things that was covered in an Emily Post chapter like "How to Decline a Tea Party." It was a tad awkward that the first thought that popped into Maddie's head was, "Hate to dash off, but I want to go have sex with your son to make him feel better about you getting married."

Maddie turned to face Janet. "I'm really happy for you."

"Thanks, sweetie."

"Have you set a date?"

"Oh, nothing like that. No. Phil's going to try to tell his mother and see if she is well enough to leave the home for an afternoon, and then he needs to check with his two daughters over in Brattleboro. That's where they were raised, where his wife was from. Probably early next summer."

"Oh. Okay. Well. Let me know if there's anything I can do to help you get ready or anything."

Janet looked winsome. "You'll be back at school by then, sweetie, but thank you."

"Yeah." Maddie took a very deep slow breath. Back at school. So what was she doing standing in this woman's kitchen when the man she wanted to spend every spare moment with was stewing in his own confused mess of feelings a few yards away?!

"So. I think I'm going to go up and see how Hank's doing. Do you mind?" Maddie was pointing up toward the garage in a stupid gesture, as if Janet didn't know which direction the garage was.

"Yes. That's a good thing."

Maddie squeezed Janet's shoulder as she walked past. "It's all going to be good."

Janet smiled, but she looked at Maddie with a skeptical gaze.

A few minutes later, Maddie knocked lightly, then opened the door to Hank's apartment. He never locked it during the day, and she'd gotten in the habit of knocking and coming in at the same time. This time she felt like she should have waited for him to answer before she barged in.

She stayed there, resting the palms of her hands against the shut door behind her. Hank was at his drafting table, hunched over some drawings and using a ruler to make some straight lines.

"Hey," Maddie said.

"Hey."

"Can I come in?"

"You're in already."

"But I can go. Seriously, Hank. Look up just for one second. Do you want to be alone or are you kind of hoping I'll hang around until you finish what you're doing and we can order some Chinese food and watch a movie and fool around on the couch?"

He didn't look up, and she could feel him just seething over there in the corner. The light was beautiful, streaming into the space. The bright white paint on all the woodwork, all the effort he had put into making this place simple and beautiful and plumb.

As long as he didn't tell her to leave, she was staying. Maddie walked over to the refrigerator and grabbed a beer.

"You want a beer?" she asked over her shoulder.

"All right." He muttered it reluctantly, but at least it gave her an excuse to walk over and touch him. That kitchen departure down there had been brutal. Her body had started humming the minute his truck was on their street. By the time he'd walked in with that big happy smile on his face, she'd barely been able to sit in her seat.

And then he'd left.

Of course she was feeling all emotional from everything Janet had told her, but her body, her physical self, was becoming a demanding, forceful thing.

"Here you go." She held out the beer for him. Hank reached up to take it from her without taking his eyes off the complicated engineering blueprints he was making.

She didn't release her hold on the bottle. He tugged on it once more.

"Look at me, handsome," she whispered.

Hank looked up at her and she almost collapsed. His eyes, those beautiful dancing green eyes, were dark and frightened. So sad and confused and tormented.

Maddie pushed her way into him, forcing his swivel seat so she could spread his thighs apart and slip into his personal space. She let go of his beer bottle, and he took a sip. He kept his head down, but he didn't push her away. She let her free hand loop around his neck, then leaned in and kissed his neck, right near his ear, where she knew it turned him on the most.

"I missed you today . . . it got so bad . . ." She kept kissing him and touching his neck.

"Maddie . . ." He was still a mess. She could hear that his voice was still strained, but if she could pull him out of it, out of that terrifying locked-off place, she was going to do it. And if it meant that she was seducing him and it was just a surface solution, a short-term fix, then so what? Maybe the short-term fixes would start happening more often. And then they wouldn't be fixes, they would be Hank coping with the natural waves of feelings that were going to keep cropping up in his life.

Hank took her beer out of her hand and put both of the bottles on the coffee table behind him. "Come here . . ." He pulled her into his hard stomach with both of his strong, needy arms, and Maddie felt like she was part of him, part of something amazing and real. They went into the bedroom a few minutes later and he made love to her with a silence and tenderness that left her weeping.

"Don't cry, Maddie, honey." He was wiping the tears from her face and kissing the skin where the tears had left shadowy tracks.

Do not tell him you love him right now! The voice in her head was so loud she was amazed he couldn't hear it too, or see it in her glassy expression. He had so much passion and drive and beauty in him, and it was all clogged up in there. Except for these incredible, isolated moments when he was with her like this.

"Okay," she tried. "I won't. I'm fine, really." She was smiling, and the tears had abated. "That was just . . . really great." *Right*, that practical voice in her brain encouraged, *make it about how good he is in bed.* But it was so unlike anything she had ever said—or ever would say—that Hank looked suddenly skeptical.

"What?"

Oh, great. Now she had to backpedal, because never in a million years would she pat a guy on the back and tell him what a tiger he was in the sack. Perfect. "I just meant, it was a long week, and it felt really good to be, you know, together." At least that was true, if still a ridiculous bunch of meaningless words strung together to get him to stop looking at her like that.

She shifted into a more upright position and gave him a friendly shove on his chest. "Come on. I'm fine. I want some moo-shu pork and a couple of Tsingtaos. Let's order." Maddie sprang off the bed and pulled on her sweaty running shorts, then her jogging bra. "Let me run back and take a shower and change into sweats, and we can drive down to Ming's. Sound good?"

He was still lying there like a naked, satisfied beast, taking her in, when he said, "Did you just have your way with me?"

She put her hands on her hips and smiled with the right half of her mouth. "Maybe . . . You have a problem with that?"

He shook his head no. "Happy to oblige."

Maddie leaned down and kissed him gently. "You are so accommodating."

She scooted out of his reach before he could pull her back into bed. "Order dinner so it's ready when we pick it up!" she called up to his window as she sped down the stairs. Janet wasn't in the kitchen, but Maddie didn't want to take any chances, so she darted up the stairs and bolted into her bedroom to take a shower and switch into clean clothes before heading back to Hank's to spend the night at his place.

CHAPTER 14

I t went on like that for all of August. No plans. No dates. No mentions of birthdays or weddings. And certainly no mention of first days of school or last days of summer jobs.

Finally, Maddie couldn't stand it anymore and asked if he wanted to go camping or off to a lodge or something for her last weekend. She might have said "our" last weekend, but she was trying not to be overly analytical. It was hard enough *not* saying 'I love you' every second that it popped into her mind, which was every time he got out of the shower, or stepped out of his truck, or kissed her in the middle of the night when he wasn't even awake, and he so obviously loved her back, but neither of them were ever going to say it. Because what would be the point?

"Sure. If you want. We can go camping or to a hotel in the mountains or something." He wasn't dissing her exactly, but he wasn't looking up from the diving magazine he was reading, either.

"Okay. Can I go on your computer?"

He looked up. "Sure. You don't have to ask permission, you know that."

Maddie had gotten into the habit of logging onto her e-mail at his place on Sundays, to send the weekly all-is-well e-mails to her parents and her brother Jimmy. "Okay, let me see if I can find any last-minute specials. What are you in the mood for? Ocean? Mountains? Lake? City?"

He looked up. "City?"

"I don't know . . . Boston might be fun . . . Go to a baseball game, ride the T, get drunk and stay in a really expensive hotel and not care."

He kept staring at her. "I choose city. I want to see you with skyscrapers in the background." Hank went back to reading his magazine, as if nothing had happened. When he'd basically just told her that he wanted those memories as badly as she did.

Damn. Did she call in a favor and get the suite at the Ritz or stick to the bet and only use the money she'd made at Phil's? She had saved nearly four thousand dollars over the past twelve weeks. She clicked on the hotel Web site to see what it would cost if she didn't call her father's secretary the way she usually did.

"Holy hell!" Maddie cried out.

Hank laughed. "What's the matter?"

"An executive suite at the Ritz-Carlton in Boston is $745 . . . a night! If we spend Labor Day weekend there it would be . . ."

"Two thousand, two hundred and thirty-five dollars," Hank said.

"And that's not even including taxes and parking and meals. I mean . . . who stays there?"

"You."

She looked over her shoulder at him.

"Well?" he asked. "Have you ever stayed there?"

"Yes." She wasn't going to lie about it.

"In a suite?" he asked.

"Yes." Her spine stiffened involuntarily. Hank got up off the

couch. Of course, *now* he would lose interest in his diving magazine, because he saw an opportunity to give her a hard time.

The photos of the suite were up on his big, flat-panel computer
screen. "Have you stayed in that one?" He began caressing the tender skin at the base of her neck, under her pony tail.

She began melting into him. "*Mm-hmmm.*"

"Go to the next one up . . . we're not executives. Go to the Park
View Suite . . ."

Maddie used the wireless mouse to click on the pictures and
the floor plan. Her fingers were shaky because he kept up that sexy
touching the whole time.

"That's the one," Hank said. "I want to sleep with you in that
bed."

The groan that escaped Maddie was completely his doing. "Let
me see how much it is . . ." Her voice was raspy. She had to bite her
teeth together to hold her concentration. She clicked away from
the photo section to the reservation section. "Yeah, that's not
going to work," Maddie muttered.

"How much?" Hank had begun kissing her neck as well as
touching her.

"Three thousand . . . six hundred . . . a night . . ." She was starting to slither off the stool. "I can't afford that."

"My treat," Hank whispered as he reached his hand up under
her T-shirt and pulled her back into him, his strong hand flat
against the quivering muscles across her stomach.

"That's over ten thousand dollars, Hank," she said, thinking he
must have misheard.

"You're worth it, beautiful." He pulled her up into his arms and
had her naked and flat out on the sofa in under a minute.

❦

So they spent Labor Day weekend at the Ritz-Carlton in Boston. For the rest of her life, Maddie would look back on that weekend as the last weekend they were together in their innocence. Before everything else happened.

Maddie packed up all of her measly possessions and said goodbye to Janet and Phil and Sharon on Friday morning. The drive from Blake to Boston took about three hours. As Hank's big, silver-gray pickup truck pulled up in front of the modern glamour of the Ritz, Maddie's heart started pounding. She had thought it might be odd to see Hank so far out of his element, but it turned out she was the one going through some sort of weird urban reentry. She'd thought the Ritz would feel like coming home. Not like she had been Eloise or anything, but it was sort of a family tradition that the Posts would go into Boston a week or two before Christmas and shop and see a show and spend the night at the Ritz. In Maddie's mind, it was always the original Ritz, over on Arlington, which had changed hands years ago, but the feeling was the same at the new, modern building across the park. Checking into a hotel always felt . . . promising.

"Ready?" Hank asked. He reached across the front seat and pulled her hand into his. The valet car-parker had already pulled open the large truck door and was waiting at attention for Hank to step out.

"Yes," Maddie said. "I'm so excited."

Hank leaned in closer and whispered so his lips touched the curve of her ear. "Good, because I love it when you're excited."

He might as well have put his hand between her thighs: that was how much it turned her on. Before she could gather her scattered thoughts, Hank had hopped out of the car with a jovial,

"Thanks!" to the car-parker. He talked to the guy for a few seconds while Maddie tried to become a little less flustered.

"Just the two bags in the backseat," Hank was saying. "I'll grab the backpack." He reached into the backseat and pulled out his canvas rucksack, then winked at Maddie. "Hustle up, I want you in that bed, pronto," he said from the backseat.

Maddie jumped out of the car, her door also held open by a uniformed attendant, and followed Hank into the soaring glass-and-marble lobby. He took her hand, and they walked together to the check-in desk.

"Hello, may I help you?" The days of checking the Social Register to see if someone was of a high enough quality to stay at the Ritz-Carlton were long gone. Maddie was in her usual tight black T-shirt and shorts, and Hank was in a . . .

Hank looked like a frigging movie star. Maddie sized him up from a first-glance perspective and she smiled and turned to the smiling attendant. Maddie's look of smug satisfaction pretty much exuded, *Yeah, I'm with him.* She hadn't really noticed anything different about his appearance. Sometimes he wore the white-collared shirt and trim khakis that he had on today, instead of his usual uniform of gray T-shirt and cargo shorts. So what? But with his aviator sunglasses and backpack slung easily over one shoulder, Maddie realized, he looked exactly like a younger, hotter James eff-ing Bond checking into one of those tropical resorts after spending the morning chasing bad guys in his Aston Martin.

"Gilbertson," Hank said. "The Park View Suite."

Maddie gazed up at him like a silly teenager. He looked like a rock star, so she might as well swoon a little.

"Excellent," the professional attendant said. "Will you be using the credit card that you used to reserve the room?" She looked from Hank to Maddie without a blink. Clearly there was no snobbery. Despite the glamorous surroundings, it all felt particularly egalitarian. All who could afford to stay here were quite equal to one another.

"Yes, here's the card and my ID." Hank passed his cards across the cool marble, and the woman took them and put the information into the computer. A couple of minutes later, she passed him a small gray packet holding the room cards. "You have access to our club level, so please feel free to join us for a complimentary cocktail after five. The gym and the pool are open until midnight. If you need anything at all, my name is Jane," she said, then gestured behind Maddie and Hank to the valet. "And this is Vince, who will show you to your suite."

"Great. Thanks, Jane."

The woman smiled at Maddie, then back at Hank. "Have a great weekend."

Hank pulled Maddie along as she called over her shoulder, "I think we will!"

They rode up in the elevator in a simmering silence. The bellman looked up at the digital numbers. Up. Up. Up. Every passing level cranked up Maddie's adrenaline until she was set to burst when the doors finally opened at their floor.

Hank hauled her out behind the bellman's luggage cart. Kind Vince opened the door for them and set their luggage on the racks in the bedroom. He gave them a brief tour of the large suite, pointing out the safe and the refrigerator, and asking if there was anything else they needed.

Hank handed him a twenty-dollar bill and the man (*finally*, thought Maddie) left.

When Hank came back into the living room from the darkness of the small hallway that led to the door, he said, "Get undressed, Maddie." He kicked off his shoes and pulled his button-down shirt up over his head. He tossed it on the back of one of the upholstered chairs. Maddie froze. Hank looked so predatory and delicious, she didn't know whether to run toward him or away. He began to unbuckle his belt, her eyes glued to his hands and their deft movements.

"Maddie!"

She looked up into his eyes. "Uh. Yeah?"

"Take. Your. Clothes. Off. Now."

"Oh, right." She fumbled with the button closure of her shorts and then bent over awkwardly, pulling off her sneakers and socks, then pulling off the shorts. She pulled her T-shirt off and let it drop on the floor next to the shorts and shoes. She stood there in her bra and underwear and stared at Hank's naked form as he moved around the space.

He looked like he was doing forward recon. Opening cabinets, looking in closets. Then he pulled open the refrigerator and took out a bottle of champagne.

"What do we have here?"

Maddie stared at the flinch and ripple of his shoulder muscles as he popped the cork on the champagne bottle. He pulled two glasses from the small cabinet next to the refrigerator and poured.

He walked to where she was standing. She realized that she had foolishly thought that Hank would be entering *her* world, or some stupid idea of the world of luxury and privilege that she had grown up in and around. What a fool.

Hank was a total master of his surroundings. Of course he had some secret huge bank account that he never touched. Of course he could stroll into one of the most expensive rooms in one of the most expensive hotels in the world, and it would belong to him.

"Drink." He put the cold glass against Maddie's lower lip and tilted it into her mouth. He poured slowly but he didn't stop. Maddie nearly lost the rhythm of swallowing, then closed her eyes and relished the spark and *ping* of the bubbles as they slid down her throat. "That's my girl." When he pulled the empty glass away from her lips, Maddie opened her shining eyes, and Hank filled her entire field of vision. His face, his smiling lips, his broad naked shoulders. His chest.

"I am, you know," she whispered.

"What are you?" He put both of the glasses on the dining room table behind Maddie and then began touching her . . . lightly along her shoulders, down the length of her bare arms, dragging his knuckles across the lace of her bra.

"I'm your girl. I'm yours." Her voice was so quiet she almost hoped he wouldn't really hear her.

"I know." He dipped his head to hers and began kissing her, so slowly, with light tenderness, and then his hands gripped her waist and pulled her against him. She cried a low moan into his mouth. That set him off. Almost angry, he plunged deeper into her mouth, then lifted her up and carried her into the bedroom.

"Did you bring a sexy dress?"

Maddie was like a loose pile of useless muscle and bone. They'd been in that luxurious bedroom for over two hours, and she wasn't sure she could stand, much less put on a dress and go out to dinner. Hank was in the huge marble bathroom, freshly showered, naked and shaving. Back to business as usual. How was that even possible?

"Maddie?" He was pulling at his jaw to get a closer shave.

"*Mm-hmm?*"

He smiled into the mirror. "Get out of bed and into the shower. I need to see you against skyscrapers, remember?"

Maddie carefully peeled herself off the mattress, then sat at the end of the bed until she was certain her legs would carry her the short distance to the bathroom.

She let her fingertips drag across Hank's lower back when she passed behind him on the way toward the shower. "Yes. I brought a dress. I don't know how sexy it is." She turned on the hot spray and stepped into the steaming glass shower enclosure.

He finished shaving and turned to watch her in the cascading water.

"Cut that out," Maddie said. "Go get ready and wait for me in the living room. Let me get all pretty and surprise you."

"Okay, okay." He tossed the hand towel on the marble counter next to the sink and left the bathroom, pulling the door shut behind him.

Maddie had never been one for extensive makeup to begin with, but she only had the bare minimum with her, in any case. After she got out of the shower and had twisted her hair up into a towel, she opened up her small cosmetics bag and set about making herself up. She took her time with the mascara and eye shadow and put a little bit of powder on her forehead and under her eyes. She didn't need to add any color to her cheeks, seeing as Hank kept her in a perpetual flush. She added some sexy, dark red lipstick.

She took the towel off her head and flipped her head over. She didn't have any hair gel or mousse, so she decided to go with a loose-curled look. Her hair was dry and shimmering down past her shoulders a few minutes later.

"Can I come out now?" Maddie called.

"I'm in the living room," came Hank's muffled reply. "You're all good."

She stepped out into the empty bedroom and went over to her duffle bag. She pulled out a little black dress that was made of that stretchy material that never wrinkled. Maddie laid it on the bed. She reached back into her bag and pulled out her favorite red bra and underwear set, then slipped them on and pulled the dress over her head. She wished she had a pair of killer heels for once in her life, but settled on the shiny silver sandals she'd worn that first day in Blake, and hadn't had on since.

As she put on a pair of silver hoop earrings and her wide silver cuff, she was overcome with a strange melancholy, imagining how good it would feel to get ready like this, for Hank, for the rest of her life. She gathered her disintegrating feelings and took a good long look at herself in the full-length mirror that was leaning against the far wall. Good enough.

She walked out into the living room.

"Not a lot to work with, I'm afraid." Maddie gestured down at herself, feeling prettier than she had all summer, but still rather plain compared to what she could have looked like with open access to her full arsenal of clothes and shoes.

When Maddie looked up and saw Hank in a coat and tie she nearly lost her footing. He was up from the couch and standing in front of her with that silent speed that she now recognized as distinctly his. He held her upper arms.

"You look phenomenal, Madison Post."

Maddie congratulated herself on her good sense to forget the blush. Her neck and cheeks were hot immediately.

"You too, Henry Gilbertson."

"I made a reservation somewhere. As a surprise. Is that okay?"

Almost unable to look at him, Maddie peered over his shoulder as if she were more interested in the sunset view outside the window. "Sure. Whatever you decide is fine."

"Fine?" Hank touched Maddie's face and gently made her face him.

"Yes. Really, really fine." She was about to become an emotional mess and she didn't want to ruin their awesome weekend with some sort of preemptive bawling about how life was so unfair and why-did-she-have-to-go-back-to-her-senior-year-at-college-and-never-see-him-again?

"We're going to have a great time. Trust me."

Maddie tried to smile, but for some reason seeing him like this—in all his glory—was a hard pill to swallow. *Sure. We're going to have a great time. Until Monday. And then we're never going to see each other again.*

"Come on." Hank took her hand in his. "Stop being such a sad sack." He led them to the door of their hotel room, but before he opened it out to the public hallway, he stopped in the narrow entryway. "Take off your underwear."

Maddie looked up with wide-eyed confusion. "What?"

"You heard me. Off."

The bastard. He knew exactly how to get her mind off all that maudlin, I'm-going-to-miss-you-like-hell thinking.

She shimmied off the red lace and held it up by one finger. "Are you going to be all kinky and carry it in your pocket?"

"Nope." He took it from her hand and threw it like a slingshot back into the living room. "Why do I need the underwear when I've got you?"

He opened the door and held it open for her. "Off we go."

She felt more naked than she'd ever felt in her life.

CHAPTER 15

"Breezy out here, isn't it?" Hank taunted, walking ahead of her down the hall and pressing the elevator button.

"You are a lunatic," Maddie said.

"How lucky for you, since you're obviously in need of a little lunacy."

She shook her head. The elevator doors opened, they stepped in, and then they closed. He was almost a stranger, dressed like Jason Statham and joking like that. But he was right. She needed to be wild and free this weekend. It was great. They were great. But there was no place for her in Blake, Maine, and there was no place for him during her senior year at Brown. But after . . .

"Stop letting your mind wander. I'm right here." He pulled her into a kiss, and they were still making out like a pair of teenagers when the elevator doors opened.

"Madison Post! Is that you?"

Maddie was too dazed to pull away from Hank altogether. She held onto his hand and stepped out into the lobby.

"Hello, Mr. and Mrs. Lodge. How are you?"

Mr. Lodge was sizing up Hank. Mrs. Lodge was sizing up Hank.

"Oh, pardon me," Maddie said. "This is Henry Gilbertson. Henry, I'd like you to meet Lila and Theodore Lodge—"

Ted Lodge, a fit, good-looking man in his early sixties, extended his firm hand toward Henry. "It's a pleasure. You look familiar."

The elevator doors closed, and Maddie repressed a sigh that her parents' friends the Lodges were still on this side of the silver doors. Ted Lodge was a good guy, old Boston Brahmin, modest in his way. But Maddie wasn't in the mood to stand around explaining what she had been doing sucking face with Hank when they'd seen the doors open—

"Your name sounds familiar, too," Ted pressed. "Are you the same Henry Gilbertson who invented the patent for the deep-sea fiber-optic tubing?"

Maddie's head spun. "Yes, Henry. I've been meaning to ask you that."

Hank stared down at her, and she could have sworn he was thinking about the fact that she didn't have any underwear on and she best be watching herself if she knew what was good for her.

Hank's look silenced Maddie and he turned back to Mr. Lodge. "Yes, sir. I was on the team that developed that. And you are at Ocean Works Laboratories, if I'm not mistaken."

Lodge looked proud to be known for something other than his old Boston ancestry. "Yes. Yes. Quite happy about what we've gotten up to down there in Woods Hole. If you have any time this weekend, I'd love to talk to you about what you've been doing with the depth/pressure components of the—"

"I'm so sorry to interrupt, sir, but we don't have more time to talk just now. Madison and I have a dinner reservation at seven thirty—"

"Of course, of course," Mr. Lodge said. "Wonderful to see you, Madison. Wonderful to finally meet you in person, Major Gilbertson. I hope we'll get a chance to speak soon."

Mrs. Lodge was making not-very-subtle googly-eyes at Madison that might as well have spelled "N-I-C-E C-A-T-C-H" in skywriting.

"Nice to see you, Mr. and Mrs. Lodge," Maddie said.

Hank said his good-byes and fended off Mr. Lodge's encouragement to meet up later in the weekend with, "Sorry, but Maddie and I are going to be flat out for the next few days."

"Bye, dear. Say hello to your mother for me," Lila Lodge called after them.

"As if that will be necessary," Maddie muttered, once she'd put a bit of distance between herself and the Lodges.

"What's that?" Hank asked when they were standing out on the sidewalk. "We need a taxi, please," Hank said to the doorman, then turned back to Maddie. He kept his hand on her lower back, which made her slightly less churlish.

"I said, *'As if!'* There's no way in hell I'll need to tell my mom I bumped into Lila Lodge at the Ritz in Boston, because I'd lay odds that Lila is in that elevator right now dialing my mother's phone to let her know."

"Let her know what?"

Maddie threw her hands up. "Oh, forget it. I don't care what Lila Lodge says or does."

"Me neither," Hank said, close to Maddie's neck.

The taxi pulled up, and Hank held the door open, then smirked at Maddie. She realized she was going to have to maneuver in and out of the car very carefully if she didn't want to flash half of Boston while she was at it.

"You are so going to pay for this," Maddie said as she slid into the taxi. She held one hand at the hem of her dress, at the back of her thighs, to make sure the fabric didn't fly up in the late summer wind.

"Mistral, please," Hank said when he got in after Maddie. The driver took off, and Hank settled the palm of his left hand between her legs. Maddie closed her eyes and muttered, "Did we just bump into someone in the lobby, I can't remember . . ."

Hank smiled and looked out the window at the passing tourists and pedestrians and children. When he was here like this with Maddie, everything seemed possible: bumping into mutual friends in hotel lobbies, going to dinner on a Friday night. He felt like he might be a whole person after all.

While caressing the soft, warm skin of her inner thigh, Hank felt connected . . . to everything. He knew it was wrong. He was using her in the most rudimentary way. She was his ticket. When they were together, he was somehow able to look people in the eye and talk to people and just be. When he was at work and he'd seen her the night before, and knew he was going to see her again that night, he could manage just fine. But. The abyss was beginning to stretch before him. He had a few plans in place to put the misery at bay. He would travel. He would stay busy. He needed to make this weekend count. To make himself take everything he could from what he and Maddie had and savor it. For the future. Long-term savings.

Because after this weekend, it was back to business. Any type of relationship beyond this summer just made him feel uncomfortable in his own skin. He didn't want to meet her family. He didn't want to meet her roommates. He didn't want to attend her graduation. Hank wanted Maddie in his bed, and with him, like this, soft and pliable in his hands. He didn't want to have to navigate the rest of it. The family gatherings. The parameters of commitment. It wasn't that he wasn't up for the challenge—who wouldn't want to be with someone who made him feel the way she did, after all?

It was more that he despised the idea of all those eyes on them, all those opinions, all that input.

It had taken him a lifetime to get used to his mother's constant inspection, and even now it made his skin crawl. It had taken him weeks to trust Maddie enough to let her look at him like that. Like she was right now. But for the whole world to look at him? No way.

And Hank could tell that Maddie was going to be out in the world. She was a part of everything. She would probably make the Olympic cut in two years for the women's crew team. She was going to be someone public and important.

"What is it?" Maddie asked.

He looked back from the passing sidewalks and smiled into her dark violet eyes. "Just you." He smiled and kissed her cheek. "I was just thinking what an accomplished person you're going to be."

Her face pinched together. "So . . . why would that make your face so dark and stormy?"

Squeezing the inside of her thigh, Hank said, "I wasn't dark and stormy. Just thoughtful. You're amazing, that's all."

Maddie wanted to slap him. Slap him awake. Wake up! Wake up to the fact that I am this way when I'm with you, you idiot. You make me feel like this. You make me feel like I can accomplish anything when you look at me like that. But then I see that the reason it makes you so wistful and distant is that you won't be there to share in those accomplishments, will you? Because that would be too exposed and miserable.

Taking a deep, quick breath, Maddie turned to look out her side of the car. "Thanks." She couldn't think of anything else to say. Thanks for thinking I'm amazing, because it's going to be very short-lived, so you might as well revel in it now. Because when you drop me off at the train station on Monday afternoon, and drive away, and don't wave or look in the rearview mirror, I'm going to be shriveling up inside and setting my mind to rowing as fast as I can, and studying as robotically as I can, so I can finish this chapter of my life and hope that missing you doesn't destroy me.

She sighed. Again.

"Enough!" Hank was smiling. It wasn't a fake smile, exactly. It was more of . . . an effort.

"Okay!" Maddie tried to brighten along with him.

"We're here," the cabbie called from the front seat.

Hank pulled a few bills from his pocket and paid the fare, then stepped out of the car and held the door open for Maddie. He smiled (no effort) when she had to swing her feet out, knees tight together, and then dip her head and stand in a gymnastic attempt to get out of the cab without letting her legs split open.

"Very funny," she said as she passed right by him and walked straight into the glamorous restaurant.

The maître d' showed them to their table immediately, and Hank reached across the narrow table for Maddie's hand. She was fumbling with her napkin and looked up to see his gorgeous, demanding expression.

She reached her hand out slowly and absorbed the relief that passed through both of them when they were back in contact like that. She resolved not to sink into any misery about the future, and opened the menu.

"Oh, this is heaven. Look at all this *meat*!"

Hank smiled. "I figured you'd be ready to eat half a cow after spending the summer under my mother's roof."

"*Mm-hmm*," Maddie said, without looking up from the menu. "You figured right. I feel like I could rip flesh off bone with my bare hands."

"Good."

They ordered all the richest things on the menu—foie gras, escargots, corn chowder with lobster, then rack of lamb for Hank and tenderloin for Maddie.

She ate every bite and loved the feeling of Hank's eyes on her mouth while she did. Her plate was nearly scraped clean, thanks to the final swipes of bread Maddie had dragged across the surface. She swallowed the final bite and stared at Hank's soft, tender eyes.

"Did you like it?" he asked.

She nodded. "So much," she whispered. And then she was crying right there in the stupid restaurant and had to put the napkin up to her eyes and dab some of the ice water around her eyes to stop from being all splotchy and red.

The waitress came over to clear their empty dinner plates. "Oh my gosh," she exclaimed, mistaking Maddie's weeping for joy. "Did you just get engaged?"

Maddie must have looked up with the wrath of the gods shooting from her eyes. "No!"

"Oh . . . sorry." The woman grabbed the plates and scurried away.

Hank was smiling.

"How can you smile at a time like this?"

"A time like what?" Hank asked.

Maddie rolled her eyes. "Please don't be coy. It's like the giant elephant in the room—with a giant ticking bomb around its neck—which neither of us is talking about. I'm leaving on Monday. That's three days from now." She looked at her watch. "That's actually two days and some, not counting when we'll be asleep, which will be never if I can help it. Because I don't want to miss a minute—"

"Maddie—"

"What?!" Her voice had gone up an octave, and the two guys at the nearest table looked over simultaneously to make sure everything was okay. She smiled and waved at them like an insincere politician. "What?" she whispered, turning her full attention back to Hank.

"Just . . . let's just have such a great weekend, okay? You know I can't do anything more than that. You know I feel like shit about it, but would you rather have me make a bunch of lame promises, like I'll call you every Sunday at four to check in, or I'll come down to Brown for homecoming—" He jerked his head back and curled his lip at the absurdity. "Look, it sucks. I agree. Maybe I'm weak. I don't know what the hell I am, but this is it."

"I know." Maddie looked at the table and tried to be mature about the whole thing. "I've known all along, but I just kept hoping something else would miraculously happen that would make everything . . . possible." She reached across the table. "I don't want dessert."

"Good. Me neither." Hank raised his hand to the very penitent waitress as she passed nearby. He asked for the bill.

For the next three days, they clung to each other. Maddie was surprised they were able to have such a lighthearted good time— they ate oysters at B & G, they went to the Isabella Stewart Gardner Museum and stared at paintings by John Singer Sargent. On Saturday afternoon, Maddie asked if Hank would mind if they spent a few hours at the Houghton Library at Harvard. It would save her a trip in the fall. There was one bit of research she wanted to see in person, and it wasn't eligible for inter-library loan.

They decided to walk from the hotel over to Cambridge. It took about an hour, but it felt good to be out of the hotel room and near the river and just holding hands and walking along together. They got to the Houghton Library around two o'clock, and the librarian wouldn't let Maddie into the stacks after all, because she didn't have a letter from her dissertation advisor.

Hank was standing to the side with his hands in his pockets. Maddie made one last attempt, but the librarian merely shook her head slowly and seemed genuinely apologetic. "I'm so sorry, but I can't help you."

Maddie walked back to where Hank was standing. "Let's go. I'm sorry I dragged you all this way."

"Do you really want to see this book?"

Staring into those green eyes of his, Maddie wasn't sure if Hank was going to whip out a gun and blow his way into the stacks or if he had more traditional means for getting them in. Maddie shrugged. "It's not the end of the world. I just wanted to hold it in my hand, if you know what I mean."

"Give me a second," Hank said, then leaned down and kissed her on the cheek. He walked over to the librarian and she smiled up at him. They spoke quietly for a few minutes, then Hank handed Madison a temporary visitor's card.

"How did you do that?"

"I have my ways, Post."

"I'm starting to see that."

"The research project in Woods Hole has a reciprocal agreement with lots of libraries. We got lucky."

She grabbed his hand, and they walked into the reading room of the Houghton Library. Maddie got a thrill at the idea of the place, just being under the same roof as pieces of history that were thousands of years old, papyrus scrolls and medieval books of hours. She requested the manuscript from 1610 that she was looking for and, a few minutes later, a librarian set it on one of the angled reading stands.

Hank sat next to her and watched as she put on the archival gloves that the librarian had provided and carefully opened the book. She read the sections that were of particular relevance and took a few brief notes on a couple of note cards. After about an hour, she looked up at Hank.

"Aren't you bored?"

"Not at all. I could watch you all day."

She took off the gloves and set them next to the book. She got up and told the librarian she was finished and thanked her for her assistance.

They walked out, and the late afternoon sun was starting to cool down a bit.

"You want to sit under a tree for a few minutes?" Maddie asked.

"Sure. You getting wistful?"

"I think so."

They walked over to an English oak in front of Harvard Hall. Hank sat with his back against the trunk, and Maddie slipped easily between his legs, leaning her back into his chest and looking up at the green-and-blue pattern of sky and leaves.

The two of them were quiet, and the warm air settled around them. Their breathing was easy and gentle. To Maddie, it felt really safe.

"I love you, Hank," Maddie said, out of nowhere. "I don't want to have all this time pass and not have said it out loud. You don't need to say anything because I'm pretty sure you love me too, but you probably won't ever say it and I think I'm okay with that." She was crying again, not bawling or anything, just tears flowing down her cheeks. But even the tears had become such a normal occurrence in the past twenty-four hours that she barely noticed. He squeezed her so tightly, and she knew he couldn't say it, but he could feel it, which was something. In fact, maybe he felt things very deeply, and that was why he tried so hard not to feel them at all. She reached her right hand up and touched his cheek. He turned his lips into her hand and kissed her so sweetly, and then she felt the moisture of his tears between her fingers, and the two of them just rode it out, sitting there under the English oak in Harvard Yard, their hearts breaking to the hushed rhythm of the leaves that scratched and whispered above their heads.

When Maddie finally had the courage to open her eyes and the most intense emotions had subsided for the moment, she turned to face him. He had wiped his tears away but he looked kind of disoriented. Wrecked. "Let's go back to the hotel. Maybe I can take your mind off things." She smiled and stood up, holding out her hand to help him up from where he was seated on the grass. He reached overhead and took her hand, not that he needed any assistance doing anything he wanted with his body.

"Let's see if we can get a taxi. I want my mind taken off things right away."

"Thought so," Maddie said, and squeezed his hand in hers.

They never left the room again until they checked out on Monday morning. They ordered room service and watched movies naked in bed, and Maddie felt like they were John and Yoko during their bed-in. Neither of them really said much, Hank because he couldn't really, and Maddie because she had said everything that she wanted to say. She had told him she loved him. So that was done.

It was liberating to be able to shout it out as loud as she felt like when she had spent all these weeks, especially in bed, making sure that she never let it slip out. Now she had become all full of I-love-you swagger, telling him how much she loved his mouth and his green eyes and his sensitive ears and his amazing shoulders and how he knew her body and moved around her in that stealthy, knowing way. And he didn't seem to mind all her enumerations and recitations of why she loved him. At first he looked like he was tolerating it, but after he saw that she wasn't going to let up, he got into the swing of it. He would smile or do something that would demonstrate why said body part was indeed lovable, which usually involved touching Maddie. So everybody was happy.

Until Monday at noon. Then, nobody was happy.

CHAPTER 16

Monday. At. Noon. Just the sound of it was like being penciled in by the Grim Reaper. For the rest of her life, Maddie would never schedule appointments for Monday at noon. Bad. Bad. Bad.

The poor people at the Ritz must have thought the Park View Suite had not lived up to the unattainable expectations of Mr. Gilbertson and Ms. Post, for the dismal expressions both of them sported when they checked out.

"It was the absolute best!" Maddie exclaimed when they asked if they'd enjoyed their stay, but she had to turn away quickly before she started crying again.

When they left the hotel and were standing on the sidewalk waiting for the valet to bring the truck around, Maddie looked up at Hank and said, "I think I'll walk over to North Station and take the train home. Give me a little time to decompress, you know?"

"Oh, come on, Maddie. I'll drop you in Weston, it's not a big deal."

"Where? At the end of my parents' driveway, by the mailbox? Or will you come up the drive and then come in and stay for dinner and pet the yellow Labrador retrievers and talk fiber optics with my dad? Or maybe you'll stay over, and my mom will put you in the blue guest room—"

"Maddie. Stop."

She looked away, toward Boston Common. This was definitely the way to go. Leave the hotel. Say good-bye. Don't get back in the truck. Don't have to say good-bye again. All of a sudden, she felt like she'd been saying good-bye ever since the first day she met him.

"Hank. Let's just say good-bye. Here. Okay?"

He looked so tormented that she almost wanted to help him, but it was all his deal, all that torment. She'd tried to talk to him. The man simply refused. The minute the conversation turned to his time in the military or hey-what-a-coincidence-that-you-are-also-an-inventor-of-things-Ted-Lodge-sells or what kind of research have you done at the Houghton Library . . . Maddie knew all of these things were facts, but until he chose to share them, none of it really amounted to anything.

Maddie could feel how badly he wanted to touch her, to stop her. She moved into him, dropping her duffle bag from her shoulder and hugging him as hard as she could. "I love you so much, Henry Gilbertson. Now let me go." Her words were clear, but she had sort of exhaled them into his chest, through the fabric of his gray T-shirt. She looked up and smiled. "This is what you wanted, remember?"

He stared at her, his eyes raking over her like a digital scanner, taking in every detail. "Madison." The desperate way he said her name nearly leveled her; it was a plea and a defense all rolled up in one.

She smiled and shrugged her way out of his arms. "Well," she pulled the duffle bag back onto her right shoulder, "when you figure out why you think you can't have me, maybe you should give me a call."

He smiled too, tight and sad. "I'll try to figure that out."

"Good." Maddie nodded. *Agreed*, she thought stupidly, *glad we got that settled*. "Okay, then." She took another deep breath. "Here I go."

And she did.

She turned and starting walking, and she felt like she might be able to make it to the end of the short block. After that, it would probably be conceivable that she could head north and cross the green expanse of the Common. From there, she might even be able to feel her legs beneath her as she followed Joy Street over Beacon Hill and down again—how apropos, that descent on Joy. And then she would find her way to North Station, the way she always did. And everything would be normal. By the time she got home to Weston, she would be just like she always was. Maybe even better. A senior at Brown. Captain of the crew team. All that promise.

Maddie called her mom from a pay phone at North Station to let her know she'd be on the 1:20 train into Kendal Green.

"Oh! Maddie! We've missed you so much! I can't wait to see you, honey! Your brother is a horrible person for putting you up to this! I'll be at the train station with bells on!"

"Thanks, Mom. I can't wait to see you, too."

A little while later, Maddie stepped out of the train into the leafy suburb of Weston. Her mother, Laura Post, was standing next to the old station wagon, one elbow resting on the roof. She was tall and beautiful, much fairer and more feminine than Madison, who'd inherited her father's dark chestnut hair and strong shoulders. But it was Laura who had passed down all that unbridled enthusiasm. She waved wildly to Maddie, as if Maddie might not see her when, in fact, they were the only two people in the vicinity.

Maddie pasted on a smile and walked to the steps that led to

the parking lot. When she reached her mother, she dropped her
bag and hugged her so hard she almost crushed her.

"Oh, sweetheart, let me look at you. You are so gorgeous! Look
at how long your hair has gotten, and you seem . . . softer somehow."

Maddie burst into tears. "Oh, Mom. I missed you so much."

Her mother hugged her and patted her back and let her cry it
out, the two of them standing in the hot sun at the empty station.
"Well, you're home now. And now we know that e-mails on Sunday are not enough. You were a beast not to call us one time in
three months. Not even to let me hear your voice."

Wiping at her tears with the handkerchief her mother had
handed her, Maddie picked up her bag, put it in the back of the car,
and walked around to the passenger side.

"Is everybody at the house?"

"Yes," her mother said without taking her eyes off the road.
Her mother had always been an extremely cautious driver. Laura's
twin, Maddie's aunt, had died in a car accident when the sisters were
in their twenties, and the lifelong consequence was that Laura Post
drove exactly at the speed limit and obeyed every rule of the road.
After she had stopped at the railroad tracks and looked in both
directions, and then into her rearview mirror just to be safe, Laura
accelerated across the tracks and began talking again. "We've finished lunch, but I made you a plate and left it in the fridge. I knew
you'd be hungry."

Maddie stared out the window and was sort of resentful that
her mother was right. Life would just go on, hungry, tired. The
usual. Eat, sleep. Everything was all so much the same. She couldn't
breathe for a second when she pictured Hank alone in his car,
driving north on I-95. He was probably crossing into Maine right

about now. That would wear off too, Maddie told herself. The picturing him all the time. Soon enough, she wouldn't know his schedule or where he was or who he was with. Chances were pretty good that he wouldn't even be in America much longer.

He hadn't said as much, but he'd hinted around future projects and other opportunities enough for Maddie to get the drift. He needed to keep moving. He needed to stay isolated and safe. Untethered.

"What is it, sweetheart? Do you want to drive around and talk a little bit before we go home?" Her mother didn't look away from the road, but Maddie knew she was concerned.

"It's such a cliché, I guess. But I got my heart broken in Maine."

"It wasn't that Zander, was it?"

Maddie shook her head and kept looking out the window. "No. I never saw him again after he was a jerk on the Fourth of July. I told you about that, right?"

"Sort of," her mother answered. "But you were pretty vague. Just that you had seen him and he'd been with some of his friends, and you hoped you didn't bump into him again."

"Anyway. No. It wasn't Zander."

"Was it the man you were with at the Ritz this weekend?"

Maddie's head whipped around to face her mother's profile. They were driving right on past the lane that led down to their house. "Did Lila Lodge call you? What a witch."

"Why is she a witch? She said you looked gloriously happy and you were with some stunningly handsome man."

Oh, please don't start with the gloriously this and the stunningly that, Maddie thought miserably.

The silence filled the car. Maddie was reminded of one of those scenes in a movie where a car flies off a bridge into a river and the water rises up around the trapped passengers. The air pocket was becoming smaller and smaller as the water neared the ceiling of the car's interior.

"Breathe, Maddie."

This was her mother. Her loving, caring, supportive mother. Why was Maddie trying to drum up a bunch of hatred and resentment? She breathed, as she was told.

"That's better." Her mother never pretended to have any grand philosophical perceptions about life. She was what was commonly known as a go-getter. Over the years, she had become a fierce activist, raising awareness about domestic violence. Eventually—though it had begun as charity work—she became the executive director of the largest advocacy group in Massachusetts. She was no-nonsense. Raised in the corridors of privilege, at the center of the northeast establishment, Laura Standish Post was practically ascetic when it came to her own comfort. Wealth meant responsibility. Advantage meant obligation. It didn't mean fancy cars or marble countertops in the kitchen.

They drove around in silence for about fifteen minutes.

"You ready to face your bothers?"

Maddie smiled. Ever since she was a little girl and couldn't say her *R*s, she had called her three older brothers her "bothers." The term had entered the family lexicon.

"Sure. Let's go. I'll dive in the pool and rinse off all this moping of mine."

"Can't be that bad if a dip in the pool will make you forget about him."

Maddie tried to laugh. "Oh, it's that bad, but at least I'll be refreshed and miserable instead of sweaty and miserable."

Her mother took a quick look at Maddie. "Just get through this afternoon and then we can spend the rest of the week reading and moping together. I cleared my schedule so the two of us would be able to spend some time together before you head back to school next week." They had pulled in front of the house, and Laura turned off the engine and faced Maddie. "Sound good?"

"That sounds perfect, Mom. Thanks."

Maddie looked up at the eighteenth-century farmhouse that had been in her father's family since it was built. The gray clapboard could probably use a new coat of paint, and it looked like one of the dogs had clawed her way through the screen door again. The sounds of children's laughter and splashing were coming from around the back. Maddie's oldest two brothers each had three young children, and the squeals of glee as they played in the pool carried.

It had been wrong to make Hank feel like he wouldn't have fit in here. To describe all that WASP-y yellow-Lab and blue-guest room stuff, as if he wouldn't have been a part of all that in about three seconds. She'd apologize to him for that . . . if she ever saw him again. She just couldn't have borne the pain of seeing him woven even deeper into the fabric of her life. This was *her* mother and *her* house and these were *her* nieces and nephews. Maddie needed to keep some things separate, or the whole world would remind her of Hank.

Laura got out of the car. Maddie followed a few seconds later, pausing to pull her duffle from the backseat. "I'll go up and change then meet you outside, okay?"

"Sure. See you in a few minutes. Take your time."

"Thanks for picking me up at the station, Mom."

Her mother gave her a quick hug at the bottom of the stairs.

"Of course. I'm so happy to see you." She touched Maddie's cheek as if needing to feel that she was actually real. "So happy." But Laura Post's face didn't look happy. She looked like she wanted to take all of her daughter's heartache and carve it out of her with a sharp scalpel and take it on herself.

"Thanks, Mom," Maddie whispered, then turned quickly up the stairs to avoid a new onslaught of the ever-present weeping.

When she climbed the second set of stairs and turned into her third-floor bedroom, Maddie finally collapsed. She dropped the stupid duffle bag on the floor with a thud and stared around at the slanted walls and pretty vintage floral wallpaper. The sheer embroidered curtains reminded her of the ones in Janet's living room in Maine. The lace canopy that hung from the spindly posts of the Queen Anne bed looked unfamiliar. She had slept under that delicate protection her entire life and now she barely recognized it.

Maddie pulled open the second drawer of her dresser and grabbed a bathing suit. She changed and pulled on an oversize T-shirt and flip-flops to walk down to the pool.

When she headed out of the back door and walked the short distance across the grass, her brother Jimmy looked up to see her approach. He smiled and set one of his nephews down from his lap, then stood and walked to meet her halfway.

He gave her a big hug, lifting her up off the ground and spinning her around once. Jimmy had always been a bit of a jerk, so when he was warm and genuine like this, it always threw Maddie off balance.

"What was that for?" she asked lightly.

"For a job well done. You really did it! Not a single cry for help. I underestimated you."

"Well. Thanks, I guess." She smiled up at him, and he must have seen the storm just below the surface of her eyes.

"We'll talk later, okay? I owe you fifty large. Fair and square."

Maddie's gut lurched, and she stumbled where the grass ended and the slate perimeter of the pool area began.

"Whoa!" Jimmy grabbed her. "Watch where you're going, tiger. You didn't think I'd welsh on my part of the bargain, did you?"

"I guess I just sort of forgot about the money part of the bet."

Jimmy's eyes widened. "Forgot about fifty thousand dollars? Madison, you slay me!"

"Donate it to the VA hospital, Jimmy."

"What?!" He stopped and looked down at her.

"You heard me. Donate it to the VA hospital in Augusta. Set up a visiting doctor's chair or something. Just do it. As you just pointed out, I won fair and square."

He stared at Maddie for a few seconds, then gave a firm-lipped, single nod of respect. "Done."

"And no more calling me 'Sis.'"

Jimmy smiled. "I'll try."

By that time, Maddie's dad had gotten up and walked over to where the two of them were standing. "Get over here!" He pulled her into a tight, brief hug. It was pretty effusive by William Cabot Post standards.

"Hi, Dad."

"Hi, sweet pea."

She smiled at the old nickname. He must have really missed her if he was slipping into that.

"Aunt Maddie! Aunt Maddie!" Her two nieces, ages four and six, came running over. "All the bothers and mothers are so boring,"

Anabel, the wise six-year-old, informed her, taking her aunt's hand in hers. "They don't want to swim with us anymore, and we need you." Maddie got tugged toward the pool.

"Okay! I'm in." She pulled off her T-shirt, kicked off her sandals, and dove into the pool with a grateful splash.

CHAPTER 17

Hank had to pull off to the side of the road just after he crossed into Maine. It was after two, and Maddie was probably safe at home by now. He should have insisted he drive her there. He would have been able to see that she was safe and back where she belonged.

Who was he kidding? It wasn't for her safety; it was for his insanity. It would have given him the chance to picture where she was, which he was feeling the need to do. He couldn't picture her anywhere now. He didn't know if she lived in a brick house or a clapboard, if it was down a long manicured driveway or a winding country lane overgrown with oaks and white ash and wild rhododendron. What did her bedroom look like? Was it pink and girly or modern and filled with rowing trophies?

He was finding it hard to breathe. His truck was on the shoulder, and the pounding of other trucks passing by, close and fast, threw him into a horrible spin-cycle of memories. He was back on the side of the road in Bahrain, having done his job, sitting quietly at the wheel of an unmarked civilian SUV. He'd followed orders. He'd remained completely undetected while he attached C-4 and high-velocity gelatin explosives to the bottom of a known terrorist transport boat. Once they'd set their course and headed out to sea, they would be unaware of any pending threat right up until the detonation destroyed them all and sent their stray parts into the food chain of the sharks and other beasts that would remove all evidence of their existence.

Hank sat on the side of that dusty highway in Bahrain for nearly an hour, trying to calm down, trying to let the swish-and-thud of the passing speeding cars work as a sort of meditation. Breathe in. Breathe out.

Only it didn't work that way. Since then, the swish-and-thud had been a horrible reminder that he had been an integral part of a killing machine. He had taken all of the obedience and precision he had learned in the military and done what was expected of him. And it was the right thing to do. It wasn't a case of innocents dying. The men on that ship had done abominable, hideous things. They had taken videos to make sure that the world would know the extent of their cruelty. They wanted people to know. That way, they could be the pirates that the modern age required. Ruthless. Insane. Inhuman. Effective.

So it wasn't guilt, exactly. Hank was an effective warrior. He had pride in that. It was more the . . . detachment, the level of compartmentalization that was required to do the necessary evil. It didn't slough off like dead skin. It had become a hard, real part of him. Not even a shell, because a shell would imply that he could maybe outgrow it and move on. At that moment, on the side of the road in Maine, Hank realized that he could separate himself from that hard protective covering. It was going to hurt like hell, but he could do it.

A sharp tap on Hank's car window penetrated his disoriented fog.

He looked up slowly. A Maine state trooper was standing, one hand on his gun, looking down at Hank.

Hank rolled down his window and felt the force of hot air and dust against his face.

"You all right?" The officer's reflective sunglasses caught the light and helped bring Hank back to the present.

The adrenaline from reimagining himself back in the black water—attaching all that plastique in the midst of all that watery silence and pitch darkness—was still pulsing through him, and his tongue hinted at the rusty taste of it, but he nodded yes.

"Just a migraine," Hank said. "I think I'm okay to drive now." He looked at the clock on his dashboard and had a hard time accounting for the fact that he'd been sitting on the side of I-95 for over an hour.

"Where are you headed?" The officer looked more concerned than adversarial.

"Up to Blake."

"May I see your license and registration, please?"

Hank leaned over to the glove compartment and pulled out his registration, then took his driver's license out of his wallet and handed both of them to the officer.

"Wait here, please."

Hank let his forehead rest on the steering wheel and waited for the trooper to run his information through the system. About ten minutes later, he was back standing close to Hank's truck. "Sorry to bother you, Major Gilbertson. Take as long as you need until your headache passes, but you'd be much safer about a half-mile up the road at the rest stop."

"I'm fine now." Hank took the items back from the trooper with a small smile. "Thanks for checking on me."

"Drive safely." The trooper gave him a quick salute. Former military.

Hank nodded and rolled up the window. He took a deep breath, turned the radio to a station that wouldn't remind him of anything, and accelerated back onto the highway.

When he pulled into his driveway an hour later, his mother was sitting on her front stoop talking to Sharon MacKenzie and her two daughters. He almost kept driving rather than have to hear all that gaggling about Maddie and how-was-their-weekend-in-Boston? He pulled up to the closed garage door, turned off the engine, then leaned over the front seat to grab his luggage out of the back.

When he stepped out of the car, the two little girls waved, and Sharon held her hand above her eyes to prevent the glare. "Hey, Hank." She waved but didn't make a move to leave her conversation with Janet.

Janet just looked at him and smiled, sad and knowing as usual, then went back to talking to Sharon.

"Hey, ladies." He figured that included the girls and the women. He turned to walk up to his apartment . . . which was going to feel like an empty reminder of everything that he had just walked away from by not being able to make any sort of long-term commitment to Maddie.

After he tossed his key in the dish and shut the door behind him, Hank looked up to see a present on his countertop. He set down his luggage and walked slowly to the kitchen area. Maddie had run back into his place Friday morning before they left for Boston, claiming that she'd left her hairbrush in his bathroom. She'd come out empty-handed and told him she must have already packed it.

He approached the gift like an undetonated bomb. It was

wrapped in beautiful white paper with a wide blue ribbon. It was a cube, about the size of half a brick.

There was a pale blue envelope beneath it. He pulled the card out first, before gearing up to open the present. It was a child's birthday card, with a cartoonish drawing of balloons and big bubble letters that cried, "YOU'RE 6!" He smiled and opened the card. There was a little rhyming couplet about the years going fast and having a blast, and then a written message from Maddie on the left-hand side.

I was in a rush at the drugstore when I went to pick out a card to go with your present, and I figured, you are basically an emotional six-year-old, and with the whole explosives/blast pun, that you might smile when you read this. Also, you were so juvenile not to let me celebrate your birthday properly. If you had just let me bake you a cake or something normal like that, I might not have gone overboard with a far too expensive present. As it is, when I found this on eBay I thought it was fitting that it cost the same amount that I earned the entire time I lived here—the entire time I was with you. So it seemed right. M.

PS I also love that it says "antimagnetic" on the back, because that is SO you.

Hank set down the card after letting his fingertips skim over the slants and scrapes of Maddie's vicious handwriting. Her penmanship was just like she was, fast and to the point. He stared at the box and wondered if he had the courage to open it. He took a deep breath to fortify himself, then reached for the blue ribbon.

He pulled it open slowly and could practically feel the ghost of Maddie nearby, jumping up and down and clapping her hands and saying something like, "Oh! I hope you love it! Open it! Open it!"

Once he'd taken the ribbon off, he coiled it neatly and slipped it into the drawer in the kitchen where he kept string and tape and scissors.

He removed the white wrapping paper, slowly at first, then tearing it harshly to get the box out. It was a worn leather watch case, obviously old but well taken care of. He opened the hinged top with a mixture of dread and hope.

She had given him the Swiss watch, the vintage Blancpain Fifty Fathoms. He had no idea how much they went for new, but he knew that Maddie had saved up four thousand dollars over the summer. She used to give him a weekly update on her finances, explaining how miraculous it seemed to her that her pile of cash grew and grew just by putting in her tips every night and leaving it alone. She cashed her paychecks and added that money to the coffee can on Saturdays.

At first he had found it sort of ridiculous, ribbing her for her financial cluelessness.

"I'm not clueless!" she had cried. "I am actually really financially responsible. I have assets. But this is different. This is so . . . tangible. There is such a difference between money that I make and money that I . . . received."

Maddie had never really hidden the fact that her family had money, but she'd never explained why she had no access to any of it that summer, either.

He held the watch in the palm of his right hand, letting the balance and weight become familiar to him. He touched the sharp ridges of the rotating bezel and moved the numbers around the dial. The band was made of some kind of rubber or composite. He turned over the watch to look at the back. Sure enough, the words *Fifty Fathoms* were engraved in an elegant script, with the word *ANTIMAGNETIC* in smaller caps just below. He rubbed the pad of his thumb over the cool metal words until the metal warmed under his skin. He liked knowing that Maddie had touched the watch.

He removed the cheap, reliable diving watch he'd used for years and set it on the counter, then put on the expensive Swiss replacement. After staring at the way the watch rested on his wrist, as if it had been made for the turn of bone and skin, he shook his head and walked over to his desk. He turned on his computer and logged into his e-mail. All of the decisions that had plagued Hank for the past few months seemed easily dispensed with all of a sudden. He replied to the head of the excavation team at the University of Cyprus. He replied to the administrator in charge of the NATO project in Athens. He replied to his contact in the R & D department at Ocean Works Laboratories.

Life would go on. He refused to wallow. And if he got his shit together he might even be well enough to get in touch with Maddie when she graduated. Or sooner.

CHAPTER 18

The Head of the Charles was always a nightmare. Maddie had been in the lead boat for Brown all three years, but it was always a crapshoot until a few hours before the race. The coaches were prone to rearrange the lineups right until the last minute, working on the best possible odds, given the weather, the course, and the competition. Maddie had kept herself so busy for the past six weeks that she hadn't had time to think about Hank, except when she was asleep and couldn't force her subconscious brain into submission.

All of her time was spent training, rowing, or studying. Sleeping and eating were part of training, nothing more. She fell into the robotic routine with a dismal sort of gratitude. At least she was going to have something to show for herself. She was in the best shape of her life, and her thesis advisor had pretty much told her she was going to graduate with honors if she wrote the paper he thought she was capable of.

That small bit of research she had done at the Houghton Library that day with Hank—and Hank himself, if she was honest—had inspired her to fine-tune her research to a very particular aspect of naval antiquity. She was in the midst of applying for a grant to spend the year after she graduated in Cyprus, studying the historical significance of the great galley ships—the penteconter, the bireme, and the trireme, ancient vessels powered by oarsmen.

Two hours before the first race, Maddie found out she was going to be in the lead boat. The coach gave her a quick pat on the back, and Maddie smiled up at her. Her parents were somewhere in the crowd, and Jimmy had said he was going to come, but it was too chaotic to see anyone until after her set of races was finished.

She was in the Women's Four. The boat was so familiar, the turn of the fiberglass, the way the seat molded to her bottom, the feel of the oars in her hands. The race itself always dissolved into mist in her mind. Maddie always remembered the final inhale before the gun went off, and then she was just . . . off. And then it was a steady, grinding series of pulls and breaths and muscle that hurled her body into a space of pure motion. And then it was over. And they'd won. Her teammates were hugging and crying, and Maddie looked up and thought she saw Hank in the crowd, but then the man turned and it wasn't him, and then her friend Stephanie in the seat behind her grabbed her shoulders and shook her and was screaming her congratulations, and Maddie smiled and tried to look back where she thought she had seen Hank, but the crowd was moving and shifting like the water all around her, and Hank was gone.

Or her dream vision of Hank was gone. She let herself cry, because everyone was crying for joy from having beaten the crap out of Princeton—finally—and she thought it was as good a time as any to completely let her guard down. When they got back to the boathouse, the coaches and the rest of her teammates were hooting and clapping, and everyone was thrilled. Maddie felt like she was in a tunnel, she was present, but everything was distorted, and the volume seemed to increase and decrease at odd times.

"Hey, beautiful!" Strong arms grabbed her and pulled her into a hug, and Maddie's stupid, gullible heart flew into a crazy, joyful dance. She whipped around, and her brother Jimmy was holding her and patting her back and congratulating her on her grand achievement.

He so wasn't Hank. She hugged him back and cried.

"Wow. Since when did you turn into such a bawl-baby?"

Maddie laughed and wiped her face. "Since we just kicked ass, that's when."

Jimmy smiled and gave her one last squeeze. "You know, I'm not really supposed to be here, but Mom and Dad are so happy for you, and I wangled my way in. Great job!"

"Thanks, Jimmy. I'll see you at dinner tonight."

The imaginary sightings went on like that for the rest of Maddie's fall semester. She knew it was part of her emotional crack-up or whatever it was that she was going through. It just seemed so impossible that she had been with the right guy and it hadn't worked out. In that, at least, Hank was right: Maddie was spoiled. She had been raised to believe that with hard work and integrity, things would work out for Ms. Madison Post. She no longer believed that.

She knew it was spoiled to think that way, with all of her privileges and a future that was basically laid out before her, but inside it felt shadowy and thin compared to how she'd felt in Hank's arms last summer. By Christmas, Maddie was entirely capable of masking her disappointment. She suspected that many people lived their entire lives masking their disappointment. Perhaps that's all that was meant by grand philosophical euphemisms like "The Human Condition."

Or "Adulthood."

Maddie's nieces and nephews were at just the right age for the perfect holiday celebration, jubilant and enthusiastic about the cookies and milk for Santa and the carrots and celery for the reindeer, and not overly concerned about the quantity of presents under the tree. Everyone descended upon Maddie's parents' place for the holiday weekend.

On Christmas morning, they were all sitting around opening presents, the fire crackling, the paper ripping, when Maddie's mother looked up. "Oh, dear, I forgot that something came for you in the mail last week, Maddie."

Laura got up and left the living room, where all the grandchildren were tearing through their gifts and sitting cross-legged on the floor in their pajamas while their parents sat in their bathrobes drinking coffee and watching the clock for when they could have the first eggnog or Bloody Mary.

Returning to the living room a few minutes later, Laura handed Maddie a small box wrapped in brown paper. It was covered in foreign stamps, and her name and address were spelled out in a beautiful masculine script. It felt like him already.

Maddie looked up. Her mother was smiling, and her father looked away as if it were none of his business. Feeling a little idiotic, all she wanted to do was hold the unopened package. She loved the way it was so meticulously wrapped and the way each of the stamps had been placed with exquisite care at the upper edge. It was so Hank.

Her two oldest brothers were busy talking to each other about which college football game they were going to watch first, but their wives, Isabel and Georgia, were staring at Maddie expectantly from across the room.

"A secret admirer?" Georgia said with a raised eyebrow.

Maddie took a deep breath and opened the package. She did it carefully. She wanted to preserve the brown paper and all those stamps and his handsome handwriting, and frame it or do something special with it eventually. After she'd removed the paper, she opened a small cardboard box, which had tiny wood shavings that were keeping an even smaller box delicately afloat in the packing material. She took out the small jewelry box and opened it.

An ancient silver coin winked out at her. Maddie touched it cautiously with tingling fingertips, feeling the ridges of the ancient profile, then gently took it out of the box and held it up to the light.

Her mother gasped. "Oh, darling! What is it?"

Maddie folded her fingers around it in a possessive move that surprised her mother and herself. Her unspoken answer: *It is mine.* She held it like that for a few seconds, then opened her palm and held it out to her mother.

"Here," Maddie offered. "It looks like there's a description in the box. I think it's second- or third-century BC. You hold it while I read about it."

Laura Post took the artifact out of her daughter's hand and examined it closely, pushing her reading glasses up her nose to have a closer look. "How gorgeous."

There was a small folded piece of pale blue paper tucked along the inside edge of the cardboard box. Maddie unfolded it and began to read. An academic description of the gift, in Hank's strong confident hand, told of the face of the goddess Athena on one side and the full form of Herakles on the reverse. It was from 280 BC and . . .

And then Maddie couldn't read it very clearly anymore because it was all stupid beautiful things that he could never say in real life about how she was his goddess and he was trying to complete his labors and how he hoped that she would wait for him for just a little while longer because they were two sides of that coin and—

"Is that a description of the coin, Maddie?" Her father reached for the thin airmail paper, and she folded it up quickly and tucked it back into the box. "No, it's nothing." She wiped her cheeks with the sleeve of her robe, and everyone was kind enough not to ask her why she was a weepy mess. "Apparently the coin is Lucanian," Maddie explained. "Third century BC." She asked her mother if she could have it back for a moment, and then Maddie passed it to her father.

While her enthusiasm and bravado had come from her mother, Maddie's love of old, beautiful, solid objects had come straight from her father and his parents' side of the family. This house. Everything in it. Old. Beautiful. Solid. It was a strange kind of wealth, really, because it felt like everything had always been there. There had never been any evidence of acquisition. Everything was just there.

Maddie's paternal great-grandparents had been antiquities scholars at Harvard. Everyone always joked that her great-grandmother had been the smart one because the woman's husband had only spoken four languages and she had spoken six. They went on long, dangerous trips. They were nineteenth-century adventurers.

William Post took the coin from his daughter and held it in the palm of his hand for a few seconds. "May I?" He held it up to indicate that he wanted a closer look.

"Yes. Let's." Maddie stood up too, and she followed her father out across the front hall and back toward his office, which overlooked the snowy expanse of the backyard and the adjacent conservation land. It was a glorious winter scene, all crackling black branches against virgin snow.

"Have a seat, sweet pea, and let's see what we've got."

This was always the way. Objects bound Maddie to her father. She would find something in the woods or down near the stream that ran between their property and the Wallaces' next door, and she would run home and wait until her father got back, and then she would present it to him for inspection. He always encouraged her and brought her into his mysterious and secret world. His study.

At the moment, he was looking through a large, handheld magnifying glass. He had set the coin—about the size of a quarter—onto the green, papery felt of his desk blotter and had turned on a desk lamp that shone down upon it. "It's quite something, isn't it? Look at the detail on Athena's helmet. *Mmm-hmmm.*"

Maddie sat in the chair next to his desk, her hands held palms together between her thighs, in her old pajamas and her flannel bathrobe and ragg wool socks. She was waiting for her turn.

"Come see," her father finally said.

She jumped up and took the hand lens that he held out for her. He had a metal pointer, like a surgical instrument in the shape of half a tweezer and twice as long. "See here," he began. "Do you notice the Scylla here?" He was pointing at the figure atop Athena's helmet.

"Yes. She's beautiful."

"She looks terrifying, if you ask me!" Her father laughed. He loved to make these long-dead characters come to life. "But I suspect Herakles," William paused to turn over the coin to show the over side where the hero stood, "thinks she's worth fighting for, don't you?"

Maddie stared at the small piece of history, thousands of years old. Thousands! She sighed. "It's a spectacular gift. I don't really know how to . . . think of it."

Her father sat back in his old, creaking leather chair on the casters. "I think the person who gave it to you is very clever . . . and knows you very well."

She could tell that her dad was skimming around the pronoun. "He. It's a he. He knows me very well." She smiled up at her father, then continued speaking while her attention returned to the coin. "I think you'd like him . . ."

"I *would* like him hypothetically? Or I *will* like him when I meet him?"

Maddie smiled but didn't look up. "I hope the latter."

"So do I! So do I!" William Post pushed away from the desk on the wheels of his chair and stood up. He clapped his hands together, then opened his arms wide. "Merry Christmas, Madison!" She hugged him back. He patted her twice quickly, and then it was over. She set the magnifying glass back onto his desk, picked up the coin, and turned off the table lamp.

As they walked back toward the living room, her father said, "I'm afraid the sweater your mother and I got you is going to be rather anticlimactic."

She smiled up at her father and held the coin in the palm of her hand for the rest of the day.

That night, Maddie re-read Hank's letter over and over. If anything ever happened to it, she had it committed to memory for all of eternity. He had been in Greece. Obviously. But other than that, he said he wasn't able to tell her details. He didn't use the word deployed, but it sounded like that was the case. He said it was going to be better for both of them if they met up again in August when he got back. And then his tender request that he wanted her to wait for him. It was so glorious. Maddie's face hurt from smiling when she read the words, and said them over and over in her mind. *Two sides of the same coin.*

CHAPTER 19

Everything made sense again. Maddie spent the rest of her Christmas vacation baking with her mother and babysitting for her nieces and nephews and working on her senior thesis and generally being in a stellar mood. She got back to school in January and felt like she was in the final segment of the longest race she'd ever rowed. The combination of the ramped-up academics to finish her senior year, waiting to see if she got the grant, counting down the months and weeks until Hank resurfaced from wherever he was—it all began to wear on her.

She watched the news with an intensity that set her roommates on edge.

"What is your problem, Post?"

Maddie was sitting in front of the banged-up television in the living room that she shared with three of her friends in the off-campus house they rented together. She was biting her nails. The habit had started sometime after the Head of the Charles. It helped, somehow.

"No problem," she mumbled. "Just watching the news."

"You are not a poli-sci major. Since when did you get so interested in the Gulf War?" Her roommate Deeanna was a bit of a pain lately.

"It's not the Gulf War, you idiot."

Deeanna stared at her. "What did you just call me?"

Maddie looked up from the television. "I called you an idiot. The Gulf War ended before we were born. The only active combat zone right now is Afghanistan. I am watching the news about Afghanistan." Maddie rolled her eyes and went back to nibbling her fingernails and trying to see what she could see when the news camera swept over the landscape between Kandahar and Kabul.

The news clip finished, and Maddie turned off the television.

Deeanna was still standing there with her hands on her hips. "What the hell has gotten into you?"

Maddie stood up and raked her hair back into a ponytail, pulling a rubber band from her wrist, where she always had an extra. "I'm sorry. You're not a total idiot." Deeanna was one of the top pre-med students at Brown. It wasn't a lie. "But you seriously know so little about American history that I sometimes worry for you."

Deeanna smiled. "Isn't that what Wikipedia is for . . . all those silly dates?"

Maddie shook her head. "Let's agree to disagree. I think all those silly dates pretty much define our humanity. You go cure cancer. Together, maybe we'll make the world a better place."

They walked into the kitchen and had a couple of glasses of wine that Maddie poured from the box of cheap dreck they kept in the fridge.

Deeanna stared at Maddie's pale, exhausted features. "Are you ever going to tell any of us what this is all about?"

Maddie stared into her wineglass. "Probably not. It's bad enough thinking about him all the time, I don't think I could bear—"

Her roommate made a fist pump. "I knew it! I told Leah that you met someone and you were heartbroken—"

Opening her mouth to defend herself, Maddie was immediately cut off.

"—or temporarily heartbroken or whatever."

"Yeah," Maddie said. "That's about right. Temporarily heartbroken. But I think I'm on the mend."

Sort of.

After Maddie had begun to do a little research on the role of military divers and the jobs they tended to have after they retired from the military, Maddie became mildly obsessed with where Hank actually was. If he thought it was safer not to be in contact, it had to be pretty hairy. By the beginning of April, Maddie was reaching the point of desperation from not having had any word from Hank. And then Janet's wedding invitation arrived.

Maddie tore it open, then picked up the phone.

"Hello?" Janet answered on the third ring.

"Hi, Janet. It's Madison Post. How are you?"

"Maddie! What a treat to hear your voice, you sweet thing! Did you get the invitation already? I hope you can come. It's probably right around your graduation and impossible and—"

"No. It's perfect. I get out of school the week before, so we will all have something to celebrate."

"Well, I'm sure Hank has told you, but it's such a shame he won't be back in time."

Sure Hank has told me? Madison began to get a creeping feeling that she was going to regret the next few minutes for the rest of her life.

"Oh. Have you heard from Hank?" Maddie asked.

Janet obviously heard the hint of false disinterest in Maddie's voice.

"Well, of course. I mean, yes. He's been very good about staying in touch. But he said he's too far away to come back in June. His assignment finishes in August, and I just didn't want to wait that long to get married. You understand! Phil and I are so ready to tie the knot."

Maddie felt like she was suffering repeated punches to the gut. *Very good about staying in touch*? What the hell?

"Maddie?"

She must have stayed silent for too long. She tried to recover her equanimity. "I'm here. I'm so sorry, I was distracted for a few seconds. I'm so happy for you." But her tone was empty, and she figured Janet could probably hear that too. They talked about Phil and what a brutal winter they were having in Blake, and then Maddie asked about Sharon and the girls, and then finally if there was anything special Janet wanted as a wedding present.

"Oh, nothing special, sweetie. We have everything we need. It would just be wonderful to have you here if you can make it."

"I'll definitely try," Maddie said. Somewhere in the course of the conversation, she'd gone from definitely going to definitely trying. They made a bit more small talk, then one of Maddie's roommates, Leah, came into the living room of their apartment and Maddie begged off the call and said good-bye.

She stared at the phone and tried to process that Dumpster full of information that she'd just gotten. Hank was able to write letters to his mother and not to her? His *goddess*? She felt like a stupid, stupid girl. Why did every other Army wife have Skype and e-mail and you-name-it to stay in touch with their loved ones? Was she even a *loved one*? Had Hank once said he *loved* her? Or did it just make him feel good to send her precious ancient coins and tell her how great he thought she was? And to wait. That must be so much easier than actually showing up and being in someone's life like a *normal* person.

She almost pawned Athena and Herakles, with a mind to giving the money to Janet and Phil. And what was up with not even going to your own mother's wedding? Who *did* that? Except the most heartless, disconnected beasts? And Hank Gilbertson.

He'd set this whole stupid situation up this way. Sure, he probably thought it was best to keep Maddie focused on her final year of school and her studies and her athletics and every other damn thing, but that should have been her decision, not his. Who was he to make all of these unilateral wait-for-me-to-complete-my-labors type of statements?

Maddie was still storming around the living room when Deeanna came back from her chemistry lab. "Another bad day in Candyharr?"

Looking to the ceiling to keep the rage from flying in her roommate's face, Maddie counted to three and said, "Kan. Duh. Har. It's pronounced Kandahar. And yes, as a matter of fact, I am having a particularly shitty day. Anything else?"

Deeanna smiled and walked into her room. "Nope. That about does it." She shut the door quietly, and Maddie realized that all three of her roommates were closed up in their respective rooms and she was standing alone in the middle of her living room. In the middle of what was supposed to be the best year of her life at one of the best schools. In her prime.

Here she was, pining away for the ghost of a guy who had nothing better to do than string her along while he wrote regular letters to his mother while she, Maddie!, sat home and bit her fingernails and watched YouTube videos about the construction of the bridge across the Panj River into Tajikstan.

The resentment boiled up inside, fierce and fast. She yelled so her voice would penetrate all three closed doors. "I need to go out!!!"

Within seconds, all three of her friends poked their faces out of their rooms. With an eyebrow raised in sarcasm, Emily said, "Oh, has Madison Post decided to come back to earth?" She looked from Maddie to Deeanna to Leah and back again.

"Yes!" Maddie tried to corral her enthusiasm. "I am back and I want to get bombed and pick up the first hot guy who hits on me. Give me twenty minutes to get tarted up, and we are out of here."

The other three turned back into their rooms until the sounds of closet doors opening and closing and makeup caps popping on and off were drowned out by the stereo being cranked up to full volume with a rapper pounding out a steady thrum of lust-inspiring aggression.

Maddie got her wish.

She got completely drunk and picked up the first guy who hit on her. Unfortunately, or rather, fortunately, the guy was a friend of Deeanna's, and there was no way he was going to take advantage of a completely unconscious Madison Post. He helped her stumble home and got her into bed fully clothed. He felt like he had achieved new levels of chivalry when he tossed a blanket over her passed-out body.

When Madison woke up the next morning and realized she was alone and fully clothed, she was mildly disappointed. She almost wished she had gone through with her first drunken one-night-stand. At least then the pain of Hank's strange silence would have been overshadowed by the requisite regret and shame she would have felt if she had actually slept with the guy who was just then passed out on the floor next to her bed.

He was kind of cute, actually. His name was Sam and he sat in the back in one of Maddie's Latin classes. He wasn't stupid. And he wasn't a pig. He was just sort of there. When he began to wake up, Maddie was still staring at him, and his glazed expression didn't really register where he was or who she was.

"Hi," Maddie said. "I'm Madison Post. We're in Latin class together. I think I threw myself at you last night."

He had light reddish hair and it was all flattened out on one side. He looked like a stray.

"Hi. I'm Samuel Pruitt. Nice to meet you, Madison."

She reached her hand out from under the too-thin blanket in order to shake his hand. "Nice to meet you, Samuel."

They talked a little bit more, and Maddie felt like the least she could do was offer the guy some breakfast in thanks for not sleeping with her despite her—*ahem*—gracious offer to do whatever he wanted to his body or hers. He was just reminding her of all of her generous propositions.

"How charming." Maddie cringed, but they both laughed and through the odd set of circumstances, Maddie had made a new friend.

After she'd made him an omelet, there was a quick double-tap at Maddie's front door. It was only about nine thirty on Saturday morning and all of her roommates would be asleep for hours. The only reason she was awake was that she was used to getting up in the dark every morning for crew . . . and there had been a guy snoring on the carpet next to her bed. She rubbed her achy forehead and pulled the front door open. Sam was coming up behind her, his sneakers in one hand, his winter coat in the other.

"I should probably go. It was great to meet you—" He leaned in to kiss her cheek as Maddie pulled the door open, figuring she could show Sam out and sign for the UPS package or whatever else it would be at that unusual hour.

Sam froze.

Maddie froze.

Hank was, as always, frozen in place. Unmoving.

"Hank?"

"Wow," he said with a slow glance at Sam and then back into Maddie's eyes. "You remember my name."

Sam looked from Hank to Maddie, then slipped past Hank. Sam's floppy red hair bounced around as the poor guy hopped onto the cold front porch and pulled on one sneaker and then the other to get out of that loony bin as quickly as his legs could carry him.

"Do you want to come inside?"

CHAPTER 20

Hank stared at Maddie and wanted to rip his own heart out. She looked ragged. Her hair was lank, she was too thin. Her eyes had dark circles under them, and her lips looked chapped and drawn. "I don't know . . . maybe this isn't a good time . . ." He stood where he was and let her take the responsibility of telling him what the hell had just happened.

"Up to you," Maddie said with a dismissive wave of her hand. She left the front door open and started to walk back toward the kitchen. "Either come in or don't, but shut the door to keep out the draft, please."

What had happened to her? He walked in slowly, pulling the front door quietly behind him. He knew she had three roommates who were probably asleep behind the closed doors that led off the living room. He followed Maddie back toward what must be the kitchen. She was pouring a cup of coffee, and he could see her hand was shaking as she tried to hold the carafe steady over her mug.

"Here, let me do that," Hank offered.

Maddie slammed the carafe back into place on the heating unit of the coffeemaker and swung around to face him. "I can make my own cup of coffee, Hank."

"Maddie. It's me. What the hell is going on?"

"What's going on?" Her voice was shrill. Deeanna had woken

up and wandered into the kitchen in a too-short nightie and nothing else. She walked over to the coffeepot, reached up for a mug, started to pour, then turned to Hank and said, "You the one she picked up last night?"

Maddie growled. "Deeanna. Shut. Up. Get out of the kitchen and leave us alone."

"Touchy. Touchy. I need milk in my coffee." She shuffled over to the refrigerator and topped off her coffee with a splash of milk, then shuffled back toward her bedroom.

"And put on a bathrobe!" Maddie cried after her.

"Whatever, Maddie."

Hank stared at her.

Maddie stared at him. "What? I'm a college senior. You send me one stupid letter and I'm supposed to wait around like an idiot? Haven't you ever heard of the Internet? Or the telephone? Or the US Mail?!"

At least she was getting worked up, he thought. When Hank set aside the boiling rage that accompanied the thought of her picking someone up at a bar the night before, he was relieved to see her get that fire back in her cheeks.

"I couldn't. I was on totally high security—" he said in a defensive tone.

Maddie slammed the flat of her hand on the cheap kitchen counter with a loud *thwack*! "That is such a lie!" Her voice was rippling with anger. "You are such a screwed-up liar! You just say shit, and I am such an idiot that I actually believe you—"

He reached out to touch her, anything, her hand, her cheek, to hold on to her upper arm.

"Don't! Don't touch me!" She pulled away from him. "I talked to your mother yesterday."

He let his hand drop away from trying to touch her.

"Yeah. Remember her? Your mother?"

Hank's face fell. He felt so guilty that he had taken the few precious days he had to come to Providence instead of going to see his mother who had dedicated her entire life to repairing the damage she thought she had done.

"I thought—" He was going to say he had thought Madison was more important, but he stumbled when he saw the rage in her eyes. It was so unfamiliar. Especially directed at him.

"You thought what? You thought it wouldn't strike me as odd that you send me one letter," she held her index finger up and put it close to her face, "*one* stinking letter, and then your mother just blithely tells me that of-course-she-hears-from-you-all-the-time-and-didn't-I-hear-from-you-all-the-time-too?!"

Hank stared at Maddie, his face impassive. "Is that what this is about? You're jealous of my mother?"

Maddie stomped her right foot on the ground. "How *dare* you try to twist this around?!" Another roommate could be heard plodding down the hallway to the kitchen. "Ugh! Just come into my room so we can talk without half the neighborhood coming and interrupting us." Maddie sort of shoved Hank into her bedroom and pulled the door shut just as Emily was turning into the kitchen.

Hank saw the pillow and the pallet of blankets that was on the floor next to the bed and he reminded himself that Ms. I-have-condoms-falling-out-of-my-bag had also happened to be a virgin. "You have a dog?"

Maddie looked where Hank was looking, then rolled her eyes in disgust. "No! I don't have a dog! Well, not counting you, I don't. That's where Sam the Latin nerd slept last night."

Hank took off his black windbreaker and set it on the back of her desk chair.

"Why are you taking your jacket off and making yourself comfortable? You are not staying here."

"Because I only have forty-eight hours, and I don't want to waste it bickering." He stood with his hands on his waist. He was wearing a black woolen sweater with canvas patches at the shoulder. He supposed he looked military and foreign all at the same time. "Come here, Maddie."

He saw the flash of longing in her eyes, then her immediate attempt to squash it. "No." She folded her arms to cover her breasts. He could tell her body was already betraying her. He pulled her desk chair around so he could sit in it, then bent over to untie his laced-up combat boots. They were polished and immaculate. He had wanted to look sharp for the NATO officials on the flight they'd been kind enough to offer him a seat on. But mostly he wanted to look good for Madison when he imagined her opening her front door.

Part one of that vision had turned out great: the NATO officials had congratulated him on a job well done. Part two of that scenario hadn't turned out at all the way he'd planned. But if anyone knew how to move forward after unexpected circumstances, it was Hank.

"Why are you taking off your shoes?! Seriously, Hank, you can't just walk in here after—what, six months—"

He stood up, and Maddie gasped. He pulled the dark sweater over his head and began unbuttoning the cuffs of the gray button-down shirt. He towered over her. "Seven months." Maddie looked down at the floor. He touched her cheek. "Three days." She whimpered a lame protest. "Twenty-two hours." He traced the contours of her lips with his finger. "Seventeen minutes," he whispered finally.

Maddie looked up at him, still clinging to her defiance. "But why not a single call? Why did you have time for other people and not for me?"

He wanted to kiss her so desperately. He leaned in—

"Hank! Tell me!" Her voice was cracking.

He kept his fingers at the back of her neck, in that warm place beneath the fall of her beautiful hair. "I wrote to my mother in advance . . ."

"You what?" She wasn't able to follow his words when he touched her like that. Her eyes were already beginning to cloud with lust.

"I wrote fifty-two letters in advance," he repeated.

"So . . . why didn't you . . ." She moaned when he reached his hand under her long-sleeved T-shirt.

"I couldn't write to you in advance . . . it felt like a fraud. My mother just wants to know I'm alive. You? I couldn't . . . I just wasn't able to bring myself to do that."

He leaned in and kissed her neck, and someplace in the back of her mind she thought she should be fighting harder to tell him something or demand something. Her head was still fogged from drinking too much the night before, after being so torn up about him just the day before. Wrecked. It was too much.

"Hank. Please stop." She said it so softly, but he felt it more powerfully than if she'd clocked him.

"What is it?"

"I just need to look at you and touch you and know you're real. It's been so long, Hank. Really, really long."

His brow pulled tight. "I've thought of you every minute, Maddie. I've been working on a project, so completely immersed, and you are always with me. I think of things that I'm going to tell you, and stories about the stuff I'm doing, and what I'm going to do to your body . . ."

She swayed into him, her lips barely an inch from his. "I don't trust you, Hank."

Maybe it *would* have been better if she had clocked him. He felt the wind get knocked out of him after he heard those words. He set her a little bit farther away from him. "*You* don't trust *me*?! I just knocked on your front door and some good-time-Charlie kisses you good-bye, and *you* don't trust *me*? This is unbelievable!"

Maddie moved away from him and sat at the foot of her bed. She looked around her bedroom and tried to see it through Hank's eyes. There was evidence of her infatuation with him everywhere. The jewelry box with the coin in it was sitting on her bedside table. A picture of the two of them that Janet had taken over the summer was framed and sitting atop her dresser. A movie stub. A fortune from one of the Chinese fortune cookies from Ming's. Small scraps were tucked into the edge of the frame of her mirror. The brown wrapping paper with the Greek stamps and her address in Hank's handwriting was in a shadow-box frame over her bed.

He looked at all the evidence and then smiled down at her. "Really? I think you've missed me as much as I've missed you. And you're too stubborn to admit it."

He kneeled at the end of the bed, pushing her legs apart so he could see her eye-to-eye and lean into her. Whatever had happened on the phone with his mother, Maddie had been devastated. Hank took a deep breath.

"I'm so sorry, Maddie. I . . . I don't have any idea how to do this right. I took the assignment because the pay is amazing and it ends in August and I thought, maybe, if you still cared about me, we could be together then. I'll have enough saved to go . . . wherever you're going. To Cyprus for the fellowship, or to California to train for the Olympics. Because you're going places and you're not going to be easy to keep up with, you know?"

Her eyes were still closed, and the tears were beginning to seep out. "You kept everything from me, Hank. Not just where you were these past few months, but all your feelings. Everything. The whole time."

He leaned in and kissed her neck and reached under her shirt again, lightly touching her stomach. "I might have been quiet, but you always knew how I felt. You've always known that I loved you, since the minute you walked into my mother's living room and you were supposed to be some little old lady. But you were you." Hank took a quick breath. "And I was a mess. I just . . . I'm better now, I swear. I'm talking to the right people—"

Maddie opened her moist eyes and stared into his. "You are?"

He laughed. "Yeah. I am. Big man meets shrink. You good with that?"

Maddie nodded and smiled, but she was still sad. "I'm glad someone is there for you."

"It's all because of you, Maddie. You were there for me."

She looked like that wasn't correct either.

He shook his head. "No, that's not right. It's not because of you in that way that leaves you with the burden. It's thanks to you . . . for making me see it was possible . . . that everything was possible. I had no incentive to really connect with other people after I left the Army. You were amazingly incentivizing . . ." Hank kept one hand under her shirt and one hand at the back of her neck. And waited.

Reaching up to touch his cheek, Maddie finally released her arms from the defensive posture across her chest. "I missed you so much . . ." She touched his cheek, and his eyes softened. The relief of her touch. The relief of being there with her.

Hank had been worried that he might have concocted the power of their connection. Now he knew for sure it was entirely real. She took his hand from her neck and put it to her chest. "I can feel my heart starting to beat again," she said softly. "I felt sort of dead when you were gone. It's not healthy. It's wrong. I feel like I'm disappearing when we're not together."

Hank pulled her hard and fast into the solid wall of his stomach and chest, then heaved them both onto the bed, nearly crushing her beneath his desperate body. "You could never disappear."

"My body needs you. I need you. I worried about you all the time. If anything happened to you—" Her words flew out in a rush.

He lifted her hands so he could look at the ravaged cuticles and nonexistent fingernail tips. "I'm supposed to be the one looking out for you, not the other way around."

Maddie smiled and looked embarrassed. "I became rather knowledgeable about military deployments in Afghanistan."

"Oh, you did, did you?" He was kissing her neck and unbuttoning her pants. "What's your favorite river?"

"The Panj. Or maybe the Arghandab."

He smiled. "Why those?" He leaned back on his knees and pulled off her jeans, then pulled off his own shirt.

"Because they usually show soldiers, so I can picture you there." Her voice was getting reedy as it always did when she was losing her focus on the words and transitioning into the world of their pleasure.

"Forgive me, Maddie." Hank leaned his lips into the warm turn of her neck. "Please," he whispered near her ear.

She arched up into him and then turned her lips to his. Their forty-eight-hour clock was ticking and she didn't want to waste another minute.

CHAPTER 21

Maddie rolled over into her pillow and thought she had been dreaming about Hank again. The pillow smelled like him. But she was alone in her single bed in Providence. Disoriented, she got up and pulled her robe from the closet. She wrapped the belt around her waist and rubbed her eyes as she opened the door into the kitchen. Hank was sitting at the table in his gray button-down shirt and military-looking pants and drawing something, or taking notes, and talking to Deeanna.

Taking a few seconds to just stare at him, here in her world. Not in the Ritz-Carlton or on the perimeter. Really here. At her kitchen table with her roommate. Deeanna saw her first and she gave Hank a quick tap with her elbow. He stopped what he was doing and looked up at Maddie.

His smile spread across his face, and Maddie was almost embarrassed that Deeanna had seen such a display of . . . everything.

Maddie pulled her bathrobe more tightly around her because that smile made her feel naked. She walked over to make a new pot of coffee. "How long did I sleep?" she asked.

"It's almost one," Hank said.

"In the afternoon?!" Maddie almost dropped the glass coffee carafe into the ceramic sink. "Why didn't you wake me up?"

When no one answered, Maddie finished refilling the water,

poured it into the coffeemaker, and turned to look at them, folding her arms across her chest. "Well?"

Hank stood up, and Deeanna looked at the paper he had been working on and pretended not to pay attention.

"Because you were tired," Hank said, snaking his arms around her waist. She pretended to stay irritated.

"We've wasted precious hours," Maddie mumbled, keeping her arms crossed, but starting to dip her lips to his chest to get a kiss.

He smiled and hugged her close. "We're good. Pack a bag. Jump in the shower. We've got plans for the weekend."

When Maddie looked up, her eyes were alive and expectant. "Really?"

"Unless you're too busy?"

"As it turns out, I've had a lot of time to devote to my studies lately." She smirked.

"Then let's go." Hank turned her around and pushed her toward her bedroom. "Hurry up!"

She stumbled in with a stupid grin, looking around at her messy room. The clothes that she'd worn the night before, and slept in— the same clothes that Hank had taken off her with slow, deliberate care that morning—were strewn all over the floor. The makeshift pallet that poor Sam Pruitt had slept on was still crumpled next to the bed. The bed . . . looked like it had gone through a tornado.

Maddie smiled when she looked at the mangled sheets and remembered how good it felt to be there again with Hank—

"Why are you still standing in the middle of the room in your bathrobe? Chop chop! Let's go!" Hank was smiling but he wasn't joking. "It was fun to have a toss in a single bed for old times' sake, but we've got places to go . . . places with big beds and no one around for miles—"

"Okay! Okay!" Maddie ran over to her closet and pulled out her duffle bag. She packed, jumped in the shower, and threw on a pair of jeans and a sweatshirt.

When she came out to the kitchen, Deeanna was bent over another piece of paper talking to Hank. He had put on his sweater and his shiny boots while Maddie had been in the shower, and he looked so great.

"What are you two up to?" Maddie asked, leaning over their shoulders to see what they were working on. She rested a hand on Hank's shoulder, and he touched his cheek to the back of her hand for a second. The paper they were studying was covered in an incomprehensible spray of numbers and arrows.

"Oh." Deeanna looked up. "Henry was just telling me about some of the mesh composites he's been working on. I've been talking to my chemistry teacher about some ideas I had about that sort of thing for vascular reinforcement, and I just thought I'd run them past Henry . . . while he was here . . ."

Maddie looked from one to the other. "Miss Candy-harr and Mr. I-Clean-the-Bottom-of-Boats for a living? You two are ridiculous."

Deeanna pretended to be offended, then smiled and pulled together her homework papers. "Thanks, Henry. It was really great meeting you. Sorry about the are-you-the-one-she-picked-up comment earlier."

Hank was standing and reached down to shake her hand. "I think we'll probably see each other again." He looked quickly at Maddie, then back to Deeanna. "It was good to meet you, too. Say bye to Emily and Leah for me."

"Will do. Have a good rest of the weekend, you guys."

Maddie smiled, and Hank took her hand and led her back toward the living room and out the front door.

When they'd walked down the few steps to the street, Hank turned to Maddie and smiled. "I don't even know what kind of car you have."

"I don't have a car."

"You don't?"

"Nope."

He led her toward his black rental car. "What do you do? How do you get around?" He took her bag and threw it in the back, then opened the passenger door to let her get in.

"I run everywhere."

He smiled down at her, then shut the door and walked around the front of the car and got in.

He started up the car and headed down the hill from her house.

"Oooh!" Maddie clapped her hands. "Are we going to the Ritz? Please-please-please!"

"God I've missed you like hell."

Maddie looked out the window and furrowed her brow and stared at the row of houses in her neighborhood. "I was right here the whole time."

"I'm so sorry, Mad. It was all wrong. I had to get some stuff sorted out. You of all people knew that. But we're going to be good, right?" He reached for her hand, and she gave him hers.

"It's going to be good," she said, bringing his hand to her lips. She set their clasped hands down on the armrest between them. "But . . ."

Hank took a deep breath and blew out a loud sigh. "But?"

"But . . . where the hell have you been? When will I see you again? Where are you going to be next year? How am I supposed to plan for the rest of my life?" That last bit might have been going a bit far. Or not.

Somewhere along the line, this whole summer-fling-thing had catapulted headlong into love-of-my-life please-don't-ever-leave-me territory.

Hank smiled slowly. *Victorious* was the word that came to mind when Maddie looked at him just then. "Thinking about the rest of your life, are you, Maddie?"

She looked a little guilty. "Well, yeah . . . but also where you've been and all that other stuff. But, yeah, all right, I admit it. I want to be with you. There. I said it. I want to live in the same house. I want to sleep in the same bed. Eventually, I want to sleep in the same bed and make lots of little Hanks and Maddies, and if that makes me some sort of jumping-the-gun weirdo well, then that's just—"

Maddie stopped when she realized Hank was smiling so broadly that he was almost laughing at her.

"Are you laughing at me? At a time like this?"

They were on the highway by then. Hank slammed on the brakes, pulled the car to the side of the road, and pushed the gear handle into park. He unbuckled his seat belt, then hers, and pulled Maddie so hard and fast into his arms that she pretty much melted there on the spot. "I want every single one of those things," he said hot and fast into her ear. "I want them yesterday. I have a ring in my pocket right now and we are driving to a beautiful house on the Cape so I can propose to you somewhere gorgeous and memorable, because I want to do everything right by you, Madison Post. I want to make you so happy that you never have that look on your face that I saw this morning when you opened your front door and you were not happy to see me. If I ever see that sadness on your face again, I think I will . . . behave very badly." He kissed her again. "That redhead escaped with his life."

Maddie was crying and laughing and kissing him. She had wriggled into his lap, on her knees, holding his face in her hands.

When she put her lips to his, she transferred all of the pent-up desire and commitment and love that she had been harboring for the past eight months without him physically there to receive it all. "Please don't ever leave me again, okay?" she whispered. She scraped her fingertips across his scalp, loving the tingle of his short hair against her skin.

"Okay." He smiled, but it was thin. "I have to finish this assignment, sweetheart, but I swear, in August I'll be done, and we'll be set, financially at least. We can do whatever we want." He helped her get settled back on her side of the car. "Let's get to the Cape and get those clothes off and just take care of one thing at a time."

"All right. But I don't like it." She pouted, and he smiled.

Hank looked into his side mirror and his rear mirror, then over his shoulder before pulling back out onto the highway. "You don't like the idea of being naked in an empty house with me to entertain you?"

"You know that's not it. I don't like you being all secretive and unavailable. I know I'm just being grumpy and selfish. But we don't need the money. Is that wrong of me to say?"

"It's not just the money, and you know it. I'm not going to marry you and live off your inheritance. Neither are you, for that matter. I know you would never do that. Why would you expect me to?"

Maddie twisted her mouth into a frustrated pinch. After a few minutes of contemplating the truth of what he said, she threw up her arms and cried, "Oh! Of course you're right! But I am just so sick and tired of waiting-waiting-waiting for everything."

Hank burst out laughing. "Maddie! You're twenty-one years

old! What are you even saying? What have you ever had to wait
for?"

She gave him a guilty smile. "Well," she bounced her left knee
impatiently, "it feels like twenty-one . . . thousand. It was a nightmare. Honestly, I can't tell you what it's been like to watch that
damn television and see all those soldiers and not know if you're
there or somewhere else, and if you are working with explosives—"

"Maddie—"

"What? You don't think I can look up the job description of an
Army Diver Engineer . . . right there in little letters after all the
other good deeds, like building bridges and fortifying dams and
all that structural stuff . . . explosives."

Hank kept staring straight out the window.

"Are you going to deny it?"

"What's the point?" Hank shrugged. "I work with explosives."

Maddie was becoming impatient, then realized that Hank's
face had changed and that something about the conversation was
becoming far more difficult for him than discussing minor things
like, oh, getting married.

"What is it?" Maddie asked in a softer voice.

"What is what?" Hank asked back.

"Why don't you want to talk to me about the explosives? Something happened—"

"Maddie. Of course things happened. I was in the Army for ten
years. Six of those years I was actively deployed in the Middle
East." Maddie could tell that Hank had probably practiced saying
those sentences. He sounded like he wanted to add all sorts of epi-
thets, and she had to give him credit for keeping it even-keeled.

"Oh-kaay." Maddie stretched out the two syllables. "Sooooo."
She tried to think of the best way to get him to tell her a loose

outline of what had happened. "Why don't we just approach it like an interview, just hand me your résumé. I don't want an emotional hazmat situation any more than you do. But I would like to at least know where you were, just loosely." He stayed quiet. "If you can." She squeezed his hand gently to encourage him.

"We'll talk about everything, I promise. Let's just enjoy the drive for now. Okay?" Hank asked.

"Of course." Maddie felt guilty for pushing him. "Whenever you feel like it." She looked out the car window and saw that they were getting toward the more remote reaches of Cape Cod. She loved the feelings of isolation and space this place had always evoked for her. "What a gorgeous day."

The spring air felt new, and the weight of winter had been scrubbed from the landscape. The ocean was still that metallic gray of those freezing months, but the dunes and grasses were a stunning, vibrant green. They listened to the radio and drove the rest of the way talking about nothing in particular, what they wanted to make for dinner, how her thesis was going. Maddie felt like the urgency she had felt even a few minutes before, wanting to know everything right that instant, had begun to abate. They had the rest of their lives for everything to unfold.

Hank pulled the car up in front of a small general store when they pulled into Wellfleet. They filled a hand basket with some vegetables, milk, coffee, a bottle of wine, and some pasta. A few minutes later, they were back in the car, and Hank turned it down an unpaved lane that ended at a quintessential shake-shingle Cape Cod home, with the sea extending beyond it in every direction. The trim around the windows and doors was a bright white against the patina of age that the salt air had imparted to the cedar shingles over the passage of time.

They grabbed their luggage and the groceries, and walked into the house.

"No key?" Maddie asked.

"No. My friend has someone who lives nearby and checks on the place and opened it for us."

"You were pretty confident I would just fall into your arms, huh?" They were unpacking the groceries in the old farm kitchen. The red countertops looked cheerful and enduring, like someone had thought they would be a really good idea in 1960.

"Either that or I'd need to drown my sorrows in a lost weekend of blackout drinking. So, I figured I'd need this place either way." He was joking, but Maddie felt the idea of Hank at that level of misery lance through her. She walked up behind him where he was setting the fruit and vegetables into a large wooden bowl on the counter.

"Let's forget the blackout drinking part and have our own lost weekend." She began to unbutton his pants, reaching around from behind and undoing the belt buckle. He stopped organizing the produce and put his hands flat on the counter and his forehead against the wood kitchen cabinet.

"Maddie . . ."

"*Mmm-hmmm.*" She had her hips pressed against his ass and her eyes closed, the better to feel the metal of his belt buckle against her trembling fingertips as she unfastened it.

"Maddie . . ." he whispered, strained.

"*Mmmmmm.*" She turned and rested her cheek against his back.

He whipped around, buttoned his pants quickly, and lifted her up into his arms. "Let the weekend begin!" He strode out of the kitchen and into the living room. "We're not going to make it to the bedroom." He tossed her down on the huge sofa and undid his pants. "We're not even going to make it to getting-our-clothes-off."

Maddie laughed at his blind enthusiasm. "I love you like this," she said, breathless.

He got onto the couch and poised himself above her. "I love you all the time," he said quietly.

Hank leaned down and kissed her, driving them both higher and higher, and finally, home.

CHAPTER 22

W hen she recovered from the onslaught of their love-making, she turned to see Hank kneeling on the floor next to the sofa. He was holding a very old-looking gold ring in his hand, moving it around and around like he always did with his keys.

"What is that?" Maddie asked softly.

His eyes flew up. He looked so disheveled and gorgeous. Maddie felt languid and beautiful when he looked at her like that.

"I had imagined this on the beach at sunset, with me on my knees or something stupid like that, but I just can't wait another minute." He shrugged and looked down at his mussed-up self, as if it couldn't be helped.

Maddie started crying before he even finished talking. "You look okay," she choked out.

"Madison Post, will you marry me?"

She threw her arms around his neck and pulled him back on top of her. "You know I will . . . Yes-yes-yes-yes-yes . . ." She kissed him and pulled him onto her, loving the weight of his body pressing her deeper into the sofa.

His smile was so grand. She wanted to make him smile like that every chance she got. Forever. He laughed and slipped the wide gold band onto her ring finger.

"It's kind of clunky, and it's not really an engagement ring . . ."

She looked confused. "I mean, there's not going to be a second ring, so it's sort of a combination engagement and wedding ring."

She looked down at the ancient gold ring, trying to focus on the tiny inscriptions that swirled around the rounded gold.

"Why does this look familiar?"

"Because it's from the Getty collection—"

She looked up horrified. "I can't wear this—it's too much, it's priceless—"

Hank held her fluttering hands together to still her. "It's a reproduction, but thanks for thinking I could have pulled that off."

She smiled and breathed a huge sigh. "Thank god. After the coin, I don't know what to think anymore . . ."

They lay there quietly for a few more minutes. "It's perfect, Hank." Maddie looked up at the ring, where it sat on the hand she was extending behind his head. Solid and enduring, like Hank. "Just perfect. You give really good present."

He smiled and pulled the cuff of his shirt back to reveal the Blancpain Fifty Fathoms watch. "I learned from a master."

Maddie's eyes lit up. "Oh my god, do you like it? Let me see it on you!" She grabbed his hand and looked at the beautiful old watch against his strong forearm. She leaned in and kissed the pulse point of his wrist. "I knew it would be perfect for you."

They spent the rest of the afternoon and all day Sunday out on the beach and upstairs in the big bed, with views to eternity across the tumultuous ocean and the windswept dunes. Gradually, Hank told her in bits and pieces about the time he'd spent in the military.

He told her what it felt like to walk into the Army recruiter's office on his eighteenth birthday and sign away the next three years of his life. And how he thought he was doing something really valorous and philanthropic, but how he also hoped to get as much out of that experience as he possibly could, to wring the meaning out of it. He told her about boot camp and how much he loved the order and regulation of everything. Actions had consequences that actually related to those actions.

They were walking on the beach, the crisp Sunday morning breeze whipping around them.

"Unlike growing up in my house, where there were always consequences, but I never knew where they came from. People got hurt. My father died. I could never do anything to make it happen or stop it from happening. Then I was deployed, in Iraq the first time, for two years. And again, I'd love to tell you it was miserable and hideous and awful, but it wasn't. I felt like I was really a part of something meaningful for the first time in my life."

Maddie squeezed his hand. "I know what you mean, I think. It's how I feel when I'm hitting my stroke in the quad scull. You're a part of a machine, in the best possible way."

Hank smiled. "Exactly. And I was good at it. My commanding officer pulled me aside toward the end of my deployment and asked if I had ever considered staying in the Army and going to West Point to earn my college degree, to become an officer."

Maddie smiled and squeezed his hand.

Hank turned to her quickly. "Yeah, chicks dig that part."

"You are horrible," Maddie said, trying to pull her hand away, but he held her to him. "Just tell the story. I get it. You were hot shit and you couldn't keep the babes away with a stick."

He shrugged, implying the truth was unassailable.

"Just go on already, hot stuff."

"Okay. So, I didn't want to deal with my mom's constant pride-and-joy crap so I just . . . never told her. And then the compartmentalizing got to be sort of second nature. I was at West Point. I was writing letters to Mom, pretending I had gotten another deployment in Bahrain. It wasn't the end of the world. I told her I'd been sent to do a desk job, and she was more relaxed that I was out of the line of fire and all that."

Maddie looked out to the sea. Away from him. She hated this part almost more than whatever horrible military situation he was leading up to. How could he lie to his mother? She tried to remember all the years he had suffered during Janet's active alcoholism and to sympathize with that level of mistrust and vulnerability. But it was hard.

"I told her," he said a few minutes later, into the silence.

"What?" Maddie turned back to face him.

"I told my mom about West Point last September, after I started seeing the therapist. Keeping it from her was just juvenile and self-centered. She cried and then admitted it was mostly because she would have done anything to see me in all my finery when I graduated."

Maddie smiled up at him. "I'm glad."

"She was fine with it, Mad. I promise."

Maddie looked into his eyes and realized it was all part of him, and he was moving forward. She couldn't expect any more than that without being the worst hypocrite on the planet.

"I'm sorry I judged you."

"Oh, cut it out. I was a tool. You're not judging me unfairly."

She smiled and shook her head. "So you're all shiny and smart and a graduate of West Point, and then what?"

His face clouded again, and she could tell it was hard. But, honestly, if he wasn't ready to tell her, in even the loosest, sketchiest language, where he had been for those intervening years, he probably wasn't ready to get married—

"My final year at West Point I got into diving. I had already studied engineering, and that was when I worked on that project that was sold to your friend, Mr. Lodge's, company. It seemed like such a cool combination of physical and mental and . . . well, anyway, it seemed like everything was coming together. So they ended up sending me to Bahrain, which was ironic since I had made that up to tell my mom before I went to West Point."

"What was it like?"

"It was better than Iraq—I wasn't getting shot at like the guys in Afghanistan, that was for sure. So I worked on a lot of structural ordnance kind of stuff. Sounds boring to a regular person, but you'd probably love it. Bridges and whatever. Anyway . . ." He took another one of those really deep breaths followed by the really long exhale, and turned to face Maddie.

She said, "Let's go sit over by the dunes. You don't have to tell me."

"I want to."

She smiled and situated herself between his thighs, reminded of Harvard Yard and telling him she loved him. She shimmied her back up against his hard stomach and chest and settled into him. She reached around to pull his arms around her.

It was still early afternoon, and the spring weather felt good against her skin. She felt like she'd been in a tomb since the day she walked away from him at the Ritz in September. They were both coming back to life.

They sat there on the beach for two hours while Hank held her and told her about the bombs he'd planted on the bottom of the ship, and the words seemed to float up and away from both of them, losing their power while Hank shared the misery and guilt and conflicting emotions that went along with those actions. He talked a little bit more about what it had been like for him in September and October, when he had finally gone to the VA hospital in Augusta and talked to the therapist about how it was destroying him. And how hard it was for him to be around people.

Mostly they breathed into each other and let all the words drift and hover in the air around them. Eventually, he started to come around to the present, telling Maddie about the research he was doing and how it was within an international military operation, and that that was why he wasn't able to tell her the details. He was working on a nuclear submarine, so communication with the outside world was infrequent and difficult.

"At least I'm not handling any explosives," he said finally.

"Would you tell me if you were?"

He laughed. "After everything I just told you, you think I wouldn't tell you that? It's all strategic consulting at this point. And it'll be finished in a few months. I'll be back August thirty-first. We'll be together." He squeezed her tighter against him.

Over dinner Sunday night, they talked about long-term plans and where they wanted to be.

"Where do you want to live when you get back?" Maddie asked, then put a bite of salad into her mouth while she waited for him to answer. They were sitting in the kitchen, Maddie in one of Hank's gray T-shirts and Hank in a pair of loose athletic shorts. They had pretty much given up getting dressed while they were indoors.

Hank looked out at the dark sea. "I don't think I want to live in Maine. I think my mom is good now, especially with Phil. What do you think? Where do you want to live?"

"I think, if I get this grant, I really want to go to Cyprus for the year. Would you want to do that? Together, I mean?"

He smiled again. "I meant what I said in the car. I want to go where you are. We'll figure it out."

After dinner, they curled up in the living room and pretended to read while they distracted each other with light teasing caresses.

"What time do you have to be in class tomorrow?" Hank asked.

"Oh, not until the afternoon. I meet with my thesis advisor at four, but other than that my schedule is clear. What about you? When do you have to go?"

"I need to be in Boston for a three o'clock flight. I was thinking . . ."

"*Mm-hmm.*" Maddie was half-listening and half-enjoying the feel of Hank's lazy touch along her forearm.

"I really want to meet your parents."

Maddie turned to look into his eyes. "You do?"

"Yeah. I do. Can we stop by and see them tomorrow morning? Are they in Weston? Available for lunch or something . . . ?"

Maddie kissed him. "They'll make themselves available!" She jumped up and got her cell phone. "You are practically famous. The coin was like the best calling card you could have possibly presented. My father is dying to meet you, *the numismatist*, he calls you."

"And the soon-to-be son-in-law . . ."

"Yes, there's that." Maddie smiled and talked while she hit the button for her parents' phone number and then kept talking while she waited for them to pick up. "And my mom is all aflutter because Lila Lodge told her how dreamy you were—Hey, Mom!" Maddie smiled and widened her eyes at Hank.

"Good, good. Yes." Maddie laughed. "Let me get a word in edgewise. I got a surprise visit from Henry Gilbertson and—yes—that's why I'm calling! Mom, we're engaged!" Maddie laughed again, and Hank smiled as he watched her, loved her.

"Okay. Yeah, Boston's probably best . . . well, that's a little stuffy, but okay . . ." She put the phone against her chest and whispered to Hank. "They want to take us to the Harvard Club for lunch, do you mind?"

He smiled. "Perfect."

Maddie finished up her phone conversation and they were all set to meet the next day at noon. "I'm so excited! It's going to be all my favorite people in one place!"

Hank stood up and pulled her into a hug.

The next day, when the two of them walked toward the front doors of the stolid brick and limestone building on Commonwealth Avenue, Maddie saw her parents walking down the sidewalk from the other direction. She gave Hank's hand a little squeeze. "Here they come."

A few seconds later, her parents were up the steps and they were all hugging and introducing one another. Laura gave Maddie a big hug accompanied by a loud stage whisper, "He is so handsome, sweet pea!"

Maddie blushed and looked at Hank. Because he was handsome. And he was hers to look at.

"Mom, this is Henry Gilbertson. Henry, this is my mother, Laura Post."

"Hello, Henry," Laura said with a beaming smile. "It's such a pleasure to meet you. We've heard all sorts of wonderful things about you. This is Maddie's father, William Post."

Henry and Maddie's father shook hands, and Hank said, "Nice

to meet you, sir," in a formal military way that gave Maddie shivers.

They went inside, and Maddie's father spoke to the attendant behind the front desk, then the four of them went into the private room that her dad had reserved for them to have lunch.

"William's been very eager to meet you in person," Laura launched in as soon as they'd all sat down and spread their napkins on their laps. "Since Christmas, of course, with the wonderful coin you gave Maddie . . ."

Laura paused and looked around at the other three people, then laughed when she realized she had been talking the entire time since they had hugged at the front door. "Oh. I'm so sorry. We're all a little excited."

Maddie smiled and felt as if her whole existence had been leading up to this moment—that all the years and split seconds of her life until now had been an act of preparation to take Hank into her life, to receive him like this.

Hank and her father were now talking about the research that Hank had been doing when he came upon the Greek coin. Maddie looked from one man to the other. She felt momentarily that no matter how modern she was, there was a changing of the guard transpiring before her eyes. Henry wanted to be responsible for Maddie in the most elemental, possessive way. It felt almost physical, like she was being placed into his care.

It was exactly the opposite of how she had felt when she wanted to keep him away from the "rest" of her life, to save herself from having all those independent memories colored by her feelings for Hank. Now she wanted everything and everyone in her life to be mixed together with those feelings. She would need her parents to tell anecdotes about this lunch while Hank was away again for the next four months. Maddie would need her mother to remind her how handsome and kind and smart he was. How Maddie needed to learn patience.

They spent the rest of lunch in a happy rush of sharing information about Maddie's grant application, Hank's interests in deep-sea diving, engineering, and material physics, and eventually combining them somehow.

By the time they finished lunch it was after two, and Hank looked at his watch. "I'm so sorry, I have to be at the airfield by three. It has been such a pleasure meeting you both."

They all stood up and walked to the parking garage together. Hank took Maddie's duffle bag out of his car and handed it to her. She set it down, and he gave her a hug and a too-short kiss while her parents tried to look in another direction. They had agreed that Maddie's parents would take her back to the station to get her train to Providence since Hank needed to catch his plane.

"August thirty-first? Okay?" He traced his finger along her jaw.

"Okay," Maddie said, her eyes beginning to burn.

"Okay." He hugged her again and kissed her one last time, finally releasing her and saying another good-bye to Maddie's parents. He took another long look at Maddie, then got into the car and drove away.

"So. There you have it," Maddie said to her parents. Her mom pulled her into a hug and let her cry into her.

"You'll be fine, sweetheart, he'll be back before you know it."

Maddie pulled herself together and got into the backseat of her dad's station wagon, feeling like she was about twelve years old.

CHAPTER 23

The next few months were not nearly as miserable as Maddie had expected. Hank was right that keeping diabolically busy helped to pass the time. She'd received the grant, and they'd even asked her to lead a small team of researchers who would be in charge of drawing up and analyzing the findings for an archaeological group in Cyprus. She received the list of possible candidates in the middle of July and worked closely with the head of the Cypriot university team to decide on the best-qualified people.

By the middle of August, she was frantic with wanting to see Hank. Maddie had spent a week in Maine in June with Janet and Phil before their marriage ceremony. Hank had managed to get in a long Skype call the morning of the wedding, so that had been something. But not nearly enough.

After making some additional arrangements with her colleagues in Cyprus and Boston, Maddie decided to take matters into her own hands.

The twenty-two hours of travel with a layover at Heathrow got her into Larnaca in the middle of a scorching afternoon on August twenty-ninth. A car was waiting for her at the airport when she arrived and took her to the small house in the hills that she received as part of her academic housing stipend.

The next morning, she showered and called a taxi to take her to the university to meet with her team leader, the professor who was running the entire operation. Maddie was shown a small office. "This is where you can leave your things and write up your findings, but I suspect you won't be spending much time here as the bulk of your research will be compiled while you are at sea."

Maddie smiled. "Yes. It will."

Both women looked up at the sound of two men arguing behind a partially closed door at the far end of the hall.

"I don't care if she's Hypatia of fucking Alexandria. I have been on a fucking submarine for months and just got orders to come here straight from the docks, and I need to be back in Boston tomorrow, and I'll turn in my resignation if you don't let me out of this goddamned office right now—"

"She is going to be the head of the accompanying research team, and Lodge demanded that you be here to meet her on her first day," a more rational voice replied.

"Well, she sounds like a controlling pain in the ass and I'm—"

Maddie stood in the door, her arms folded across her chest.

Hank stared at her.

The Cypriot professor who had been showing her around smiled and patted Maddie on the shoulder. "Looks like you surprised him, yes?"

"Yes," Maddie said, not taking her eyes off Hank.

The other man, one of Mr. Lodge's top advisors on the project—and Maddie's accomplice—came around from behind his desk and shook Maddie's hand. "Nicely done." Then he left the room and shut the door, leaving Hank and Maddie alone in the small, cluttered office.

Maddie felt her heart begin to hammer. First at the mere sight of him—Hank was tanned and still sort of throbbing and fuming from his loss of temper—then at the sizzling energy that crackled between them. She twisted her engagement ring with her thumb, a comforting habit she'd fallen into over the past few months.

"What are you doing here?" Hank finally asked.

"I'm the controlling bitch who's heading up the other team. I thought we should meet."

He walked slowly toward her, and Maddie felt like her heart was going to pound right out of her chest.

"Why didn't you tell me?" He was close now, smiling and predatory.

Maddie shrugged. When she spoke, her voice was thin and sounded as desperate for him as she felt, as desperate as the need she saw in the clear green eyes staring back at her. "I figured I could tell you later."

He reached out and pulled her into his arms.

Acknowledgments

The publisher wishes to thank *General Hospital* executive producer, Frank Valentini, and head writer, Ron Carlivati, for their extraordinary creativity, support, and efforts on behalf of this book.

YOU FELL IN LOVE
IN MAINE

Now it's time to discover your *Maine Squeeze*

Fall in love all over again
this September with a new novel
inspired by *General Hospital*.